SALT & VENOM

BLOOD, BLOOM, & WATER BOOK TWO

AMY MCNULTY

Snowy Wings
PUBLISHING

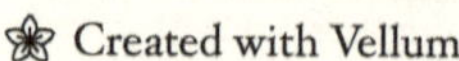 Created with Vellum

CHAPTER ONE

Blossom didn't often have time for me when Autumn was around. Though the cat was no spring chicken, she still had a youthful spring in her step, and only an eight-year-old with mountains of extra energy was up to the task of satiating the calico's thirst for prey. Usually in the form of a shoestring or curled-up ball of paper.

But Blossom poked her head up beside my bed and mewed, tapping her paw against my shoulder until I couldn't help but let out a small chuckle. As I lifted the comforter higher, Blossom snuggled right in against my side.

"At least someone won't ask what's wrong with me," I whispered. "She just *knows* something is." My fingers traced circles around one of her soft ears.

Why couldn't I just tell everyone the truth? Hashtag *ImAMermaid*. Jokes aside, I was seventeen—albeit almost eighteen—and I didn't know how to handle this on my own.

I had three parents. Why couldn't I kick and scream and have a tantrum and wind up coddled in my mom's or dad's arms?

My phone buzzed on the nightstand. Shifting so as not to bother Blossom, I grabbed it and saw the message from Calder:

Feeling better? I know last night was... a lot. I've got you, though. I promise. I need you more than I've ever needed anyone. I'll try to be a worthy prince, my champion.

A tear slipped down one cheek as I felt my face warming. I put down the phone and wiped the moisture away. Why was I crying? It wasn't like I was madly in love with the guy.

But apparently, the champion of water was kind of the prince's fiancée. So I had a boyfriend now. I'd never had one who'd lasted more than a few dates.

Now I was tied to one—cute, kind of shy though he might be —possibly for the rest of my life. We could one day lay our merbaby eggs in the blood of my fallen step-sister.

No and no. I still wasn't planning on either happening.

My phone buzzed again and I swiped away another notification from Paisley. The bits of messages I'd read from her and Lyric asked everything I expected them to, like what in the world had happened last night, was it true that Calder had lost his pants in the Homecoming fire, was I feeling all right and how was Ember, and also, back to the second point, *was* it true Calder had walked around brazenly with his elephant trunk swinging freely?

I tried not to think about that part. My face was flushing at the memory. I bet the vampires didn't have cause to go pantsless around their champion. At least not a supernatural one. I wasn't sure if that was a pro or a con, honestly. *Dirty Ivy.*

Blossom's purrs grew louder and louder as she snuggled up beside my cheek, nudging the top of her head against my chin.

"I love you too, furbaby," I said, rubbing the back of her neck and being reminded how different the cat at my new place was— Ember's cat was a scaredy-cat if ever there was one.

The thought of going back there now with how things stood between Ember and me... I couldn't. But I couldn't very well explain why I couldn't to Mom and Dad.

Even if Mom apparently had been hypnotized into accepting Orin as a family friend.

That traitorous faery.

"There she is!" screeched a voice from my partially-open door.

Autumn came trotting in—the girl had yet to learn boundaries. Thankfully for her, I was an amazing big sister. *If I do say so myself.*

"Leave us alone," I said, just a touch of my grumpy side evident in my voice. Okay, not always an amazing sister.

Autumn flicked on the light switch and padded over to the side of my bed. "Are you cramping?" she asked, twirling a strand of her long, brown hair around her finger. She had on a tie-dyed T-shirt and bright purple zebra pants. The girl could clearly not dress herself, but she was too old for my parents to be picking out outfits for her regardless.

I pushed at her gently, my arm jostling and upsetting the cat. "I'm not on my period every time I'm feeling tired," I said, grunting. "Geez, you'd have me bleeding twenty-nine days out of thirty."

"Gross." She scooped the cat out from beside me, carrying her in her arms like a big, fragile bag of groceries. My sister bounced her up and down and Blossom dug her claws into her human captor's shoulders, her yellow irises like saucers, but Autumn didn't even flinch. "Are you still sick from last night?"

"Yes," I muttered, pulling the cover over my head entirely. "Now go away. And don't forget to shut off the light."

"How did you create steam?" she asked. "When you touched that warm blanket they gave you, your hand glowed blue and steam rose out—"

"You were seeing things," I mumbled. "Now go away."

"*Fine*," she snapped. The pounding of her bare feet against the floor was loud even muffled by the threadbare carpet that ran most of the length of Mom's townhouse. "Keep your secrets."

"And stay away from Orin!" I snapped.

"Who?"

"Orin! My boss. My date to Homecoming." I poked my head out from under the blanket. Mom was hovering behind Autumn in the doorway. Great.

Autumn grinned and Blossom saw her chance to jump down, scattering off into the hallway, my little sister hot on her literal tail.

"How are you feeling?" asked Mom, her fist hovering over the open bedroom door as if it weren't too late to knock and not be invited in at this point.

"Fine," I lied, burying my head underneath the blanket once more.

She took that as an invitation because I felt her sit down on the edge of the bed. Her hand touched my shoulder through my barrier of cotton and synthetic fibers keeping me from facing reality and the fact that said reality included faeries, vampires, and merpeople. "Do you want to talk about it?" she asked.

Yes. "No."

She kept stroking my shoulder in silence.

"Don't you have work today?" I asked. She always had work and it was supposed to be a Dad day anyway. She'd been a homemaker when she and Dad had been together and though she got some "maintenance," as they called alimony for some reason, she'd had to take on a minimum-wage job at a superstore to make ends meet. Luckily, she and Dad got along well enough that he pretty much paid any and everything related to Autumn's or my expenses.

I just didn't get why they couldn't have gotten along while they'd been married, then.

Sighing, I buried myself deeper in the blankets, barely hearing Mom's response. Something about swapping shifts.

She tugged the blanket off my head and I groaned. "Hey, listen to me," she said.

"I am." *Not true.*

She stared hard at me until I was forced to look away.

"Did anyone hurt you last night?"

"No," I lied again. Not like she was thinking. Not *who* she was thinking.

"Or Ember?"

"No," I said again, my nails digging into my palm beneath the blanket. Well, *I* had hurt her. "Things just got hectic in the chaos."

"So hectic that boy lost his pants?" Her eyebrow arched.

"They were wet," I said. "And on fire," I added. I supposed the latter would excuse it where the former wouldn't. Even if that was just a little white lie to add to the mountain of them.

"Wet... *and* on fire?" Mom asked, her neck bending forward even more.

Don't test me, woman, I thought. *You have no idea...* "Wet *after* being on fire."

Mom took in a deep, audible breath. "Who was that boy, Ivy?"

"Calder Poole," I said, the name coming out like a petulant toddler forced to reveal the fact that she'd dug her hand into the cookie jar. "He's on the swim team. Or he was... He just transferred."

"Okay..." Mom said. "And is he... Do you know him well? I don't remember you ever hanging out with him before."

"That's because I hang with the baseball team, owing to Paisley's boyfriend being captain of it. Doesn't mean I don't know him." An itch took over the tip of my nose and I rubbed it into my pillow.

Mom kept patting my shoulder. "He was there with someone else and he just happened to help you and Ember—after his pants caught on fire?"

"He was there with me," I said, not wanting to get into the debate about why someone from a different school was there without a date from Union High. It wasn't like he'd transferred that long ago anyway.

"But I thought you and Orin...?" Normally, Mom would be having a fit that I'd dated an "older" guy. Ha, try older than dirt, not a couple of years older. But Orin had made her think he was a dear friend of ours somehow. For some reason.

"He's just a friend," I said. "*Was* a friend. And I'm not working for him anymore."

Not the right thing to say. "Ivy, I know you might need time off, but I *told* you it's important to start working as soon as possible. Look at what happened to me. When your father left—" Her phone rang, playing the *Jurassic Park* theme song, which I knew meant Dad. They'd gone on their first date to see that movie as freshmen in high school. I didn't know why Mom would want to be reminded of that.

"Take some time off," she said, letting the phone continue to ring a moment. "Just keep... what happened to me... in mind. A part-time job would be good for you even throughout college." Her lips pinched as she stared straight at me, and I flinched. She turned away and answered the call. "Yes?"

I ran a finger over the edge of my nightstand, ignoring the buzz that came from my own phone as I picked up half a conversation between my parents.

"That's great!" said Mom, a smile on her face. She lowered the phone to whisper to me, "Ember got the all-clear. She's home and feels fine."

I flinched. Not that I *wanted* her to be ill, of course, but... But... She was the enemy now. She'd sealed the deal before I had.

I'd missed some of Mom's side of the conversation. "He wants you and Autumn to still come over tonight," she told me, Dad clearly on hold. "They're going to order in."

"No!" I shouted, sitting up and practically whapping my poor mother across the face with my blankets.

I could hear the muffled sound of Dad's voice—he'd probably heard that.

Mom shrank back. "Sunday is usually spent with your dad—"

"Right. Oh, right." Covering my face with my hands, I winced. My throat was dry. "It's just... Mom, I barely feel like moving. Maybe Autumn can go and I..." I didn't say anything more.

Mom turned back to her conversation and spoke in a hushed voice. Then she held the phone out to me. "Your father wants to speak to you."

"Tell him I'm sick or something," I said.

"I heard that, young lady," came Dad's voice from the speaker.

"*Ugh,*" I said, bringing my knees up and resting my forehead atop them.

Mom spoke to him again and then hung up a few moments later. "We agreed both you and Autumn can stay here an extra night," she said. "Ember's dad is in town anyway. I get the feeling things are... tense between him and Noelle. They thought maybe having a crowd would make things less awkward."

"They're inviting him to dinner with them?" I asked. All the more reason not to bother going. Like I needed another awkward thing happening inside my own home when all I wanted to do was sleep for the rest of my life.

"He's staying at a motel, but yes, he's coming over for dinner." Mom sighed as a crash echoed from downstairs—the townhouse was cramped, but there was a kitchen, living room, and half-bath on the first floor. "Autumn?" she called out.

Autumn's giggling rang out even from a floor and several rooms away.

"We'll talk more later," said Mom, patting my shoulder again. She stopped when she reached the hallway, looking back at me over her shoulder. "And you're at least eating dinner with your sister and me," she said sternly. "I'm not letting you sleep the whole day away." She flicked the lights off.

Groaning, I rolled onto my side, nestling myself beneath the covers again. My phone buzzed on the stand beside my head and I reached over, holding the power button and confirming I wanted it turned off so the thing would finally go quiet.

CHAPTER TWO

Don't ask me to explain, but ditch with me? I texted to both Paisley and Lyric.

It took half a minute for a response. *First period?* asked Paisley.

We haven't ditched since sophomore year, added Lyric. *I think? Not this early in the day anyway.*

All day, I answered.

Yeah, I knew I was asking for trouble with the truancy officers, but they weren't known for being the most skilled at their jobs. And frankly, merpeople and vampires and all that made me care a lot less about getting grounded.

Heck, if I could convince them to let me "serve my sentence" at Mom's house, I'd never even have to see Ember.

I guess? typed Paisley.

I'm in, said Lyric. *Just let me inform my bae.* She paused a moment or two. *No, actually, she'd bite my head off for this. We don't have a class together until seventh anyway. I'll just get my mom to call me out sick.*

It's not playing hooky if you have permission, added Paisley, but I didn't care whether they got permission or not. I just needed a ride and a distraction, away from the venom-soaked halls of Union High.

"Don't be surprised if your father has a few things to say," said Mom as she turned the corner and Union High came into sight a few blocks away. We'd already dropped Autumn off at her school and it was a Dad day, which meant Ember picking up Autumn after school... I bit my lip. I'd have to convince one of my friends to do it. Not that I thought Ember would hurt *Autumn*, per se, but if this was war and the vampires were still butthurt over what had gone down during Homecoming, who was to say what they would stoop to with or without their champion?

Calder had insisted this was to be a proxy battle between human representatives of each species. But Ember hadn't exactly been going it alone at the pool. My guess was the final blow had to be struck by the champion, but almost anything else was fair game. Almost. The one guy—*faery*—who might have cared about the rules had already overstepped his bounds.

Mom must have taken my sullen silence for a response because she continued unabated. "He called again to check in last night and wanted to talk about that Calvin—"

"Calder," I corrected.

"—and Orin, but I told him it was ridiculous to punish you over dating Orin when he was such a good family friend." Her face lit up and I cringed. "He said he had *no* idea I'd known the guy and asked why I hadn't mentioned that before and I..." Her tongue ran over her front teeth as she focused intently on the road. "In any case, he wants to talk to you."

"Got it," I said, saluting her as we pulled up to the end of the block. Mom knew to drop me off far away, unlike Dad when he'd still dropped me off up until a few weeks ago.

Had it really only been that long since he'd gotten married, since my life had gone from dull to insane? I didn't want to think about it.

"Love you," said Mom, putting the car in park and leaning over to kiss my cheek. She had her brown store apron on already. No doubt she was running late. "Call me if you need to talk." The way she said it, it was like she knew I was in for trouble when I finally sat down with Dad.

"Okay," I muttered, in no mood to be a good daughter. Slamming the rust-edged tan door of her sedan behind me, I shifted my tote bag's straps up my arm and pumped my legs to carry me down the block. The bag was missing a few books since Mom had had me bring them to Dad's on Saturday before Homecoming, thinking I'd be headed to his place afterward. But that was just less to lug around anyway.

Once I was sure Mom's sedan had made a U-turn and headed away, I veered right, walking straight to Lyric's car in the parking lot.

They were both already waiting there, Paisley's arms wrapped around her baseball team captain boyfriend, Grey.

"Hey," said Grey, nodding at me. I looked around. Half the baseball team—though Devam was pointedly missing—was lingering around Lyric's car. My eyes went wide.

"Oh, don't have a conniption," said Lyric, pressing her key fob and unlocking the front door. "We told them it was a girls' day out."

Yeah, but maybe it would have been an easier secret to keep had we not informed our whole usual clique about the suspension-level offense we were perpetrating here. But who was I kidding? Paisley couldn't keep anything from Grey if her life depended on it. "'Kay," I said glumly, sliding into her back seat.

Ashton and Charlie let out an "ooo" sound as I slammed the door shut behind me, giggling like they were witnessing the class valedictorian breaking the rules for the first time. *Oh, please.* They knew me better than that.

Paisley and Grey exchanged a kiss that turned into three or five and I let out an impatient growl. Finally, Paisley disentangled herself and headed for the passenger side door. I clicked my seatbelt in like it was a dagger I was stabbing into the plush of the seat.

"Someone's a bit testy today," said Lyric, looking over her shoulder at me. Like she didn't usually get annoyed by Paisley-and-Grey, the two-creatures-in-one they became when they tangled themselves together. "Still feeling sick after Saturday?"

"Yeah," I said, happy for a vague enough question I didn't have to lie about for once.

Paisley shut the door behind her and strapped herself in.

"Where to, Miss Hooky?" asked Lyric, turning around and adjusting the rearview mirror.

"The lake at the park," I said, digging my phone out of my bag and swiping at its screen. He'd been too chicken to come near Union High to pick me up, of course. Well, if he didn't want witnesses, that would just have to mean no fishy business so long as I had friends along.

"The *lake?*" asked Lyric quizzically.

"Pond," I spat, the exchange digging deep into my sense of annoyance just then. Ember and I had argued about the same thing.

"*Oh... kay*," answered Lyric, then we were off.

Paisley kept talking all the way there, Lyric's replies just enough to keep the conversation going, allowing me to drift off and stare out the car window, letting my mind go blissfully blank.

———

"Oh. Oooohhhh," said Paisley as we pulled into the little gravel parking area for the park. "Now it makes sense. I guess." Paisley shifted to look over her shoulder at me. "So best we can tell is you ditched your date for Calder before things got crazy on Saturday, right?"

"Right," I said, unclicking my seatbelt as Lyric put the car in park and shut the engine off. The place was truly empty on a weekday morning. The only other vehicle in the lot was Calder's old blue pickup truck and he was sitting on the picnic table nearest the lake, playing with his phone and frowning.

"Let me guess," said Lyric, fluffing her hair in the mirror and dropping her key fob into her purse. "Parents weren't thrilled with the whole found-half-naked thing and wouldn't let you see him again, prompting you both to ditch school for your next chance at a tryst."

"Something like that," I said, climbing out. Lyric and Paisley followed suit, and I bit my lip as I looked between the lake and my friends. "So now you know. If you guys want to leave, I don't mind..."

Lyric arched an eyebrow. "So much for *girls' day out?*"

"Yeah," said Paisley. "Grey would have totally skipped with me. Though he didn't want to miss gym."

Of course he didn't. "Did they get the gym cleaned up after...?"

"Still working on it," said Paisley. "So they were going to have a free day outside. The guys were going to get some practice swings in."

Jocks. So predictable.

"Hey, who're *they?*" said Lyric, her face lighting up as she stared over my shoulder.

A fairly buff young guy with light brown skin and wavy brown hair was walking toward Calder with a tiny, pale white redheaded girl a few steps behind him, her thick hair practically sparkling as she flicked it over her shoulder.

They were both in jeans and plain T-shirts and their hair looked wet. Like freshly, sopping wet.

Merfolk. I didn't particularly remember these two from my day under the lake, but there had been a lot of faces to take in that day —a lot of things to wrap my head around.

"They're probably *with* each other," said Paisley, bumping her hip against Lyric's thigh.

"And I'm with Rae," said Lyric. "Stop harshing my window shopping, Pais," she added, grinning. "Never hurts to look."

Raelynn might have begged to differ, but... "Can you stay?" I asked. The thought of facing Calder with two new merpeople and no one there to stop them from doing their fish-tail party trick was suddenly terrifying to me.

Paisley shrugged and Lyric grinned, striding forward toward the other teens.

"He *is* awfully cute," muttered Paisley as she passed by me.

I took a look at the new guy. He was. Though Calder was maybe one iota cuter. My cheeks burned as the thought crossed my mind.

Calder's head swiveled toward me and his face lit up, his arm shooting over his head as he waved at us. "You made it!" he said as I awkwardly stepped into place beside Lyric and Paisley in front of the picnic table. It was just then that I realized Calder's Union High letter jacket had been replaced with a letter jacket in purple and gold—Central High.

"You joined the swim team fast," I blurted out, like that was what we needed to focus on just then.

"I had connections," he said, bumping his fist against the new guy's.

Lyric brushed her hair behind her ear and extended a hand out to the redhead. "I'm Lyric," she said.

The redhead looked to Calder with an eyebrow raised, almost as if asking permission. He nodded. "Laguna," she said.

Lyric grinned, her eyes shining. "*Nice.* Sexy. Aquatic. Like a mermaid."

Ha ha ha ha. If only she knew.

Laguna's pale face flooded with bright red color and she took a step back, her long hair falling over one eye, almost like she was retreating beneath its thick curls.

Calder rushed to step between them. "We all have creative parents." He nodded toward the guy with him. "This is Bay."

"Paisley," said my other friend, flicking a hand up in a sort of half-greeting.

"And you're Ivy," said Bay, his grin showing off some pearly white teeth. This guy just oozed mythical merman. Even more than Calder.

Calder jumped down off the picnic table and wrapped an arm around my back, settling his strong, sturdy hand on my side. I jumped but quickly fell into the half-embrace, dropping my tote to the ground and fidgeting with my hands in front of my pelvis as I let the small crowd around me take in the spectacle of me being all mushy with a boyfriend. Well, low-key mushy, but mushy for me.

"Do you guys mind if we have a minute?" Calder asked Lyric and Paisley, the gleam in his eye so at odds with the panic that marred his face anytime the bloodsuckers were around. "Thanks for bringing her, by the way. And ditching."

"Sure..." said Lyric, crossing her arms. "So I take it you're all from Central?" she asked Bay and Laguna. Laguna took another step back until she caught Calder's eye and sighed, putting one stiff arm in front of a stiff leg and walking away.

Bay fell in beside her, skillfully ushering my friends toward the sandy beach. "Yup," he said. "We always wished Calder had been with us, too. We grew up together..." His voice went quieter as the group descended the slight incline and made their way to the beach.

Paisley checked over her shoulder once and I did my best to smile, knowing that in most situations, I ran the risk of looking like a deranged clown when I tried too hard, but it apparently was passable enough because she turned back to the group and jogged a few steps to catch up to them. Laguna broke off slightly from the others, crouching in the sand and digging to unearth something that gleamed in the sunlight when she held it up.

"Glass," Calder said. "Glass thrown into the lakes and the rivers, worn down over years... It can be pretty, actually, even if it's a reminder of humankind's polluting ways." He tugged on me, so I turned to face him and he pressed his lips to the top of my temple.

My heart beat so fast. I thought I was better than that. Better than the typical teen who thought with parts other than their brain.

"Are you okay?" he asked.

How many times was I going to be asked that question? And would I ever be able to answer in the affirmative without lying again?

"No," I said. My voice was quiet, hoarse.

"You're not alone in this," said Calder. "Mom wants to meet with you—"

"Just give me a second to process all this first." I held my hands to either side of my head, as if to emphasize that my brain was about to explode. Then I cleared my throat, letting my voice grow stronger. "All right?"

"Okay," said Calder quietly. His one word was quiet, accepting, not demanding I change my mind. "Bay and Laguna are—"

"Merfolk," I said, finishing for him.

"That obvious?" Calder grinned.

"Wet hair aside, do you even *have* any friends who aren't merfolk?"

"Touché," he replied. He stepped back and took my hand in his, prompting me to follow him in an ambling stroll through the grass, away from the beach and our friends. We didn't say anything for a while and I shivered despite having a coat on.

"Here," said Calder, letting go of my hand to take off his coat.

"This seems familiar," I said, clutching the soft material of the jacket as he slipped it over my shoulders like a cape.

"If I recall, you were very adamant about not letting me give you my jacket last time we tried this."

"Touché," I spat back at him. Around me, the quiet lake surrounded on three sides by a wide expanse of brightly-colored trees took my breath away for a moment, the oranges, reds, and yellows clashing with the murky green of the water below the tree trunks. A little peal of laughter caught my attention as Lyric chased Paisley along the beach, dragging Laguna by the arm, clearly against her will, to follow suit. Bay laughed and then kicked up his legs, overtaking all of the girls to touch a tree trunk at the beach's edge. They'd been racing.

"Aren't you cold?" I asked, taking in the merfolks' T-shirts and feeling the quiet, chilly breeze.

"We tolerate the cold better than most," said Calder. "It's not exactly tropical down there." He nudged his chin toward the lake.

"If I were a Midwest mermaid, the first thing on my to-do list would be to move to tropical waters."

"Well, you are now. Is that what you want to do? Head for someplace perpetually sunny?" Calder grabbed hold of a light post and swung himself around it, right out of a scene from *Singin' in the Rain*. I shuddered when the dated reference made me think quickly of Dean Horne, enemy vampire, and his out-of-time cohorts.

"I don't know." I shrugged. "I hadn't gotten my post-high-school plans gelled yet before... Before..." I gestured at my legs, like that would explain it all.

Calder stood straight, the smile falling off his face. "Well, I can understand that," he said softly. "Not making plans. Not knowing what the future will bring, not really."

"You made no plans?" I asked. "What if... What if I'd never moved into that house? Never become the champion? What then?"

He didn't answer.

"Well, there's one thing," I said, only half-teasing. "Your mother made it clear I'm supposed to make merbabies with you or something."

He shook his head. "That's the idea behind choosing a champion—choosing the girl you want to be with." He cleared his throat as I felt myself go unnaturally still. "But once this is all over, you're free. From me. From my family. I don't care what she says. There won't be a need to have another merprince if it's over once and for all."

I appreciated him not making a big deal about us being together, not making it seem like some grand, destined thing. But I thought about that. About his people needing a prince. A lot had come together to have two champions in that house at the same time. "What if you'd been a merprincess instead?" I asked. "Or what if your mother had been the heir in the time of champions?"

Calder's forehead wrinkled as he took his time answering. "Then the champion would have been a guy, I suppose. Or a girl or a person of any other gender if that was what she preferred."

I thought about that. It didn't seem right that Dean had been an heir for decades while the merfolk had cycled through several. "Then if Ember had had a brother..." Actually, I was pretty sure Dad had said she did have a brother. An older one, not from Noelle.

He shrugged and went back to leaning away from the pole. "There have never been two young people of the right age in that house at once until you."

"I still don't get why you or the vampires couldn't have just *moved* people into that house if it's so important. Like explain what's up and pay the families of the lucky chosen champions to step into those roles willingly."

He chuckled. "You really think people would have responded to that ad? 'Looking for two teens to fight on behalf of creatures from fairy tales. By the way, there might be casualties'?" He shook his head as I tensed at that last word. "In any case, the faefolk didn't think that level of pre-planning would be fair."

Acid coated the back of my throat. Like impatient Orin cared about fairness.

"Hey," said Calder, stopping his little dance and standing up straight. His hands slipped over the thick material of the coat I'd borrowed and cradled my elbows. "You're not alone in this, okay? And you don't have to focus on the parts that don't concern you. I've got you."

It felt weird that he had to keep telling me this over and over. Was I that easy to read? I chewed on my bottom lip.

"I have something else I have to ask of you," he said. His gaze drifted over my head to the group now kicking sand at one another on the beach—well, minus Laguna, who had gone back to digging holes in the ground. "And I'm not sure you're going to like it."

Time seemed to slow down then, my instinct telling me to run away, to go where none of these supernatural creatures could ever find me. "I'm listening," I said, my voice cracking.

"I need you to transfer to Central High with me," he said, nodding his head just slightly. "And you're not going to be crazy about my idea for how you can convince your parents to let you."

So many awful ways to decipher what he meant shot through my mind. But once he'd told me, I could honestly say I really hadn't expected *that*.

CHAPTER THREE

Our day playing hooky had led the lot of us to the town's sole used bookstore, the gravel in its parking lot kicking up dust and making it seem even more like the last bastion in the middle of nowhere. True, there was the diner down the road, but that was it for miles that bled into endless, endless farm fields and stretches of shoulder-high grass. I wondered if the truckers stuck going along this stretch went mad at the unchanging scenery.

I was battling an anxiety attack just pulling up to The Hollow Tree.

"It's a weekday," I said. "And a morning. You really think he'd open the store?"

Calder shut off his truck's ignition. "You'd rather look for him in your dad's back yard?"

"No thanks." Though the house was likely to be empty this time of day, so maybe that wouldn't have been such a bad thing. But there was the more important issue, anyway. I didn't *want* to find this faery. "Orin's not going to help us."

"He will if we convince him it'll aid in the war." Calder opened his door, as if that were the end of it, just as Lyric pulled her car into the lot with a bouncing Paisley in her front seat and a grinning Bay in the back—he seemed to be belting out a song. Whatever it was, it went quiet as Lyric turned off her car.

Laguna shifted beside me to slide out after Calder. I jumped. Even pressed up against her shoulder, I'd almost forgotten she'd been there between us. She'd picked Calder's truck over Lyric's car without hesitation, even though there wasn't a seatbelt for a second passenger, when Calder had announced our plan to go get my "last paycheck." Or first for that matter. My employment hadn't lasted long.

I was also looking at this visit—after Calder had twisted my arm to get me to agree to it—as a chance to slug the faery who'd pretended to be my friend. But I hadn't said that part aloud.

Sighing, I opened my door and jumped out, my sneakers kicking up more dust in the gravel. The Hollow Tree's gnarled wood sign was swinging in the breeze above the hood of the truck, the creak of the hinges as foreboding as the bumps in the night in the spookiest of haunted houses.

I trusted this faery as far as I could throw him—and as far as I knew, being a mermaid didn't grant me any super strength.

Poor oblivious Paisley had no fear, though. She bolted out of the car—grabbing hold of Bay's forearm as he slammed the car door shut behind him—and dragged him up to the bookstore entrance.

"There's a kitty here," she gushed. Her eyes were practically watering in anticipation of the toll the cat would take on her allergies. But she didn't mind.

I expected her to find the door closed, though—Orin had no love for work, he'd made that plenty clear—but she strolled right in, setting off the bell above the door.

Joy.

Lyric was texting as she strode past us, a frown on her lips the only thing making her not resemble a no-nonsense fashionista or businesswoman. "I'll be in in a minute," she said. "Bae is freaking out about me 'going home sick.' Don't know whether to tell her the truth and get yelled at or continue to put up with her molly-coddling."

"Relationships built on lies drop like flies," I said, feeling sagely as I passed her and stepped up to the porch.

Calder rapidly blinked as he ascended the step beside me and I froze. "In... general," I added. True, my friendships weren't exactly going to last by my own judgement, but I hadn't expected Calder to care about that. He was the one who wanted me to stop seeing them on a daily basis.

All to avoid Ember and the hallways full of vampires.

"Ha ha," said Lyric dryly and Laguna quietly pushed between Calder and me to enter the store, the welcoming bell ringing out even as the door shut behind her.

"So you have permission to enter now?" I asked, remembering all those days he'd parked himself down the road at the diner waiting for me to get off-shift in hopes I'd talk to him.

"Guess so," he said, holding the door out for me. The bell took on an ominous tone it'd never had for me before, and I cautiously stepped inside.

A sneeze was the first thing to catch my attention, and I practically jumped out of my skin, my right hand going cold at my side as I awaited the attack. Duh. Paisley. Allergies. I needed to stop being so jumpy.

The door shut behind me as Calder entered and the bell rang out once more.

"She's *purring*," said Paisley across the quiet stillness of the room, then she sneezed again.

"Skiving off school, are we?"

This time, I really did jump out of my skin. Well, not *really*, but it felt that way. My hand went up on instinct, glowing blue, the frosty condensation steaming in the air.

"Bit knackered still, I see," said Orin, grinning as he didn't so much as flinch. "Bags under the eyes and all that. So full of the collywobbles you're about to harm the observer?"

Calder's hand rested atop my wrist, bringing warmth to my appendage. I let the ice flow out of me as I dropped my inbuilt weapon.

"You just wait," I said, my voice carefully controlled. "Wait until this is all over."

Orin whistled, one hand in his pocket, the other carrying a

worn book as he brushed past us and made his way toward the cashier's counter.

"What are you even doing open this time of day?" I asked, struggling to focus on anything other than wringing his neck for spurring this whole thing on like he had. And then hypnotizing my mom into liking him.

"Just wagging off. Might have had a feeling someone was going to be here, all right?" He put his book down—opened—on the counter and plopped his elbows on either side of it, using his fists to support his cheeks as he stared down. I didn't even want to look at that smug, glib face.

"Easy," said Calder quietly. Had my irritation been that obvious?

I opened my mouth to speak, then bit my tongue. When I heard Paisley sneeze again, I remembered my excuse for coming here. "I want my paycheck."

Orin snorted and pulled one fist away from his face—first to flip the page and then to punch a few buttons on the register without even looking at it. He pulled out three hundred-dollar bills and held them out, never once looking up from his book.

If he thought that was going to deter me from taking them—more than I was owed at that—he had another think coming. "I quit," I said, snatching the bills from his outstretched hand and stuffing them in my jeans pocket.

"Figured," he said, that quasi-cockney lilt injecting as much nonchalance as possible into that word. His fist rested against his cheek again.

Ugh.

"We also came to ask for your assistance," said Calder.

"I'm listening," said Orin, not at all appearing to be.

The clomp of feet pounding drew my attention as Paisley and Bay headed upstairs, Bay shaking his head as he looked our way, but a grin stretching across his handsome features all the same. *Uh-oh.* Paisley and Grey were hitting that seven-month itch...

A thundering clomp of books flooding onto the ground sounded from nearer the register, over at the window, and we all turned—even Orin—to see Laguna flushing red and scrambling to stack a pile of used paperbacks into her arms.

"Oy, Ariel, be careful with the merchandise, yeah?" Orin's brow crunched.

"Her name's Laguna," I said.

"He knows," added Calder. "He just likes teasing people."

Orin's voice grew louder, his gaze probing mine directly. "I do, don't I?"

Calder was undeterred. "Would you help convince Ivy's parents to let her transfer to Central High with me?"

Orin leaned back, his arms crossed over his chest, his book finally fully forgotten. "Help 'convince,' you say? Like dialing up my ol' pal Morning Glory and telling her I have just the idea for her daughter's academic growth and development?"

"You can command people, can't you?" I asked, my nails digging into my palms. "Don't deny it."

"Wasn't going to," said Orin, and with a little flourish of his hand, a tiny gust of wind turned the page in his open book, his gaze shifted slightly downward to read it.

I slammed his book shut and kept my hand atop it. "Do you want this war over with quickly or not?"

Orin simply scratched his chin. "Don't know. Been thinkin' about it and maybe I'd miss my books and the idiot box too much."

My voice took on an edge. "Would have been nice of you to have this attitude a couple of weeks ago when you decided to mess with us by knocking out the town's power." That had actually been just over a week ago. Dang, time was flowing fast.

"My mobile was charged," he said, pulling out his phone from his pocket and shaking it in the air. "And I can read by firelight in my cozy cottage while blood and water go at it."

"Don't give me that," I snapped. "You were probably observing the chaos you wrought and were disappointed to find it petered out into nothing that night."

He shrugged, sliding the device back into his pocket. "You

could say it laid the foundation for what was to come, yeah? Girls bonding with their princes—"

"I'll *bond* you," I said, fully aware that made no sense at all.

"All right, all right," said Calder, putting a hand on my shoulder. He didn't seem irritated by Orin at all, a fact that made my blood boil for some reason.

A brief sense of quietness fell over the store, broken only by the muffled sounds of footsteps on the loft above us and the quiet sliding of one book after another onto the shelf Laguna must have knocked them off of. Really, she ought to have sued him for shoddy stocking. The books could have fallen on her or tripped her. Then she could take his rich butt for all it was worth, shut this place down. I pinched my lips together to suppress a smile as I tossed my head back and glared at Orin.

He chuckled as if he had any idea what I was thinking.

"You know Union High is vampire territory," said Calder.

"And whose fault is that?" Orin scratched his cheek again.

"Mom doesn't like to directly involve innocents like that," said Calder. "She wouldn't have lured a principal, nurse, and janitor away and turned them into bloodbags to take their places."

Orin snorted. "Don't forget a few members of the school board, too." *How many people did the vampires keep on hand to feed from?* "You know, as the *impartial* observer," Orin continued, "I have to say it's almost bent as a nine-bob note for you to imply the merfolk are nothing but corkers. Who says you're so high and mighty?"

Calder slammed a palm against the cashier's counter and Laguna dropped a few more books to the ground in response.

Orin turned to face her. "Oy, love, just leave them—"

"We're giving them Union High without a fight. All we ask is that you let us have the champion of water at our school. All the merteens go there already. You know I only applied to go to Union because there was a chance Ember might get a sister—"

"Whoa, whoa, whoa," I said. "You should have gone to Central High? But you live near my dad's new place. Union territory."

"The districting lines are very weird," said Calder, glancing over his shoulder at me. "They zigzag all over that neighborhood. Demographics."

Sure. Merfolk on this side, vampires on another.

"But your mom's place is firmly in Central's district," added Calder, and I wanted to ask how he *knew* that. I hadn't invited him over there.

"Google," said Orin, answering my unasked question. "And paranormal boyfriend stalking."

I pinched my lips together. Now wasn't the time to lay into Calder, not when it would send a satisfied grin to Orin's self-assured face. Calder flushed as he realized his mistake. Clearing his throat, he said, "In any case..."

"Sure, I'll give ol' Morning Glory a call," he said, and I had to look away, watching as Laguna finished arranging the books in her hand and took a step toward the nearby window, slowly stroking Feilia, who was seated atop the back of the cushioned chair in a sunbeam. "But I haven't, er, properly *introduced* myself to *Mr.* Sass yet, yeah?"

That drew me back to the moment. "Watch it."

Calder chewed on his lip but said nothing.

"I'll 'convince' Morning Glory," Orin said, undeterred. "Then you let me in to convince dear ol' dad, all right?"

"Stay away from them after that," I said quietly, staring at the worn paperback he'd been working on. *Sense and Sensibility.* Maybe it was a lesson in empathy for that traitor.

"Hmm?" asked Orin, but he'd known what I'd said.

The bell over the door chimed and Lyric strode in, her scowl sending such negative vibes into the place that Feilia jumped up and scampered away into the back room, scurrying over Laguna's feet in her attempt to escape.

"You get what you came for?" asked Lyric, her arms crossed tightly over her chest. She didn't even spare a smile for Orin, who should have definitely fallen into her guidelines for "window shopping."

"Yes," I muttered, glaring at Orin for good measure. He winked and I scoffed, turning on my heel. "What's up?" I asked Lyric, ready to wallow in normal teen problems for a change.

"Rae figured out I was lying about being sick," she muttered.

"How?"

"I don't know. I don't exactly lie well under pressure, okay?" She flicked some of her hair over her shoulder. "And I got sick of her worrying about me."

"Better to have her angry at you," I said, nodding. That was Lyric anyway. She didn't like being taken care of. That was why she and Rae usually made such a great match. Rae was only too happy to lean more on Lyric than Lyric did on her—though Lyric got sick of that, too. High school relationships seemed like such a pain.

Reminding myself I was in one now—in a bizarre, twisted way—I reached out and gave Lyric a side hug. "Let's do something *you* want to do for the rest of the day," I said.

She glanced over her shoulder. Calder shuffled his feet behind us and Orin wriggled his fingers in a cheery wave. *Ugh.* "What about your secret boyfriend?" Lyric asked.

"I'll see you later," I said loudly to Calder this time. Merfolk business could wait. We just had to collect Paisley and blow this joint, wasting the rest of the day away until we had to own up to ditching class.

No sense in losing out on all the fun we could have until then.

CHAPTER FOUR

When Lyric offered to let me stay at her place—even if just for a few hours, if I didn't want to spend the night—I was tempted. But we'd gotten all the fun we were going to have today out, just messing around at the mall, at Paisley's before her parents got home, then seeing a movie. Though Paisley had been texting her boyfriend up a storm—the only time I'd seen her stop that for more than a waking moment was when she'd been hanging out with Bay— Lyric and I were pointedly ignoring our phones. Every few buzzes, we'd check and frown—Lyric likely receiving messages from Raelynn, me, from my parents. I just wanted to make sure none were from Calder, none were about this ridiculous paranormal business.

Parents could wait.

Until they couldn't.

And then I'd realized with a start that I'd never asked Lyric to get Autumn home, leaving her to Ember's mercy. I'd texted my sister right away then and had felt my stomach muscles relax when she'd texted me back that she was at Dad's. Dad had gotten off work early to pick her up. He'd tried picking me up, too.

Thus all the frantic messages while I'd been at the movies.

"You sure you want to do this?" asked Lyric, pulling up in front of my dad's house. Since school was out now, Paisley had gone off to attach herself at the hip to Grey, her flirtation with Bay seemingly forgotten. I looked down the street to where I knew Calder's merfolk mansion must have been, somewhere a ways down the road and walled off by trees.

"Yeah," I said. "I can handle this. Can't ignore it forever."

"Okay," said Lyric. She put the car in park and leaned over to kiss my cheek. "It was nice knowing you."

"Ha ha." *Easy for her to say.* She'd gone the route of calling her mom and faking illness so she could get an excused absence called in. Her mom wasn't typically home until late, so she wouldn't even notice.

Shutting the car door behind me, I steeled myself and clutched the handles of my tote bag harder. Just as I took a step forward, the garage door opened and I jumped back, fist at the side and at the ready.

Ember surely wouldn't attack in front of our parents, would she? Unless she'd convinced them to go on a date night or something.

"Finally." It was a much deeper voice than I'd expected, extremely familiar and not carrying any of that old-school movie accent. "Where have you been, young lady?"

I wasn't a 'young lady' unless I was in trouble. Not that I'd been such a bad kid until lately.

Dad was wiping his hands with a greasy faded red rag, a speck of grime no doubt from his never-ending motorcycle tune-up project across his cheek as well. *So glad to see you were so worried about me.*

He tossed the rag on a box marked "Goodwin Suppliers," reminding me as to the nature of Ember's mom's business—something like supplying all the restaurants and offices in towns with napkins and staplers and all that.

"Your mom said she called in sick for you."

I blinked. She did? Did I owe that to Orin as well?

Dad continued. "But I got a call from the dean this morning that you didn't show up for class."

"Right," I said, sliding the straps of my tote bag up my arm. "Sick."

"She said she forgot to call it in until the morning was almost over." He emitted a little *hmm* noise from deep in his throat. "You could have answered my calls and told me that, then."

"Sorry," I said, scraping the driveway concrete with my toe. "Sick." As if speaking more than one word at a time would make me less of a liar.

"You're feeling better?" he asked.

I nodded.

He stared over my shoulder at the road behind us, but there was nothing there for him to use to discern where I'd been. "Who brought you here?"

It might have been a test. Mom was still on shift, no doubt. It wasn't her day to have us.

"Lyric," I said, glad to be telling the truth for once. "She came to check on me after school." Right back to the lies.

Letting out a deep breath, Dad gestured with his grimy hands for me to follow him into the garage. I flinched at the touch of his hand on my shoulder, wondering if I now had a stain I'd never be able to get out. Dad didn't seem to notice. "What's this your mom tells me about you wanting to transfer to Central?" He hit the garage door button as we passed it, and a sense of dread washed over me, like he was trapping us in the perfect little confined space for bloodsuckers to go to work on our carotid arteries.

I shrugged. Orin had done his job, I supposed. I didn't know what was in it for him, unless he really thought this would bring the end of the battle about much more quickly.

"It's your last year of school," Dad continued as we lingered in the doorway leading back into the house. My ears strained for signs of other life inside the house, but all I could make out were the voices from one of the Cartoon Network cartoons Autumn devoured.

"Your friends are all at Union," Dad added. That was a gut punch. But it wasn't like I had much of a choice. I'd tried today, but I couldn't really focus on just being a normal high schooler anymore. Not really.

I wasn't going back to carefree days goofing off with my friends. So being at the same school wasn't as important anymore.

"Are you being bullied?" Dad asked.

"*No*," I snapped, taking a step inside.

"Now hold on a minute, young lady," he boomed. "We're not done talking here. Not by a long shot."

Autumn's head twisted to watch us as we made our way out the foyer to the kitchen and the living room. She was surrounded by brightly-colored ponies and a couple of Transformers. No one else was in there with her.

"You found her," said someone from the stairs—Noelle.

My heart thundered. No doubt Ember was right up there behind her.

"Let's have a talk," she said, gesturing to the kitchen as she reached the bottom of the steps.

A sharp spark of resentment fluttered across my chest. She wasn't my mom. She was barely my step-mother. I didn't want to talk to her about any of this.

Be more mindful of the demon spawn you raised yourself, I thought strongly toward her. Something like it must have shown on my face because her pale golden eyebrows rose. She looked way too much like Ember.

Clearing her throat, Noelle tossed her head back. "Ember is out with her father," she said, perhaps mistaking my look for not wanting to have this "talk" in front of the whole family. Whoop-dee-do. One less member there to witness it.

Though truth be told, a weight lifted off my shoulders at the news. I could feel my shoulders actually loosen. Resigned, I pounded into the kitchen.

"Autumn, dear, would you mind playing upstairs for a bit?" came Noelle's voice from the other room.

"It's fine," I said. "She can stay."

Autumn peeked into the kitchen, a devilish grin tugging at the corner of her lips.

"I *insist*," said Noelle as she walked into the room. She glowered at Dad. How quick the man caved.

"C'mon, sport," he said, guiding her by the shoulders. She groaned and stomped away but didn't flinch at his greasy hands like I had.

Letting out a breath that sent a lock of my hair fluttering, I sat down at the table and waited for Dad to finish scooching Autumn up the stairs and join me. After leaving briefly to turn off the TV, Noelle lingered in the entryway, eventually taking a seat across from Dad, the two of them surrounding me on either side of the table.

They exchanged a look and Noelle nodded.

"We want to talk again about Saturday," he said.

"What about it?" I asked. "I told you everything I could." I was getting good at this careful-phrasing-to-relieve-myself-of-the-guilt-of-lying thing.

If I started pouring my heart out about merfolk and vampires, would this family meeting end with having me committed?

"How did Ember get hurt?" Noelle asked, her lips curling into what could only be called a fake smile when I glanced her way. "She said what you did—that she slipped into the pool on the way out during the fire."

I supposed Ember had as much—if not more—to hide about that night as I did. "So why are you asking me again?" I drummed my fingers on the table.

"I just..." Noelle licked her lips. "You would tell me if anyone *hurt* her, right?" She extended a hand to cover mine and I pulled away, crossing my arms.

"If this is about Calder again..." I started.

"Is that the naked boy?" Dad asked.

"He honest-to-Pete just had to take his pants off because they were *on fire*," I spat. So much for dancing around an outright lie. But what was I supposed to say? They ripped off whenever he grew a merman tail?

"His underpants too?" Dad coughed then, choking on an attempt to clear his throat.

"He goes commando apparently," I said. *Why not? Why not just go full storyteller at this point?* Where was that annoying faery when you needed him?

"Oh. Interesting," said Dad, his face going pale.

"Okay," said Noelle, worrying at her lip. "Anyway, if your pants were on fire, you might rip off your underwear, too," she said, nodding. Something was washing over her then, like it was all making sense. Then her head cocked. "How did his pants get on fire? Did that boy *set* the fire to begin with?"

Uh, yes, but there's no way I can tell you that. I shrugged. "We don't know how it started."

"A pile of towels by the pool," said Dad, his brow wrinkling. Right. Firefighters had ways to figure out where fires started. Well, that, and there was probably a gleaming pile of ash by the pool.

I shrugged again. "Calder was with Orin and me. He ran through the flames trying to get out. You can ask Orin."

Wrong thing to say. I'd just been hoping for the faery shortcut to fixing this at this point.

"Why on *Earth* were you bringing an older boy—your *boss* to Homecoming with you?" asked Dad. He pulled his fists under the table, but I saw them clenching before he did.

"He's like twenty," I said. Twenty hundred? Who knew?

"And you're seventeen," he said.

"Almost eighteen." I shrugged and before Dad could say more, I pointed out, "It wasn't like that, Dad. We were just friends. And I quit the store anyway."

"Why?" asked Noelle, though this time Dad glared at her, like he didn't want her to encourage me to go back to spending more time around this "older boy." Ha, if he only knew.

"I've just got too much going on," I said. The truth.

Dad wiped a greasy hand over his face and left another little smudge above his brow. Noelle flinched at the sight and got up, going to the sink to wet a dishtowel that she handed to him, pointing at his cheek and brow.

"And now you and your mom are telling me you're as good as transferred to Central," he said, dabbing his face and doing a poor job of removing that grease. Noelle hadn't been around a grease-monkey for long, that was for sure. She should have known mere water could never match the power of Goop.

I am? I thought. Go Orin and his powers of persuasion. I just nodded.

"I told this to your mother, but you can't just make these kinds of decisions without consulting me," he snapped.

"Do you *care* where I go to school?"

"No," he said, wringing his hands around the dishtowel. Noelle's lips curled down as she took in the sight of one of her cute, crisp towels getting all wrinkled and dirty. "As long as it's a good school."

"Central's fine," I said. "Better than Union, people say." I guessed.

"Okay, but then I'd want to know *why*," said Dad. "You didn't even ask to transfer *before* the school year began, which would have been weird enough, but you waited until right after this disaster of a dance."

"It has nothing to do with that," I snapped. *Lie.*

"Then why...?" Dad leaned back in his chair.

Noelle brushed her fingertips over his shoulders and gazed down at me. "It's a boy," she said.

I stiffened but said nothing.

"*What?*" said Dad. "Is that *true?*"

I didn't answer.

"Ivy, for Pete's sake, if you're dating some kid from Central, you can see him *outside* of school hours." Spittle started flying from Dad's lips. "Wait, you know what, you can see him *after* I've met him and approved of you two dating."

"This isn't the eighteenth century," I retorted. "I don't need the men who court me to ask my father's *permission.*"

Dad's breaths got louder, a sudden tightness taking over his expression. "You're a *child!*"

"Barely," I said.

"You know, Dean introduced himself to both me *and* Ember's father—while he's been in town." Noelle kind of choked on that last part. "And she's eighteen. But some young men understand what it means to be a gentleman, and that it doesn't mean you're setting back women's rights just to drop by to say *hello.*"

Dean. Dean and Ember. What a gentleman, that blood sucker. "You know, Mom understands that it's not just about a boy." I snorted. "Mom understands that maybe I just feel too crowded here in this house, with this new *person* to lecture me." I offered a fake smile back to Noelle, much like the one she'd given me when she'd thought I was hiding something about Ember being assaulted. "I want to live with Mom full-time."

Dad exploded. "Now, listen here, young lady—"

But Noelle wouldn't be deterred, either. "I can't believe you would say something like that about me. Easton!!" She gestured widely, but Dad was on his feet, walking back and forth and going on and on about what a good dad he was, how most kids of divorced parents would *beg* for more time with their fathers, to look at Ember...

Oh, please.

I sighed again. To a point, this was unfair to him. It wasn't that I didn't love him or didn't like him. It was just...

A noise at the front door sent my blood pumping and I gripped the table, my right hand growing cold.

Ember was home.

The doorbell rang and Noelle, still huffing, strode out into the hallway to answer it.

Did she forget her keys?

"What on Earth?" shrieked Noelle from down the hall. "You would dare come here?!"

Uh-oh. I had a feeling that was for me. I leaped to my feet and Dad followed, still lecturing me, but I ignored him, desperate to beat Noelle to the door. But she was already opening it.

Orin stood there, his hands in his pockets, his shoulders slightly hunched. He pulled one hand out and wiggled his fingers at me. "Got impatient waiting for the right moment." His bright white teeth lit up the smooth brown of his face as he grinned at me.

Crap. He was right. "Come on in," I said, nodding.

"Now wait a minute, young lady," started Dad.

"This is *my* house," added Noelle. All the more reason for me to feel unwelcome in it.

"Now, now," said Orin, slipping an arm around her shoulder. She flinched and stumbled back at first, but then he said, "We're old pals, aren't we, Mrs. Whatever?" He didn't pronounce the 't' in "whatever," making the name sound even more bizarre.

"Goodwin-Sheppard," she said, a smile edging onto her face. Her shoulders relaxed and she visibly straightened. "But you can call me 'Noelle,' dear."

"Noelle...?" asked Dad, his expression slack.

"Mr. Goodwin-Sheppard!" said Orin, pulling him in with his other arm for a big group hug.

"Sheppard," I corrected.

"Mr. Sheppard!" said Orin. "Old friends, we are, all right?"

"Yeah..." said Dad, his face softening. "Call me 'Easton,' buddy."

I rolled my eyes.

"So we need to have a chat about Ivy switching schools, yeah?" said Orin, looking from one parent to the other. He glanced at me. "Any other odds and sods you want me to bring up while we're at it?"

Dang it, I hated this. I needed this, but I hated it. I stared at Dad, the anger washed out of his face, the memories of him always being there when I needed him at war with my need to get out of this house, away from Ember.

Clearing my throat, I opened my dry mouth. "Yes," I said, finally deciding what I would have to do.

CHAPTER FIVE

Orin nodded our way as Calder and I pulled away from the curb in Calder's truck, then he turned on his heel and trudged back across my dad's lawn, ducking around the house, no doubt on his way to the woods back there and his isolated cabin. Just before he vanished from my line of sight, he squatted and I tensed, expecting some trickery on the faery's part, but he was simply bringing a carnation from the scraggly bushes on the side of the house to his nose, inhaling it as if it were the sweetest wine.

Calder's voice startled me. "I take it that went well or you wouldn't be going out with me tonight."

We turned the corner and put Dad's house behind us. I shifted in my seat, my neck strained from the tension of watching over my shoulder. "Dad and Noelle are all smiles about my transfer to Central," I said. "And they don't think you're a flasher anymore."

"A *what*?" Calder hit the brakes a little too hard at a red light.

"Yeah, I guess I kind of forgot to tell you about that." I adjusted the seatbelt so it didn't dig so harshly into my neck. "They were mad about me bringing an 'older guy' to Homecoming, but they were also concerned that you might have done something... *bad*... to Ember?" I didn't know why I stated it like a question.

The light turned green and Calder sat there another minute, only hitting the accelerator when someone behind us honked. His jaw clenched visibly beneath his tanned skin with the slightest hint of golden stubble.

The car behind us sped up and veered into the oncoming traffic lane to get around us, some jerkwad flipping us off as he merged back. He was lucky there were no other cars in the road.

"Take a right up here," I said, as much to break the silence as to make sure we didn't miss the turn that would take us to Paisley's. I'd also summoned Lyric and Grey and Ashton and as much of the team that would bother to come on a school night because I had something to tell them.

A text didn't seem the right way to deliver the news. At least, thanks to Orin, my parents didn't have a problem with anything.

I sighed. This didn't seem right—relying on Orin, manipulating my parents' minds.

I hadn't been able to make him tell Dad I was leaving his house permanently. He'd still have Autumn anyway. I didn't want Orin messing with her mind to explain everything, and I had to have faith that Ember wouldn't do anything to a little girl.

So I'd asked Dad via Orin's *nudging* to let me stay at Mom's full-time for a "couple of weeks." This had to be over by then. I just... didn't know what "over" would look like and if I'd ever forgive Ember for effectively *dragging* me into this.

But only if both of us were still left standing... *No.* I wouldn't let myself think like that.

"Why did they think I'd...?" Calder licked his lips, unfazed by the car that had passed us. "And why Ember specifically?"

"No pants. Unconscious girl." I shrugged. It *had* looked weird if I thought about it, but it wasn't like there hadn't also been a dozen other things going on at the time.

Calder *tsked.* "Bet the vampires don't have that problem," he muttered. "Don't need to take their pants off to suck blood."

I snorted, the laughter bubbling out from my mouth unintentionally. I refrained from educating Calder about the *other* things sexy vampires seemed to get up to in fiction. Then I sighed. I sure hoped Ember and Dean weren't that far along already. Her devotion to the vampires could never be broken if he was her... *first.*

Leaning my elbow against the window, I let my mind go blank as I watched the scenery go by.

"Thank you," said Calder after a moment.

"For what?"

"For everything."

Calder's face reddened just a bit, his Adam's apple bobbing visibly. "You gave my people a fighting chance. And you're... you're giving up so much for me."

Playing with the handles of my tote on my lap, I absentmindedly let the coarse material make temporary indents on my fingertips. Switching to another school, causing me to only see my friends after class, *and* taking a few weeks off from my dad's shouldn't have seemed like a big deal, but it kind of did. But in any case, this would all be over soon... somehow... and then things could go back to the way they were.

A smile fluttered onto my face as I stared at Calder, the softness of his expression wearing down my defenses. "I couldn't leave you to those bloodsuckers' mercy." I squeezed his hand, which hung loosely on the steering wheel. Calder took a deep breath and checked over his shoulder before making a lane switch. We were in the busier part of town now and Paisley lived just a mile or so more away.

"Turn up there," I said, letting go of Calder and pointing down the road.

We didn't say anything more for a bit, so I took my position up against the window again, taking stock of the cars, the few people ambling down the sidewalks, and the gas station attendant manually switching out the price on the sign—one of the few left in the area that hadn't moved on to digital screens. We made the turn and my view changed to a guy raking the leaves in his yard, a couple of kids riding their bikes back and forth a few driveways over, and the "sold" realty sign in the yard of the house next door to Paisley's, boxes stacked on the house's porch, the front door wide open. "This is it," I said, pointing to the driveway leading to Paisley's ranch house.

Some of the baseball team guys were already there, Paisley and

Grey entwined as usual on the patio. Ashton and Charlie were taking turns tossing a baseball in the air in the yard and then rushing to be the first to catch it in their mitts, while the handful of others nearby sat in the grass laughing at something one of them had said.

Calder parked at the end of the driveway just as Lyric pulled in and took one of the few remaining spots across the street. "So you couldn't go more than a few minutes without me," she said as she trotted up beside me in the driveway. "Luckily for you, Raelynn still isn't speaking to me." Her smile faltered, but she stuck another one on, the strain obvious. "I'm a *liar*, apparently. Like she needs to know every little thing I do."

I gave her a side-hug, moving my tote to my other hand. "You'll make it better. You always do."

"You make it sound like we're always fighting," she said, but she chuckled before letting out a big sigh. "But so... How'd it go by you?"

I exchanged a look with Calder before he nodded and smiled at the guys on Paisley's lawn. "That's what I wanted you all here to tell you."

"*Okay*..." Lyric made her way to the porch, only to flinch when she saw Charlie coming toward her, his head turned up, completely focused on the ball above him. She tossed her purse up the porch steps and shoved her shoulder into the incoming boy, reaching up and catching the ball with her long arms before he could. "Ha!" she said with a wicked grin, keeping the ball above his head in an echo of "takeaway."

"Give it back, you long-limbed freak," said Ashton, jogging up beside Charlie and Lyric.

Lyric's eyebrows arched. "*Excuse me?*" She turned around and wound up the pitch, sending the ball sailing into the neighbors' back yard. Smugly, she crossed her arms over her chest. "Too bad I can't go out for the team, eh?"

Charlie and Ashton both shook their heads, but there was a sliver of a smile beneath their irritated expressions.

"Hey, guys?" I said, taking the few steps up to Paisley's patio. "Can we just—pause a minute? I have something to say."

The group did give me their attention and I felt a hot flush creep up my neck at the sudden awareness that I was everyone's focus. My eyes scanned the small group of baseball guys, and though not everyone was there—it wasn't like I was super close to all of them, anyway, just always near them by proximity of Paisley —one guy was noticeably missing. "Has anyone heard from Devam?" I asked, my previous train of thought derailing.

Calder slipped in behind Ashton and Simpson—I forgot his first name, everyone always just called him that—and glanced this way and that over his shoulder, his hands in his new letterman jacket pockets, his shoulders hunched forward.

The clank of a ramp being lowered from the back of a truck drew my attention to the neighbors' driveway. Over the fence, the newly-visible top of a white moving truck explained the sound.

"He's been sick since Homecoming," said Charlie, pounding his right fist into his catcher's mitt on his left. He grinned. "I told him about the mess he missed. He wasn't sorry he got food poisoning after all."

Food poisoning. More like he was poisoned and became the food. I swallowed. But at least someone had been talking to him since then. And it hadn't been that long. I couldn't believe the dance from the fiery depths had been only a few days ago.

"Oh," I said, and I flinched again with the sound of something large dropping on the other side of the fence. I cleared my throat, aware that I was losing everyone's focus to the sounds of a neighbor packing house. "Well, someone will tell him, I hope. But, uh, so... Tomorrow I'm transferring to Central."

Licking my lips, I took in the puzzled expressions—the similar looks on Lyric's and Paisley's faces punctuated by jaws agape. Lyric took a step back, suddenly unsteady on her feet. Paisley maneuvered herself out of Grey's arms with some effort, pushing on his chest to get free, whirling on me.

"*What* did you just say?" she asked.

I tugged on my sleeves, shuffling my feet. "I'm transferring schools tomorrow."

"*Why?*" demanded Paisley, grabbing me by the arms and shaking me. "We've gone to the same school since—forever!"

Lyric was still speechless and now she'd walked back into Charlie, and she didn't even seem to notice.

Ashton looked over his shoulder at Calder. "Something to do with the new boyfriend?" he asked.

I exchanged a look with Paisley and she winced. So she'd told everyone. Ashton didn't seem that bothered, though. So much for our little flirtation the previous year.

"It's not just that," I said, clearing my throat and weaving my hands together in front of me. Simpson and the rest of the guys who barely interacted with me were already talking amongst themselves, one tapping at his phone while the others glanced over his shoulder. "We've got a game against them in March," said Simpson, like I cared.

I supposed it was their only way to relate to me.

"So you're our rival now," said Charlie. He grinned, but Lyric looked about ready to slap that grin off his face.

"This has to be a joke," she said. She lifted her chin high and went unnaturally stiff, a slight swallow jiggling her throat. "Ha ha. Very funny."

"It's all being taken care of already," I said. "Mom and Dad both agreed..."

"Why would your parents agree to this nonsense?" Lyric tossed her hair over her shoulder.

"Come on, Leer," said Charlie, patting her shoulder with his mitt-less hand. "It's not like you'll never see her again." He motioned to Ashton over his shoulder and pointed to the fence, then they were off, no doubt to collect the ball Lyric had flung over there.

Grey slipped an arm around Paisley's waist and she flung it off like a child in no mood to be coddled. "You can't just *do* that," she said. She turned around and glared at Calder. "You can't just decide to take her to your school," she snapped. "She was *our* friend before she was your girlfriend."

There really was no getting around everyone thinking that was *why* I was making the transfer, was there?

One of the guys let out a shout and the whole wave of them, minus Grey and Calder, moved back and looked to the sky, their hands or mitts extended, and I realized their ball was soaring toward them from over the fence.

Ashton took a little leap into the air and managed to catch it in his mitt, and the whole lot of them went wild.

Calder took a wary step back from the clump of jumping and hollering boys, his tanned skin suddenly sickly.

"Nice catch," said a deep, hollow voice.

At the edge of the fence near the sidewalk strolled Dean in a dark gray vintage pinstripe suit, his sunglasses pointedly affixed in my direction. He tipped his hat slightly at me, then leaned a shoulder against the fence, crossing one foot in front of the other, his hands in his pockets.

I didn't know why I'd never thought of it this way before, but he looked like an old-timey gangster.

Before I could even blink and realize what was happening, my brain registered the speeding blur retreating from the yard as Calder bolted for his truck.

Alone.

CHAPTER SIX

I stood, slack-jawed, as Calder stared back at me right before climbing into his truck. Dean looked over his shoulder at him, too. Calder gestured for me to follow.

Did he honestly think the vampires were going to do anything to us here—in front of my friends? Orin had said neither side was to involve innocents.

Though Orin wasn't here.

Still, I clenched my hand into a fist, feeling the cold sizzle in the air against an already-chilly breeze. I shook my head.

Then Calder shook his and started his vehicle up, pulling away from the curb and down the street.

He left me.

He actually left me.

I was so dazed that I didn't notice the guys jogging over to Dean, the moment Dean had redirected his attention to charming the small crowd in front of him.

"Uh, wasn't he your ride?" asked Lyric.

Stretching out my fingers, I anchored myself back in the moment, letting the tension roll off my muscles. A chicken Calder wasn't anything new. I'd just thought now that we were a team...

"He, uh, had something to do," I said, though my friends would have witnessed the whole thing, how he'd just turned on his heel and run without a word. "He'll be back later." *Or he can kiss his champion's support goodbye.*

I scanned the area, looking for anything else I'd missed. Taking a backward step up Paisley's patio, I got a better look at the top of the moving truck: Horne Moving Co. *Stupid*, I told myself. *You knew to watch out for that.*

But honestly, I had no idea what they were doing here, next to Paisley's house—how they'd known I'd be here.

"Funny coincidence," said Dean loudly enough to get my attention. He gestured over his shoulder. "That we were hired to move your neighbors." He pointed at Ashton and then Simpson and kept pointing at the people gathered one by one, as if waiting for the real Spartacus to speak up.

"Mine," said Paisley, a slight tint of red to her cheeks as she wriggled her fingers at him. Grey slipped in on what looked like instinct, wrapping his arms around his girlfriend. She didn't push him away this time, settling in back against his chest as he stood behind her.

Dean grinned and stuck his hands back in his pockets. I could have sworn his sunglasses-covered eyes fell on me. "Quite a coincidence."

My sometimes-scaly mermaid butt.

I stared Dean down, waiting for him to say anything more, but he broke into quieter chatter with the bulk of the baseball team guys as a loud clang rang out again from the driveway behind him.

"You picked a really crappy time to transfer," said Lyric, suddenly bringing me back to the crisis at hand. The normal teen crisis, the one that didn't involve the paranormal.

The one of my own making. I shrugged, feeling my hand warm up, my shoulders relax. "You're not telling us something," said Paisley softly, and I realized she'd maneuvered the Grey-and-Paisley train to face me once more. Grey kept looking over his shoulder at the other guys, though, and after half a minute, Paisley released him and pushed him gently off into the wild.

"No one just transfers a month and a half into the school year," snapped Lyric. "Not unless they were moving to another city or something—but you're going to *Central*."

"It's just some... issues with my dad," I said. "Sort of. Look. I just need some space."

"But you're still going to see your dad half the week anyway, right?" asked Paisley.

I didn't really want to throw my dad under the bus when he hadn't done anything wrong. "It's not... It's like... I'm just taking a short break," I said. "From his... house."

"Is it your step-mom?" asked Lyric in a hoarse whisper, finally taking her accusatory tone down a notch.

"Kind of." I ran a finger over the zipper on my hoodie. I shivered at the feel of the cold metal.

"You never told us you were having problems—" started Paisley, but the guys letting out loud whoops and hollers drew all of our attention. A car had pulled up in front of Paisley's, and Devam stepped out of the driver's seat, sweeping his shaggy, black hair off his forehead before slapping hands with each member of the team, a move that led to a ritualized mutual exchange of pats on the back.

He *seemed* normal, but...

Around the other side of the car came Journey Slowe, a gigantic grin on her face, and behind her... Ember.

My hand went ice cold as I found my feet taking me back a step. Ember slid her arms around Dean and Dean leaned down to press his lips to hers.

"Guess Devam is over his food poisoning," said Lyric and I noticed her watching me carefully, so I quickly looked away. But it was too late. "Do you have some sort of problem with your stepsister?" she asked. "That would better explain why you felt the need to change *schools*..."

"No," I lied, finding myself swallowing down the word.

"Fine, keep your secrets," spat Lyric. "Not like we're not your best friends or anything." Her shoulders stiffened. "You know, I just might have had enough from unreasonable people today—"

I grabbed her by the wrist before she could leave. "Please. It's just... It's really personal, okay? Don't make a big deal of it. Just steer clear of Ember and Dean if you can, okay?"

Lyric and Paisley exchanged a quizzical look and then Lyric yanked her arm away, grabbing her purse off the porch and tossing her hair once again. "If you say so." Her lips went thin. "But I'm still going home. Long day." She cleared her throat. "So I guess I'll see you... sometime." She turned to Paisley and brightened a little. "See you *at school*."

"See ya," said Paisley, bouncing on her toes as Lyric went to her car. She had to ask the guys to back up and she gave Devam and Journey a little wave before getting into her vehicle and driving off unscathed, unbothered by any of the vampires moving house next door.

Ember's eyes met mine as she ran a finger down the front of Dean's tie. She looked like a genuine old-timey mobster moll. All she was missing was the vintage clothing. Instead, she had on a pair of skinny jeans and a baggy red sweater.

Drawing in a slow, steady breath, I picked up my feet and walked across the lawn to face my enemies head-on.

My phone buzzed from my tote bag as I hit the halfway mark and I realized at the sharp strike of pain in my jaw that I was grinding my teeth.

The thoughts *That better be Calder* and *That better not be Calder* both flew through my head. If it weren't for the paranormal stuff coloring our every move, he'd be out the door as a boyfriend, just sprinting and leaving me all alone in my time of need like that.

If he'd insisted on running—which I didn't agree with—he should have taken me with him from the start. And not left when I wouldn't go.

"Ivy," said Ember sweetly as I approached. Her dark red lips went wide, but there was no sign of the fangs I half-expected to find. Then again, I didn't always have the mermaid tail, either.

Ignoring her, I squeezed in between Ashton and Charlie to get a good look at Devam just as Paisley stepped into the circle and found her place back at Grey's side. Devam had his arm around

Journey, and both of them looked dazzling—yet *ill* somehow. Their overt happiness reeked of being pasted on over their former selves.

"Are you feeling okay?" I asked, stopping Devam mid-sentence in some inconsequential back and forth with Charlie about which baseball team should have won the World Series.

"Yeah. Much better. No more raw cuts of meat for me." Devam chuckled, his lips widening into a pearly-white smile that somehow sent shivers down my spine. "Just needed to rest it off—shouldn't I be asking *you* that?" He exchanged a look with Journey, who turned to Dean and Ember as they shimmied their way into the impromptu friend circle. I wished I had my tail so I could flick them right out of it.

"I was fine. It was Ember who..." I felt suddenly hot, despite the crisp cold in the air. Ember twirled a lock of her hair around one red-tipped finger, her gaze locked over my head.

"To say Homecoming was a disaster all around would be an understatement." Journey leaned her head against Devam's shoulder. "Who knew I'd be getting off light with food poisoning?" There was a murky, pallid tone to her brown skin, and I just didn't like that whatever had happened when she'd gone with Devam to the vampire stronghold, she had walked out in this sickening, strange state of bliss.

If I ever was surrounded by a family of bloodsuckers, I certainly wouldn't be making jokes about consuming raw meat.

Unless I was totally cool with vampires, I supposed...

Another crash from the neighbors' driveway had me gasping, and it certainly didn't help that my phone had gone from buzzing to full-out ringing just then. Only my parents actually *called* me, but thanks to Orin's help, I didn't think either would be particularly worried about me right now.

"Hey, did you know Sheppard is transferring to Central?" asked Ashton, nudging me with his shoulder as he faced Devam. Everyone laughed as I practically jumped out of my skin, turning toward the source of the touch with my fists up and my legs spread wide, like I was some boxer.

"Down, tiger," said Ashton, running a hand over the back of his close-cropped hair. But he did take a step back.

"You're leaving Union?" asked Ember, unfazed by me going all pseudo martial artist on my friend. Clearing my throat, I adjusted my tote bag's straps up my arm and stood straight, thrusting my arms tightly across my chest. "Yup."

"How did our parents take that?" *Our*, she'd said. Like we were normal step-sisters, nothing more to see here.

Shrugging, I bit down on my lip. Hard.

"Hey!" called Paisley, bringing me back to the moment. She was focused on the street, where three boys about eleven or twelve were tossing a football between them. "Alan, what did Mom tell you? *Stay out of the street!*" Her little brother was one of them.

"No one's coming!" the dark-haired boy with dirt on his jeans and an uneven hoodie drawstring dangling over his chest screamed back. He ran backward, practically tumbling over his untied sneaker lace, and caught a spinning pass, screaming and stomping his feet in delight.

"Your phone's ringing," said Ashton beside me, pointing to my tote bag. So it was. Again. Ashton's pasted-on smile as he took another awkward step back told me he was pretty sure if he got too close, I'd try some self-defense moves on him. Considering the tension in the air, he wasn't wrong.

"Thanks," I grumbled, digging through the bag, trying to somehow feel for it amidst my things while keeping my eyes on the vampire in front of me.

It was Calder, and I had a number of missed calls. I dismissed the notifications to see his earlier texts pop up instead.

Get out of there. We're not ready.

Well, gee, thanks, I thought, no time to text him back. *Maybe if you'd grabbed me before bolting out of here...*

"Alan, do you want me to tell Mom and Dad?" Paisley's voice was loud now, commanding, as she broke away from her boyfriend and strode out toward the sidewalk and the street. Alan was surrounded by his two other friends now, who were jumping in place in the middle of the cracked and fading pavement.

Paisley thought to check left and right as she stood on the curb, bending her legs and practically ready to reach out and snatch the kid. She took on a tougher persona wherever he was concerned, even though the little beanpole was well on his way to towering over her.

Alan thought it a game, running out of her reach and sticking to the street, laughing and clutching the ball under his arm.

"Stop being a brat!" shouted Paisley, and the guys around me *oohed* and laughed, like they were enjoying this little kid being a royal pain.

My phone rang again—Calder, no surprise—and I answered it, staring as Alan pointed for his friends to go long and they vanished from view around the side of the fence.

"*What?*" I snapped.

"Finally!" said Calder on the other side of the line. "Tell me you've gotten out of there."

"*No*," I said, my eyes snapping back to Dean. He merely inclined his head toward me, a knowing smirk on his lips, like he could hear my entire conversation. Maybe supersonic hearing ranked among the vampire powers I didn't know about. Or maybe he just had the keen insight of putting running-boyfriend plus we're-at-war together.

"I went to get help," said Calder, and my roiling surge of anger calmed down just a notch. So he wasn't just running off with his tail between his legs, to hide again like usual?

"You left," I said quietly, both words a struggle to get out with so many people nearby. Even if most were distracted by Paisley screeching at her brother to get his butt out of the road.

"I'm sorry," said Calder. "I just..."

But I didn't get to hear what he "just" because a car's brakes squealed, causing a sedan to jackknife. The laughter died as shouts resounded and most of the group went running to the road. I clutched the phone at my side and chased after them.

There was silence for a moment, the thundering of my heart drowning out even the sounds of rustling leaves in the breeze.

Then there was a high-pitched little laugh.

The driver rolled down his window and leaned his head out, the spittle practically flying from his lips. "Watch it, you little punk!"

Alan was fine. On his butt on the ground just a few feet in front of the car and laughing.

"It's not funny," snapped Paisley. "I'm going to kill you!" Her face reddened as I swore a vein started to throb at her temple. She rushed out into the street and lunged for her brother, but he jumped up and staggered back, clearly at ease and not caring that he'd just escaped death and was continuing to escape the threat of it from his enraged older sister.

"Go long!" he shouted over her head and the heads of the guys who'd jumped out into the street to join her. He sent the football spinning over the car, causing the driver to curse, and into the neighbors' yard, where some more chuckling echoed, and I remembered his friends had disappeared somewhere in that direction.

"Ivy, what's going on?" The faint voice from my phone broke through the chaos for a moment.

"You little—" But whatever else Paisley had to say died as the boy had already run up across the other curb, darting behind the car that had almost killed him and joining his friends in the neighbors' yard, his sister on his tail and most of the guys following behind her. Grey stopped briefly in front of the driver and exchanged a few words with him, his hands clasped together in apology. The driver shook his head and then rolled up the window, driving off once the road was clear of preteens and teenagers.

"Ivy?" said Calder from my phone again.

I spun around to look for Dean and Ember or Devam and Journey, but they'd vanished, leaving me completely alone in Paisley's yard.

"Get over here," I said into the phone. "Help or no help, it's time you stepped up, Calder."

I hit *end* before he could do more than voice a syllable of his reply, slipping the phone into my bag.

"*Alan!*" screeched Paisley from somewhere over the fence.

Something snapped and crackled in the air—like fireworks going off—and there was a loud boom that shook me to my bones, causing me to stumble in place.

"Alan!" shrieked Paisley, all traces of anger gone from her voice, replaced by sheer, cold terror.

Alone or not, I had to do this. I threw my tote bag on the ground and bolted, running headfirst into the lion's den.

CHAPTER SEVEN

There was a virtual circus in the neighbors' front yard, boxes and teenagers and besuited sunglasses-clad vampire movers all sprinkled throughout the grass, all staring up at the smoke rising from the side of the house. Dean and Ember weren't among the group, and Devam and Journey both lingered over by the open moving truck in the driveway, whispering in hushed voices to one another, their faces grave.

"Get that fire out before an eager beaver calls the fuzz!" shouted one of the vintage-style vampires, a gruff, unhealthily pale Latino man. The other guys leapt into action and ran to the moving truck, where Devam already seemed to be anticipating them, pulling a fire extinguisher out of the back and tossing it at the nearest vampire in a smooth, fluid motion.

I ground my feet into the grass, narrowing my eyes at the one who had spoken. They didn't want the cops around, did they?

Charlie had his phone out in front of him.

"Wait," I said, putting a hand on his wrist.

I didn't know why at first. And then I did. The other vampire —with smooth, golden hair and a chiseled jaw—ran past with the extinguisher and my muscles quivered, my toes curling in a way that seemed to scream I needed to rip him down into the nearest body of water and wrap my fins around his face.

End it now, I thought. "Go check to see if the kids jumped over the fence into Paisley's back yard," I told Charlie, purposely directing him out of harm's way. "I thought I saw them go that way." A complete and utter lie.

Laughter pealed from around the side of the house and I picked up my feet to discover what had happened. Mr. Chiseled Jaw sprayed a smoking air conditioning unit with the extinguisher, focusing on a ripped, thick tube of some kind with wires exposed —black soot on the unit quickly covered by the white of the foam. Alan and his friends were on the ground a few feet away, staring at the machine. They'd probably tumbled against it, tearing the wiring or messing with some of the volatile gases.

But they were all alive. And not crying or anything. Paisley hovered over her brother, grabbing him by the arm. "You're in *so much trouble*, you don't even know! Mom and Dad aren't going to let you out of the house for forty years, you utter—"

Alan ripped his arm away and stumbled to his feet along with his friends, the three of them laughing so hard, they had to clutch their sides as they barreled past the vampire mover continuing to spray the unit, then up around the moving boxes—and through the open front door of the vacant house.

"You. Are. Dead!" screamed Paisley, flicking her fists at Grey's chest as he tried to grab hold of her to soothe her.

Chiseled Jaw with the Fire Extinguisher exchanged a look with the guy who had worried about someone calling the cops and even if I couldn't see their eyes behind those cursed dark sunglasses, something cold flushed through me, replacing my anger with terror. Fight or flight. For a brief second, I empathized with Calder, whose instincts clearly always chose the latter.

But the cold was focusing on my hand and I needed to see this through.

A tangible sense of relief had seemed to lead Grey to leave the yard, joining his friends on the other side, but I knew the truth. The danger Paisley's little brother was in could just be beginning. I aimed to follow Paisley up the porch steps and into the house, screeching to a halt as another of the besuited movers stood in front of me.

It wasn't Dean, but this guy also seemed to have the vampire's knack for moving from one place to another out of nowhere.

"What's buzzin', cousin?" he said, his thin, dark lips peeling back on one side to reveal the slight tip of a fang. "Remember me?"

I assumed that meant he'd been present for the Homecoming pool disaster, but I couldn't be sure. With the sunglasses on, they were all just interchangeable, out-of-touch bloodsucking jerkwads, as far as I was concerned. I checked over my shoulder. My friends weren't there. I'd have to assume they'd headed back next door. Fat lot of help they were to poor Paisley—though to be fair, I was the one who'd redirected Charlie—but I was glad for it, considering the vampires every which way.

"Remember this?" I said, winding up my glowing hand and commanding the ice to lash out just as my fist met his solid abdomen. His thick muscles cracked the coating of ice, but the blow still made him jump back, his mouth curled open in a silent 'o' as the tiniest bit of steam started sizzling from his belly.

I was glad they felt pain of some sort, even if they were all dead.

He left just enough room for me to slip past and up the porch stairs.

Inside, I paused a moment, looking to my left and to my right. Empty rooms, cluttered by the occasional remaining box or piece of garbage. A missing light fixture in the living room, with wires dangling dangerously overhead. A scuff mark on the dining room floor, the outline of a giant area rug around it where pale wood met grime.

The distant peals of giggles, followed by Paisley's muffled indiscernible cries, led me to realize they were all upstairs somewhere. The sounds echoed unnaturally in the hollowed-out house.

I bolted for the stairs, shouts from the outdoors reminding me of my limited time here.

The upstairs hallway was dark, the air thick and heavy in my lungs as I clutched the bannister safeguarding part of the hallway from the floor below. Out of the corner of my eye, there was a flash of red downstairs along the staircase. But when I turned to look harder, there was nothing below.

To my side, there was a hard, desperate knock on a door.

"Open this door *right now*," called Paisley. "Right. Now."

I hurried through the darkness, feeling my way until my eyes adjusted better to the form standing outside a bedroom door. She knocked and knocked again, and giggling was her only reply.

"I can *hear* you!" said Paisley.

I flexed my fingers and felt the cold go, only realizing as it faded that I'd been walking to the light of the faint blue glow. "We need to get out of here," I hissed under my breath, alert as I realized how cornered we were.

I was banking on the vampires not wanting all these witnesses. On the fact that their bloodlust wouldn't overpower them at the thought of a giant mermaid-champion's-friends buffet.

"Yeah, I know," snapped Paisley, probably thinking about the fact that we were trespassing and her brother had just caused some property damage outside. She pounded her fist again. "If you don't let me in right now, I'm going to call Dad and have him leave work to come get you and you'll *wish* you had listened to me!"

A crack rang out from my left and I jumped, my fist at the ready, the blue starting to creep onto my fingers once more. I ran for the sound, into an open room beside the one the boys had trapped themselves in. I held my fist above me, using the faint light to look around, trying to get it dampened just in case I was overreacting and there was still a chance of keeping Paisley and her brother and everyone else out of this. The room was empty, the thin carpet cold beneath my feet. A sliding closet door revealed nothing more than a few hangers and a forgotten or abandoned coat. But there could have been something behind the door covering the other half. I took a step closer.

Another crack sounded to my right, this time followed by a thump and more laughter.

One of the bedroom windows had been shifted open a bit.

I ran for it, my icy hand and my normal one grabbing for the window and flinging it all the way up, peering my head to see the three boys climbing down a tree near the window of the room next to mine.

I sidestepped back toward the hallway, my gaze not leaving the boys as the last one jumped down to the ground.

"They climbed a tree and went outside!" I shouted to Paisley. *Thank goodness.* Fewer chances of being bitten by a vampire out there with the crowd and the neighborhood watch.

"Argh!" came Paisley's reply from down the hall. "I am seriously, *seriously* telling Mom I'm never watching him again. Never. Not even when he's fifty-five!" Her voice turned to muttering as she brushed brusquely past the room, something about "locking bedroom doors" and "blowing up air conditioning" and how their parents were going to flip.

I just realized that did mean the bedroom they'd holed themselves in would now require a locksmith. Or a flexible vampire mover to climb up the tree and through the window to get it unlocked. Hey, they were most likely the ones getting in trouble for all this. Good. I hoped they got sued into oblivion and got tied up in legal battles instead of—

The tinny, echoing screech of tires made me jump, and I flung my arm out, sending a ball of ice right into the wall, where it flattened like a snowball with a hard thunk.

"Blimey," came a far-too-familiar voice. "If that had gone through the wall, I'd be right chilly about now, yeah?"

I thundered over to the window, this time looking the other way, after quickly satisfying myself that the boys were no longer in the vicinity of the tree they'd used to make their escape.

Orin sat atop the roof of the house's adjoining garage, digging into a bag of chips with one hand and holding his phone with the other. An action movie blared on the tiny screen, a car chase responsible for the engine revving and tires squealing in the faint, tinny tone.

"Fancy a crisp?" he asked, lifting his bag up toward me but not peeling his eyes from the screen for a second. The Rock shifted the gears on a car, so it was probably one of the *Fast & Furious* movies.

"What in the world are you doing here?" I demanded to know.

"Observing," he said, lowering his chip bag and munching, clearly observing nothing but his tiny movie screen.

"*How* did you get here?" I asked. We'd left him outside my dad's house. Though I supposed that had been a while ago now.

"Flew," he said, his eyes probing mine and a smirk lighting up his handsome features.

I couldn't tell if he was serious or not.

There was a sliding sound from the door behind me—*the closet*!

"Ivy," said someone quietly.

I turned around to find Ember, her hand on the closet door, her bloodsucking boyfriend stepping out from the darkness behind her.

His blue eyes blazed right at me just before he pulled his sunglasses out of his pocket and slid them back on his face.

CHAPTER EIGHT

They'd cornered me. And I'd walked right into their trap. *Stupid!*

"We just want to talk, doll," said Dean, holding both palms out in front of him. "You've got moxie, walking in here. Alone. Thought you might be reasoned with."

I wanted to wipe that little kind smile off Dean's face.

Ember slid in beside him, bringing her hand up—causing me to spread my legs and ready for her fireball—but she just brought a finger to her mouth and chewed on a hangnail as she stared at me.

I glanced over my shoulder, the sound of Orin's casual crunching distracting. "Sorry?" he said. "I'll turn it down." He fiddled with the volume on his phone and then kept staring at it. Rolling my eyes, I turned back to face my step-sister and her suave and smarmy vampire prince.

"We're well beyond reasoning, I'd say." I jutted my chin out toward them. "Your grandpa of a boyfriend and his friends attacked first at Homecoming."

A knowing grin spread on his face. "You sure about that?"

Ugh. "What do you want?" I asked instead of giving credence to this liar's implications.

"Surrender," said Ember, removing the finger from her mouth

57

and smoothing her hand on the front of her sweater. "Say you submit and this is all over."

I hesitated. Calder wasn't exactly winning any points with his frequent disappearing act. And vampires seemed to have the advantage everywhere but in water—and water was something that was hard for me to come by if I wasn't prepared.

I opened my mouth, not even sure yet what I was going to say.

The screech of yet another tire—loud and piercing—made me whip around to face Orin instead. "I thought you turned that down!" But my attention was quickly diverted to the street far beyond the garage—Calder's truck was back and out poured Bay and another guy and girl—then even Laguna, the wisp of a girl, looking like she was itching for a fight.

"You're in trouble now," I said, whipping back to face Ember and Dean.

But they weren't there anymore.

"What is it about 'only the champions need fight' that has all these scaly and undead monsters so confuddled?" lamented Orin. He groaned exaggeratedly, a tragic hero in a Shakespeare play. "Guess I've got some closer observing to do." He slipped his phone in his pocket and stood on the roof without missing a beat, making a big show of bending over to grab his empty chip bag.

But I didn't have time to stand there all day watching him.

Sprinting for the door, I kept my icy fist held high, praying none of my friends would pop around the fence to see what the fuss was about. We just needed to keep it quiet, and we might not get too many nosy onlookers.

A thunderous crash—like the shutting of a moving truck door —sounded from outdoors. Maybe the moving could provide some cover for the fight.

I raced for the staircase, overshooting it and stumbling a bit as I grabbed for the handrail. Cold skin snatched my wrist before I successfully took hold of the rail, spinning me around. The besuited vampire who'd blocked my way into the house stood there, his dead skin unnaturally clammy against mine. "Payback, you dead hoofer." His fangs glistened as his mouth widened. "How about just a little snack?"

"Oy." Orin strolled down the hallway. "Your champion deals the finishing blow or it don't count, yeah, Mr. Leopold?"

The burly vampire took a step back and wiped his free arm across his lips, still not letting me go. "Wasn't going to finish 'er off, though, was I?"

Like I'd take his word for it. I focused, using the bloodsucker's cold skin as inspiration to bring the coldness rushing forth to that hand.

He shrieked and let go, and I wound back, sending another ice ball right at his abdomen. "Things are getting icy-dicey now, bloodsucker!" His back cracked against the wall and he slumped downward. I turned to go but thought better of it and whirled around to spit on him for good measure. "Never learn, do you?"

Orin seemed to be stifling a laugh. I tossed my hair over my shoulder with my icy hand and didn't even flinch when the snowy wetness coated the dark lock. "Thank you," I said, though I ground my teeth soon afterward.

"Welcome," he said, unable to keep the snicker from his voice. "Nice action hero quip, by the way." He snorted into his shoulder.

I'd never understand this guy.

Rushing down the stairs, I glanced around to find the source of all the voices. They seemed to be coming from everywhere— outside, to the right of me, behind me. I zeroed in on the most recognizable.

"I don't want to hurt you, Ember." Calder. In the kitchen.

An idea struck me just then and I fled through the dining room, bypassing little Laguna strangely holding her own against a vintage vampire who towered over her. He lunged for her and she dodged, grabbing hold of his arm and flipping him over her back like a pro.

Holy, sweet cow.

But I didn't have time for that and she seemed just fine. She flashed me a smile as I ran past, then I screeched to a halt as my waist bumped into the floating island breakfast bar that housed the kitchen sink. *Ouch.*

Ember stood in front of Calder, flames tickling at her fingers as she held her hand out between them like a normal woman might hold a can of pepper spray threateningly against a potential assailant. Rubbing my forming bruise, I hobbled around the floating island to stand beside Calder. "Took you long enough." I grunted.

"You stopped answering your phone," he hissed back, like I gave a crap about that just then.

"I didn't expect you to actually show." I sent him my best glowering, withering look. I ignored the twitch in his jaw muscles as I stepped between Ember and him, my own icy fist held out. "Are we doing this again?" I asked her. A movement from the open sliding door behind Ember caught my eye—Bay went soaring through the air and landed somewhere I couldn't see with a thud. I winced as Dean stepped inside, dusting his palms off.

So this was it. Prince versus prince and champion against champion once more. I could end it here right now. Not kill Ember, but maybe make her hurt so much, she gave up.

Nausea hit the back of my throat. I didn't want to hurt Ember. So I'd wait for her to strike first—to make it self-defense.

She stared at me, the sizzle of the flames in her palms and the hiss of crackling ice the only sound between us.

"How did you know I'd be at Paisley's tonight?" I asked.

Dean shrugged. "We didn't know. We just had a moving job."

"A likely story," I said, shifting my icy palm slightly toward him instead of Ember and finding Ember sliding her body in front of him. To protect this undead old man. How could she not see that the vampires had had their chance at life—that they added nothing to the world by being here?

At least the merfolk were on their first and only chances at lifetimes. Didn't they deserve that?

"It's true," said Ember. "Though I did get a text to come join him—I asked Devam and Journey to take me."

"A text from whom?" I sneered.

"Me, naturally. 'Allo, Deanie boy. Nice to see you less water-logged again." Orin jutted his chin at the vampire from the open entryway. With a mighty scream, Laguna slid backward on her feet down the hall behind him, crouched like a cat about to jump on its prey, her jaw clenched as she growled and seemed determined to dig trenches into the hardwood floor rather than topple from whatever vampire move had sent her skidding.

I liked this girl.

I was going to ignore that treacherous faery creature in the entryway. "Why do vampires even need to run a moving business? Surely, you've amassed enough wealth. And it's not like you need to buy groceries or anything."

Dean shrugged. "Keeps us out in the community, getting a feel for the lay of the land."

"And it helps you recruit more bloodbags, too, I imagine," spat Calder behind me. He leaned closer to me, whispering so only I could hear. "We need to retreat."

"Why?" I hissed. "I've got this."

"Do you?" he asked, louder this time.

I stared into Ember's eyes. My arm was starting to get sore from being held out so long. I wondered if the same was true of her.

When was she going to make the first move?

"We're not ready," whispered Calder, and I almost turned around and clobbered *him* with the ice ball.

"*Fine,*" I sneered, not eager to wait all day for Ember to strike first so I could feel less guilty about going at it.

I shot my ice out in a perpetual stream this time, the sweat pouring off my brow practically freezing into little icicles on my skin as I focused on the *cold, cold, cold*.

Ember flinched and her fire went flying, but I'd changed my arm's aim at the last second and I wasn't aiming for her. The stream of ice hit the faucet handle on the kitchen sink in the island, flicking it up all the way and turning on the water.

Calder screamed as he dodged and I saw his new Central letter jacket smoking, his flesh exposed at the shoulder. But I didn't have time to wait. I dropped the ice from my hand and grabbed the sprayer hose, aiming it right at Dean, pulling the trigger to send a torrent of rain-like water right at him.

He shrieked and started steaming, but I kept up the water pressure.

Ember shouted something and flung another fireball at me, but I turned the water at her and the flames melted into mist as they headed my way.

"It's wet 'n wild time now, sister!" I screamed.

I ignored the snickering coming from Orin in the entryway.

Calder had to tug on my arm and drag me away, scooping me up in his arms princess-style, which caused me to drop the hose. We bolted out the open sliding door the moment the water spray stopped—not giving our enemies a second to muster their strength to follow us.

CHAPTER NINE

The adrenaline from the fight and the odd sensation of being in Calder's thick, sturdy arms made me go numb the moment we darted around the foam-covered air conditioning unit and to the front of the house. My mind searched wildly for some kind of explanation, but I found none of my normal friends out on the front lawn, waiting—the sound of one of the guys' chuckles echoing in the air from the other side of the fence.

So none had been drawn over here by the sounds of battle.

Only Paisley probably would have noticed my absence normally, but she'd been too preoccupied with her death-defying little brother.

"Pull back!" Calder shouted to Bay, who had moved to the front lawn and was winding his arm back for a punch. He dropped the move immediately, dodging one of the vampire's own blows—the vampire had actually removed his suit coat, his milky-white arms practically as blinding as the sun—and appeared alongside us.

Bay got the passenger's side door of Calder's truck open and my merman protector deposited me in the seat as Laguna burst forth from the house and the other guy and girl I hadn't recognized earlier met up at the bed of the truck, jumping in as Bay shut my door. He joined them in the back as Calder made his way to the driver's seat and we were off.

We drove silently for a bit, Calder adjusting his rearview mirror and continually staring at it, his Adam's apple bobbing each time.

It was only when I looked in my own side mirror just as we turned the corner that I saw not all of my friends were gathered back in Paisley's yard—Devam and Journey were still at the front of the moving truck in that house's driveway.

They leaned against the hood and stared down the road at us, the slightly sickly hue of their skin apparent even from such a distance.

"What were you thinking?" asked Calder as the house vanished entirely from view.

"I could ask *you* the same thing," I pointed out. "You've got to get over bolting at the first whiff of blood." Pun fully intended. "How's your shoulder?" It didn't look like the skin was burnt too badly, but it was definitely red.

Calder batted my outstretched hand away. "Fine." His lips worked, but nothing comprehensible came out for a bit. "We need a *plan*," he sputtered out at last.

"You're telling me," I said. "But just because you have a *plan* doesn't mean you won't be attacked when you least expect it. Your *plan* needs to include an idea of what to do when things don't go according to plan." I turned around to look out the back window of the truck, at the four other teens hanging out in the truck bed, their arms clutched to the edges. "If you pass a cop, you'll probably get pulled over," I pointed out.

"They'll duck," he said with the confidence of a captain regarding his soldiers.

"So... Who are they?" The two I'd met before aside.

"Introductions later," he said. Then he went quiet, his glassy stare wholly focused on the road.

Well, I wasn't really in the mood to deal with him, either.

He'd been wrong. I'd been right. And frankly, if I'd have known the merfolk had an arsenal of kick-butt teens at their disposal, I would have called for backup earlier.

It wasn't my fault Calder had made it seem like they were all weaklings in need of protection.

After a few minutes more, I finally recognized where we were headed. "I'm not going to Dad's," I said. "Not for a while, remember? Not until this is over."

"I'm taking you to my place," was all Calder said. His tone didn't seem to allow for argument.

Fine. About time the merfolk pitched in and we figured this whole thing out.

We passed Dad's house and I stared pointedly inside, the TV room window's curtain open and Autumn on the couch beside Dad. Noelle walked in the room just as we went by, passing each of them a plate.

Something sharp coiled in my gut at the idea of missing all that for the next few days—weeks—months. Would this mess I'd gotten myself into ever end?

Why me? Why had Dad even gotten married to Noelle, moved us into that house?

It took a few more minutes of silence before I became aware that we weren't just skirting the woods that ran behind Dad's place, that the edges of the trees were cloaking a private driveway I'd never really taken notice of before. The gravel beneath the tires crunched as the merfolk in the bed started bouncing, a clunk every few seconds from their movements as we made our way between trees overhead and down, down the winding road.

At last it came into view, a veritable mini-mansion surrounded on three sides by trees, trees, and more trees—the backside of the house nestled a short distance from the river. As we pulled into a four-car attached garage, I looked out and noticed that the river continued in a trench about six feet wide all around the front of the mansion, the driveway leading to the garage and a parking area the only part of the property not cocooned in the water's embrace. Something sparkled in the dying evening light off the roof and I realized it was outfitted with solar panels—so wide and big and endless, they practically replaced the roof entirely.

There were three other cars in the garage—none flashy, despite the house's appearance, which explained why Calder's rust bucket looked more at home in a junkyard—and there was at least a dozen more cars in the parking area that could have rivaled a small strip mall's.

What did Calder's family need with so many vehicles?

He switched off the ignition and the inaudible murmuring of the merfolk behind us became louder, a couple of chuckles ringing out loudly as the truck bed's tailgate clanked open and one person after the other jumped out.

Calder didn't move. He just stared down at his steering wheel.

"I'm sorry," he said after a minute. The dampened laughter behind us seemed almost a mockery of the ghost-white color that popped against his tanned knuckles as he clutched the steering wheel.

"Okay. Thanks," I mumbled.

"And...?" he said, not looking up.

"And what?" I muttered, wishing he would drop this already.

"Don't you have something to say too?"

"Like what?"

He mumbled something that might have been a curse under his breath and let out a sharp breath in a huff.

"What was that?" I asked, with all the menace of a mother whose kid had just told her to shut up.

Calder slammed his fists against the steering wheel. "You put yourself in danger like that! And I had to put my people in danger to come *rescue* you!"

"Excuse me?" I searched down by my feet, intent on providing evidence of his own treachery, and realized I'd left my tote with my phone in it back on Paisley's lawn. *Crap.* I settled for clutching the armrest so tight, I was working its bumpy texture into my skin. "Who was it who just *ran* without me? Oh, but you sent me texts to get out of there. *So* helpful. Maybe if I started jogging down the street, no vampire would catch up to me—oh, wait, they can cross short distances in a matter of seconds. Guess I'd be screwed."

"I *said* I was sorry!"

"Yeah, and I was going to forgive you—can't expect my merman *prince* to be any help in a fight—but you turn around and blame this on me? No way, buster." I opened the door and jumped out, not in the mood for any of this. I didn't *have* to be here. Excuse me if my eagerness to put an end to this battle sooner rather than later interfered with his cowardly *plans* to take it slow, slow, slow.

The sound of Calder's door slamming shut told me he wasn't done having this conversation, but I didn't care. I lingered near the group of young merfolks, who had gathered in a circle in front of the modern-day moat. Bay had his arm dangling casually around the other guy in the group, a bulky redhead who stood tall, his own arms crossed over his chest. I realized with a start that he looked a lot like the diminutive redhead girl next to him—Laguna's brother? The other girl along—her smooth, pale brown skin; long, black hair; and dark brown eyes reminded me a lot of Bay. Perhaps this was a brother-sister combo team.

"Hey," I said as the conversation went quiet at my approach. "Thanks for helping back there."

Bay grinned, showing off his pearly white teeth. "You've got guts."

"Thanks," I said again, my voice wavering, my knees a little wobbly under his too-bright smile. Dang, now I knew why he'd had this kind of effect even on practically-married Paisley.

Calder slipped in beside me, his brow furrowed as he glared down at me, the rest of whatever he had to say swallowed down visibly before he turned to the group. "Ivy, you know Bay and Laguna. This is Laguna's brother, Llyr, and Bay's cousin, Cascade."

Brother-sister-cousin combo. Close enough.

"Hi," I said again. My eyes fluttered over Llyr's Central High letter jacket and a Central High 'C' that dangled from a keychain off of Cascade's phone. "You're all at Central?"

Cascade nodded, sliding her phone into the back pocket of her jeans. "Calder would have always been, too, but Queen Nerida thought it best he attend the school that other champion was going to. In case the opportunity arose for him to pick her as a champion."

I sent Calder the stink eye. So he'd been trying to cozy up to Ember for years before I'd even been in play? *How?* I certainly didn't pick up on her remotely knowing who he was before all of this. A chicken in battle and a chicken when it came to girls, apparently.

None of this was making me feel very special to him.

He better do something miraculous if he ever wants to make this up to me.

From the wince on Calder's face, I wondered if I was sending my thoughts loud and clear. I double-checked to make sure that no part of his skin had come into contact with me.

Good. So he wasn't reading my mind for real.

"That's all in the past," said Calder before clearing his throat. "And now we're all going to be at Central High."

The last light of the day was fading over the tops of the trees, and I jumped, my fists ready, at the loud clashes as one insanely bright light after another went on around the property. I tried to look up to get a look at the tall lampposts, but they were blinding.

"*Cripes,*" I said, squinting and blocking my eyes with my arm. "What's that? The actual sun in a bottle?"

"Close," said Calder, and I felt a hand on the small of my back. "UV ray lights. They go on at sunset."

"Oh, *that's* skin cancer waiting to happen." I shook my head. No wonder most of these guys were so tan. I peeked out from below my arm to take in Laguna and Llyr—the pale redheads must have lived on sunscreen—but they were gone.

I dropped my arm to find the others milling about before the moat and removing their clothes.

"Wait, what?" I said, trying not to stare, but dropping my arm, my discomfort forgotten entirely.

Calder started removing his letter jacket. "Do you want to go in through the garage or in the basement? The basement is filled with water."

"Whaa...?" I shouldn't have been surprised, but I kind of was. "What about the front door?"

He pointed to it and I blinked, my eyes somehow getting used to this unholy brightness. "Can you jump six feet across to get there?"

"No?" I said, searching wildly for some way to get around the moat. A splash echoed out beside me and I saw Cascade was missing. Then there was another splash as Laguna dove in. They both bobbed their heads out of the moat for a moment, their wide eyes and bright smiles bringing such life to their faces.

Llyr was bending over, picking up shed clothing, and I realized that included pants as well as sweaters, underwear, and bras.

Somehow my eyes hadn't caught sight of the stark-naked Bay beside him. I barely had time to dart my eyes away, only to watch him grab Llyr's cheeks and press his lips to the pale redhead's quickly, that "see you soon, babe" type of kiss, before he jumped in beside the girls. *Oh.*

Grinning, Llyr picked up his clothing, too, and then the two mermaids and one merman swam past us, Cascade waving at us and Laguna sticking her tail out to wriggle her fins. They shot by faster than dolphins as they submerged themselves under what I realized was something like a short glass walkway running from the garage to the rest of the house.

"The garage way," I said, though I was simultaneously enthralled at the idea of swimming into a house and wholly terrified by it. I spun around to find Calder, shirtless, his hands on his jeans' zipper.

"*Seriously?*" I said. My hand shot out to grasp his arm—the thought *What is he thinking?* forefront in my mind—and then the world around us fell away.

The water, its comforting embrace, its cool touch somehow warm against my skin, igniting my core. I felt at home here. This would make things better. This would make it all go away.

I looked down and saw my hands were tanned, my arms muscular, my chest exposed. I was Calder. This is what I—he—was thinking.

Gasping, I dropped his arm and fell back into the moment. I almost forgot I could use mermaid ESP.

Calder smirked, maybe guessing what had happened, guessing what I'd seen. He stepped back and removed his shoes and socks, then he started kicking off his pants, and I had to turn around.

"See her in safely?" asked Calder, and I realized he wasn't talking to me.

With a splash, he dove into the moat, and I felt safe to turn around again, catching sight of the way his whole body seemed to glow as he slipped by.

"Sorry to ask the champion this, but do you mind grabbing the prince's things?"

I whipped around, almost forgetting Llyr was there. His arms were stuffed to the brim with the others' clothes.

"Oh, yeah, sure," I said, scrambling to pick up the haphazard pile of clothing Calder had left behind. "This doesn't seem to be a very convenient way of doing things," I pointed out, falling into place behind Llyr as he led me back into the garage. My eyes kept watering and blinking as they tried adjusting to the dimmer, normal light inside the garage.

"Yeah," said Llyr, putting a palm against an electronic pad beside the door. "Some of us just keep a change of clothes in the cars, but then we can't bring our phones." He nudged a phone atop the pile with his nose as the door swung inward widely. "Water-proof cases help, but tails don't really have pockets."

He stepped inside and I went to follow, but I gasped the moment my foot touched down inside the short, glass walkway.

Below my feet were endless depths of water, some brown fish swimming past like a dull and lifeless aquarium display. But more alarmingly was the fact that my foot had just been submerged ankle-deep in cold, cold water.

CHAPTER TEN

"I think you have a leak," I said, my silver-studded footwear not exactly suited for this kind of submersion, even if they were—technically—boots.

"Oh, sorry about that." Llyr looked over his shoulder and stood there, totally unperturbed by the water covering his feet as he carried laundry down a spooky aquatic glass tunnel, like that was the most normal thing in the world. The light from the UV lamps outside brightened the glass considerably, warping it like some kind of aquarium funhouse. "Should have warned you. I'm so used to it." He lifted one of his feet up, the droplets pattering one after another back into the sheen of water below. He had a pair of those mesh aquatic shoes on. *Cheater*.

"Let me guess," I said, taking one exaggerated step after another, cringing as the water splashed up the calves of my pants, "a deterrent against vampires?"

"That, and we just like the feel of water." He reached the other side of the walkway and waited for me to catch up before placing his palm on another security sensor to get the door to unlock. *Sheesh*.

"I take it Calder can't have a lot of human friends swing by." My boots echoed with a clang below me. At the end of the glass walkway right before the second door was a metal panel. I stomped on it, the sound muted beneath the water, but nothing happened.

"None of us do," he said. "But that doesn't really matter. We can hang with friends at school—and besides, family is all that really matters."

That's a little creepy. "Wait. 'None of you'?" I lifted one foot and then the other onto a welcoming mat awaiting us on the other side of the door, which was blessedly dry. My foot tingled at the thought of Calder, and I quickly focused on other things—puppies, onions, feet, feet—to ensure my tail didn't make a surprise appearance.

"Yes, we all live here." Llyr was placing his stack of other people's clothing on a table next to a washing machine, sliding the extra aquatic shoes he carried on the tiled floor beneath the table and then neatly folding the rest before depositing them in baskets. "All the merfolk. Our numbers have greatly diminished in the past few centuries, but... Living together is more convenient."

Unceremoniously dropping Calder's stack on the table beside Llyr, I kicked off my boots, peeling off my drenched socks as I took in the place. The entryway with two washing machines and two dryers was long and fairly cramped, but the light—a much more welcoming, softer light than the ones blaring out there—at the end of the narrow room drew my attention. I padded over on wet feet, realizing the light was blue and shimmering, like the reflection of an indoor pool lit from down below in a dark room.

That was exactly what I found in the grand entryway of the room, a dual staircase meeting up in a big balcony overlooking a giant indoor pool.

"Who was your contractor for *this?*" I wondered aloud.

An echoing call of "whoo!" drew my attention, followed by a splash. Calder popped his head out of the pool, followed by Bay and Cascade. Laguna was already floating languidly on her back, her eyes closed and her hands clasped over her abdomen—her breasts bare but just barely covered with her frizzy, red hair.

Add that to the strip tease outside and it was clear this *family* was *very* comfortable around one another.

"Queen Nerida's grandfather had it built." Llyr made me jump, sneaking up behind me like that. "And it was mostly done by family. Many of our parents are contractors by trade."

Mermen and mermaid construction workers. Vampire movers. Sure, sure.

"And that goes to the basement?" I pointed at the pool where a grand, empty space ought to have been. I leaned backward to get a better look at the other side of the nearest staircase and saw it led off to a kitchen that jutted out from the house at a perpendicular angle.

"Yup," answered Llyr. "And so does that door"—he pointed to a nondescript door on one wall—"because we need to be able to access the furnace and the sump pump and all that good stuff, which is blocked off from the pool by a seven-inches-thick glass wall."

"Spoken like the child of a carpenter," I said, at a loss for what else to say.

Cascade swam over to the edge of the pool and clutched the side, a strand of dark, wet hair pasted across her forehead somehow making her even prettier. "Come on in," she cooed, her long eyelashes fluttering. "The water's divine."

My feet were moving before I could even blink.

"Knock it off, cuz." Bay swam up behind her and clonked her unceremoniously on the head. "That's our champion you're messing with."

I stopped cold. That siren call thing again? *Ugh.* What was the point of that? Maybe they could lure the vampires to their watery dooms.

"It wasn't on purpose," she said, rubbing the top of her head and sending Bay a withering glare.

"Oh, good, you're all home!"

Nerida walked out of the kitchen, dressed to the nines in a blouse and dress pants, reminding me somewhat of Noelle. She had on an impeccably blemish-free apron over her outfit, though, and I didn't think Noelle would have bothered with that.

She smiled. "You all look to be in one piece... Did it go well?"

The sound of splashing water behind me made me spin on my heel, forgetting for a second that that way lay a bunch of nude people. Calder was lifting himself off the edge of the pool, the top portion of his merman tail shimmering until the entire thing was out of the water, morphing quickly back into human legs.

I spun back to face Nerida, the sloshing water behind me indicating that more of the group was following suit.

"We didn't win anything," I said since Nerida seemed to be waiting for an answer and no one else was saying anything. But for the pit-pat of bare feet on the floor and the movement of the water, the place had gone awfully quiet, the laughter and murmuring suddenly gone.

"Well, I'd call an unexpected battle you escaped unscathed a win, dear." Nerida stepped forward, her arm outstretched and slipping behind my back like we were old friends. My skin crawled just slightly at the touch as she guided me toward the kitchen. "I know this conflict all comes down to you," she said. Beyond the kitchen was a dining hall with an incredibly long table—and at least two dozen women, men, and little kids sitting down at it, digging into serving bowls of food. Their soft chatter came into focus now that we were closer, ringing out along the rounded ceilings. "But we don't expect you to do everything alone." She guided me past the kitchen and into an empty seat at the foot of the table. The room went silent as all eyes turned to me, someone's spoon halfway to his mouth, another slowly putting her glass back down on the blue tablecloth.

"Hey!" shouted one man abruptly, his arms reaching outward. "*Mija*, did you kick some vampire butt today?"

Cascade slid into the room from behind me, her hair damp, but her clothes back in place. She kissed her father atop the head as she took an empty seat beside him. Laguna and Llyr and then Bay also spoke in quiet tones to people I assumed to be their own parents before taking the few remaining empty seats beside them.

Now that I thought about it, if there were this many merfolk, why on Earth were they sending their teens out to help me? Why not send the whole cavalry, or at least the fittest among those who weren't, technically, still kids? My eyes flitted over the adults of the group. There were no bodybuilders among them or anything, but they seemed capable, some lean, some more filled out. They looked like any old parents.

Actually, that explained quite a lot. My mom and dad would do a lot for their kids, but I couldn't picture them taking on vampires. They wouldn't be physically capable of it.

Calder walked in quietly and took a chair beside mine, Nerida standing behind the last remaining empty one across from him on my other side. "We celebrate the small victories here," she said loudly, her voice carrying across the room. She picked up her glass. The liquid inside was a deep blue, almost like it had been dyed with food coloring to achieve a tropical, crystal color. "After so many years of setbacks and waiting for this moment... I thank the next generation, the ones who will lead our people into a new, better life"—she looked pointedly at Calder then and he shirked under her gaze, his fingers cupping his own glass that had been filled with the bright blue liquid—"for their part in seeing to our plans for the future."

Murmurs throughout the table echoed in the grand space, and some of the adults broke out into a weird burbling call, like some kind of lovebird—or probably more appropriately, a dolphin. Glasses clinked and Nerida looked down at me, her eyes wide, her smile practically pasted on. I lifted up my own bright blue goblet, already poured and waiting for me like they'd been expecting a guest, and clinked it against hers before taking a sip.

It tasted sweet. Like nectar. With such a salty, salty tang. I gagged before I could stop myself.

"Now let's get back to eating," said Nerida, setting her beverage back on the table with a clunk. She pulled out her chair to sit down and started scooping some kind of dark green leafy casserole onto my plate. "Eat up, dear," she said. I picked up a fork and poked at it.

"Kelp," said Calder under his breath.

My eyebrow shot up as I watched him dig into his, his lips pinched. Somehow, kelp and fish—there were several blackened trout on platters, picked at and dug into, leaving behind a morbid collection of bones and flesh—made sense for merfolk, but I'd seen him dig into junk food of the more bovine variety.

"Do you mind if I use your phone?" I asked Calder then after my third or fourth bite of the stuff. I was getting used to it—it actually had a nice, cranberry-like flavor that kicked in during the aftertaste. "I left mine at Paisley's." I sighed. Paisley or one of the guys might notice it, but now that I was going to Central, it would be a bigger pain to get it back.

"Oh, I already called your mother, dear," said Nerida. I stared at her. Since when did she know my mom's number? Or figure out that was who I was going to call—since Orin had brainwashed both Mom and Dad into accepting me living with Mom full-time until all this was over? "I told her you were spending the night here with my niece, Laguna, and her friend, Cascade, two young women eager to show you around at Central on your first day." She intertwined her fingers, her pearly white teeth sparkling as she looked down the table at those gathered around us. I followed her gaze and took note of whom I presumed to be Laguna and Llyr's parents, the tanned bald man with a short, golden beard and the pale redhead with a pixie cut, her freckles even more pronounced than her children's. Glancing back and forth from them to Nerida, I pegged the man for her brother—or Calder's father's.

"I..." I looked to Calder for help, but he was gulping down his drink now, the mesmerizing blue liquid disappearing at an unearthly pace. I snapped back to Nerida. "I didn't know you even knew my mom."

"Well, I made a *point* of getting to know her," she said. She picked her cloth napkin off her lap and dabbed at the corners of her lips with it. "I met her at that store she works at—the whole-sale one?" Her face seemed to blanch. "And I took her out for coffee during her break, introducing myself as her daughter's boyfriend's mother and telling her all the good things she needed to know about Central."

"O... kay," I said, my mind running wild over the amount of time she'd have had to get this done. Orin *had* convinced Mom and

Dad to give Calder a chance, whatever their thoughts about his pantslessness had been. But even so, this didn't feel right. Mom barely had friends, and now Nerida was acting all cozy with her behind my back?

"The kids will take you to Central for your first day tomorrow morning," she said, laying the napkin beside her practically scraped-clean plate. "Then, if you insist on returning to your mother's after that, we can provide a rotating cover of guards to keep an eye on you from the street."

"*If* I insist...?" I set my fork down, the sound louder than I'd intended in the cavernous vastness of the space. The steadily moving current of the river behind the property—visible through the wide glass door at the back of the room—distracted me for a moment, making me lose my train of thought.

"Well, of course. Just look around you." Nerida swept her arms around the table as other members of the table started to get up, stacking plates of those around them—other than the group that had arrived with me, who were filling up on their last servings before those plates disappeared as well. "This place is a veritable vampire-proof fortress," she said, settling back into her chair as casually as if she'd just proclaimed her surroundings the most natural kind of home in the world. "You'll be safe here. Protected. Which reminds me. We'll scan your palm into our security system tonight so you can access the locks." She smiled broadly, threading her fingers together. "The champion of water has a home here."

I played with my fork, sneaking a glance at Calder, but he was digging his own into a piece of fish, entirely focused on the task, ever the doormat for his domineering mother.

"Thanks," I said, clearing my throat. "But I... I have a life to live," I said. Nerida's lips puckered. "And in any case—this conflict is never going to be over if I just run and hide." I nodded, convincing myself as much as her. "We need a plan." My eyes darted over the crowd of merfolk-posing-as-humans. "And I think I have an idea."

CHAPTER ELEVEN

We'd have a "war council" tonight.

After my first day of school. And I insisted I was going home after this time.

After hearing my idea, Nerida had complimented me for my *bravery*, my *leadership*, but had said she needed to discuss it with her fellow merfolk, and besides, it had been a long day and many of them had work tomorrow. She'd gathered her own plate and mine as she'd stood, instructing Calder to finish up his last few bites so she could add his to her stack. Blindsided, I hadn't gotten out more than a few words before she had joined a number of the other merfolk in the kitchen, laughing and holding conversations with them as they went to work rinsing and loading the dishes, a hostess at a house party unconcerned with the bloodsucking vampires hovering near her door.

Calder had nodded at me, mumbling something that *might* have been "sorry" again, and then retreated out the kitchen with Bay and Llyr. Cascade had been talkative enough to plaster over the knowing sense of unease that had me feeling on edge, glancing every which way and expecting to find a pale man in sunglasses. Her dad had done the palm-scan thing for me with a computer and scanner in a little office, which had made me feel like I was part of some high-tech spy thriller. He'd cracked a lot of cheesy jokes all the while about me "lending him a hand," clearly embarrassing Cascade. Afterward, the adults had all hung out in a big living room and the people my age had gone upstairs. The room Cascade shared with Laguna—college-dorm style, though with plenty of space for each to claim a corner—had had room for me on a pull-out couch. I'd stared at Laguna's glow-in-the-dark seashell stickers on the ceiling over my head as I'd lulled off to sleep, the thundering of my heart so loud, I wondered for a while if I'd ever sleep again.

In the morning, I'd showered and borrowed a set of Cascade's clothes. She liked pretty stuff, so apparently I was going to make my first impression at a new school in a puffy blue midriff bearing blouse that exposed one shoulder and a thin sea-blue cardigan that only buttoned halfway up. Central had lax dress code rules, they told me. I finished off the outfit with a pair of wave-patterned light blue leggings under a navy skirt. No more gothic punk for me, not that I'd ever been overly committed to the look. The makeup was too much of a hassle.

So sweet and cheery Ivy Sheppard, Central High student, I'd be. It wasn't like I planned to be at this school for too long anyway.

Bay was still chewing on a third extra English muffin he'd grabbed from the lavish breakfast buffet that had been available to us in the merfolk dining room as we pulled into Central's parking lot. I'd hopped in a navy-blue sedan with Cascade, Bay, and Llyr, leaving poor Laguna to sit beside Calder in his truck.

My hands felt empty without my phone. I felt itchy in someone else's clothes. Lost as I took in our surroundings.

"Have you been here before?" asked Llyr as the last of the car doors shut behind me.

"To Central?" I took a good, long look at the place, the people shuffling inside, the small groups milling about in front of the doors, their breath visible as their mouths moved. Even with rising temperatures by day's end, it was the time of year where the mornings were super cold. "Maybe once or twice for an away game? But over there." I nodded to the state-of-the-art baseball diamond with bleachers and a boarded-up concession stand. The guys were annoyed that Central had gotten the budget for such an upgrade our freshman year.

"I'll show you to the registrar's office," offered Llyr. Calder's pickup pulled in a few spots down and I bounced in place, rubbing my arms as I watched first Calder and then Laguna disembark from the vehicle. Calder adjusted a backpack up his arm and stared pointedly our way, then sent me a nod before heading inside.

Honestly?

Lately, I felt less and less like this prince had my back and more like I'd just been enlisted in a stranger's family drama. With actual combat a part of it.

"Calder has early laps," said Llyr as we made our way inside. I felt naked without my tote bag, even if the only thing I'd have kept in it before I got new books was my phone and my wallet. I was definitely going to have to figure out how to get that all back from Paisley—before the "war council" planned for today. "Early laps?"

"Swim team," explained Llyr. Bay interrupted us to wish me a fun first day and then pecked Llyr on the cheek before jogging up to Cascade and joining her among one of the groups milling about in front of the entrance. "He missed practice for a couple of days. He and Laguna and Bay..."

As if on cue, Bay nodded to the group and then fell in step behind Laguna and Calder, disappearing inside.

"Hey, you should join the team," suggested Llyr.

"The swim team?" I held the first set of doors open for the redhead. "No, thanks." Something about straining to keep my legs as legs while in the water just ruined the whole thing for me. Not that I'd ever been the most devoted swimmer anyway. Though thank goodness Mom and Dad had sprung for swimming lessons when I'd been a tot or I'd have been at a loss on how to get anywhere underwater, tail or no.

Llyr thanked me and got the second set of doors and I noticed a couple of new faces look my way as I stepped inside. Lockers on either side of the hallway ahead—classrooms being struck by the intense morning sunlight through floor-to-ceiling windows on corridors on my left and right. Pretty standard school design.

"But swimming can be so relaxing," said Llyr, smiling at a few of the staring faces as he led the way straight ahead. "Rejuvenating even." He tapped the side of his temple. "It might be just what you need to get ready for battle. It gets your muscles in shape."

"Or maybe strength won't be that important and Nerida could take my suggestion and ensure the next fight only happens *in* the water," I mumbled.

"Is that what got the adults all hot and bothered?" Llyr headed for a large staircase at the end of the hallway. Instead of going up, though, he led me to the side and around the back. "They said to keep an eye on you and make sure you come straight back after school."

Because otherwise, I'd what, lure the vampires into my trap without first consulting the rest of them? It was aggravating how nonchalant these merfolk seemed to be about it all, but my plan was no one-woman show—I'd need them on board for it to work. I checked over my shoulder, but the nearest students seemed to be out of earshot. I ran up beside Llyr to get closer to him. "I want to lure the vampires to your house."

He stopped cold, and I took a few more steps before I realized I had no idea where I was going without him.

"Oh," he said. He seemed disturbed by the very suggestion.

"Why not?" I folded my arms and took a few steps closer to him. "It's defense city."

"So what makes you think any of... Any of *them* would show up? They have more than a vague idea of what awaits them."

"Easy. We find some way to lure them there." Okay, maybe not so easy if I couldn't figure out *what* to use that they'd care about. Other than me. To end this battle. But they were probably smart enough to figure out it'd be easier to catch me outside the place and to bide their time.

Not that they'd have to bide it long. A shiver ran down my spine and I checked both to the left and to the right of me, almost expecting vampires to jump out from dark corners to send a healthy dose of venom through my veins.

But I wasn't moving into the Pooles' little fortress. I had a life.

And as amazing as the house was, I wondered if they had mold problems with all that moisture. There had to be *some* drawback.

"Hmm, maybe," said Llyr as he started walking again. "But I don't think any of our parents will go for it."

"Why not?" The words fell out in a rush.

"There are kids there," he said quietly, his eyes darting back and forth at the other students who were observing us. Maybe I *had* been a little loud. "It's our... It's our home." He cringed.

"And this is *war*," I hissed.

Llyr's pace slowed as we approached what was clearly an office, a couple of students entering ahead of us as another exited with a piece of paper in her hand and a scowl on her face. "This is it," he said, running a shaking hand through his hair.

Had I really upset him that much?

"You'll see," I said, ignoring the banalities of him taking me to an office to get my schedule and the books I'd need to start at a new school. My life wasn't going to be this for long.

"Oo, Double-L, finally done batting for the home team?" Some guy brushed past, sending me a way-too-appraising look. "Hey, baby."

"Excuse—" I started.

"Shut up," said Llyr, his jaw muscles twitching, though his tone was somewhat light. He flipped the guy the bird and the guy guffawed, practically howling the whole way.

That was more backbone than I'd probably see in Calder in a similar situation.

There was hope for these merfolk yet.

———

"Miss Sheppard. Miss Ivy Sheppard, please make your way to the registrar's office."

The bell had just rung for lunch and I'd been about to find a familiar face to ask what was I supposed to do without any cash for lunch or a brown paper bag when the overhead speaker had blared out my name.

Though virtually no one around me knew the announcement was referring to me, I found myself trying to flick two big chunks of my hair in front of my shoulders in order to partially cover up my face.

"See you around, Ivy," said a probably-well-meaning girl named Katie I'd just partnered up with in my new English class. We were studying *The Sound and the Fury*, which I'd just finished doing at Union High, so she'd probably mistaken me for a fellow smart student instead of a regurgitator of points made in my last class.

"You too," I said, pasting a smile onto my lips. My eyes darted around the room as I looked to see if anyone had put two and two together about me being the one summoned via intercom, but no one was even paying me any mind—aside from the occasional quick glance and taking of inventory of the new girl in perky patterned leggings.

It wasn't until I was almost at the registrar's office that I stopped considering all the new faces around me and started considering this was a trap.

"Ivy!" shouted a familiar voice from behind me. Calder came jogging up, Bay and Cascade at his heels.

"Honey?"

I turned back to face the registrar's. Mom stood there, her brown work apron on, my middle school mylar lunch bag in hand.

"*Mom*." I let out a deep breath and went to join her, ignoring the merfolk hot on my heels behind me. "What are you doing here?"

"I thought you might need lunch or lunch money," she said. "Though I wondered if Nerida might be hospitable enough that I needn't worry about it, but anyway..." She passed off the bag and then kissed my forehead.

"*Mom*," I hissed.

"I just wanted to make sure you were doing okay." She hadn't been this *motherly* to me since I'd been an only child.

"Hello, Ms. Sheppard," said Calder as he appeared next to me, his shallow breaths quiet but unmistakable. He must have run as soon as he'd heard the intercom.

Run *toward* a potential fight? No, that simply wasn't Calder.

"Hello, dear," said Mom, all smiles all of a sudden with the guy she'd mistaken for a pervert over the weekend. Maybe having Nerida take her to coffee had made all the difference—or Orin's little mind trick.

"I'm fine, Mom," I said, my face flushing as more and more people started brushing past us in the hallways. "Thanks for checking on me. And for lunch." I shook the bag, juggling the stack of books I'd yet to return to my new locker in the crook of my other arm.

"All right, then. I can tell when you're saying no cool kids have their moms come bring them lunch." She chuckled as she readjusted her purse. "Do you need a ride home?"

I looked to Calder and he shook his head. "No," I said. "I've got it covered."

"She may be late," said Calder. "There's swim team and then my mom invited her for dinner again."

"Swim team?" Mom asked. "Honey, you're joining swim team?"

I glowered at Calder. "I'm thinking about it," I said, covering for him.

"That's good exercise," she said, and her phone vibrated from her purse. "Oh, your father called earlier," she said. "Your stepsister found your phone last night and they want you to stop by and pick it up."

Ice flooded my veins and I exchanged a look with Calder and Cascade and Bay, all seeming to have paled at the idea.

"I don't know if I'll have time—" I started.

"Ivy, I *need* you to have your phone on you, okay? That was the deal when we agreed you could hang out so often with your friends. You always pick up your phone." She checked her screen and frowned, brushing some text away.

"Maybe I should get a new one," I said, brittle laughter breaking into my words.

Mom looked up from her phone, her eyebrow arched. "Rather than check in with your father for a few minutes? You can't..." She shook her head, her eyes suddenly going glossy. "You can't... Why can't you see him? He should... Didn't we...? Autumn is with him..."

"Maybe Autumn can bring Ivy her phone when you pick her up," suggested Calder, putting a hand on her arm and guiding her in the direction of the door. "That's today or tomorrow, isn't it?"

"Tomorrow," said Mom softly, her eyes rapidly blinking.

"I might stop by with friends to get it," I said, shooting Calder a look. I didn't like the visual reminder of how Orin had interfered with Mom's mind—mostly on my request at that.

Calder swallowed visibly but said no more.

"Anyway," said Mom, brightening. "That was work. Tara can't come back after her lunch break—family emergency—so they need me back ASAP." She threw an arm around me for a halfway hug. "Have fun at your new school, honey."

"Thanks," I said, and I watched her go.

"You can't be serious about going to your dad's," said Calder.

Over his shoulder, Cascade and Bay fidgeted. Cascade tucked a strand of dark hair behind her ear and averted her gaze. Bay bounced on his toes, flexing his muscles as he clenched his fists at his side.

"I'm not going into hiding forever, Calder," I said, feeling more confident with the thought of at least some of the team behind me. "And I'm not going to pretend certain family members don't exist because it's not *convenient* for you."

"Me?" Calder rubbed his nose. "This isn't about *me*, Ivy—"

"Then you have no excuse not to do what I say." I grinned. "After all, I am your people's champion, am I not?"

CHAPTER TWELVE

We were going to Dad's—the whole lot of us—but first I had to agree to one thing.

"Observing" the swim team to see if I wanted to join it.

I already knew I couldn't care less about anything like extracurriculars right now, my need for a few more things to dazzle the college applications or not. Too bad I couldn't add "Mermaid, Vampire Hunter" to the list of extracurriculars.

It was hard to picture ever going to college at this rate. It was hard to picture more than a few weeks from now—at least until I put this mess behind me.

"We're almost exactly the same size," said Cascade as I came around the corner of the locker room. She'd lent me one of her spare team suits, a no-frills navy-blue one-piece. Laguna already had hers on and was tucking her hair into a rubber swim cap, snapping a set of goggles over her eyes.

Cascade must have noticed me observing. "Team rules," she said. She *tsked* and tossed me an unopened swim cap package. "Though they'll probably be okay with you not using goggles since you're just observing."

A couple of the girls on the team giggled from the showers on the other side of the locker room and I lowered my voice. "So how do you...?"

Cascade plopped one foot up on a bench, showing off her gams, so to speak. "Keep these beauties intact? Focus. Should be easier for you since it's your default state."

Right. But so far, it was taking more focus than I was comfortable with to not mermaid-out in water for specific periods. Not that I'd done more than shower since Homecoming. Had that really been less than a week ago?

"Think of dry things," said Laguna, so quietly and unexpectedly, I almost yelped. "Humidity. Brisket. Deserts."

"Or Laguna's sense of humor," added Cascade.

Chuckling, I finished unwrapping my cap and slapped it over my head. My nose wrinkled. It smelled strongly of rubber, and pulling tightly on the straps that went under my chin only made it worse.

We padded toward the showers, Cascade exchanging a few words with some of the other girls on the team.

"So... Can I ask you guys something?" I lathered my hands with soap from the nearby dispenser.

"You're going to ask regardless," said Laguna quietly. She had a point there.

"Shoot," said Cascade, inviting me to say more.

My feet tingled then in the shower stream and I had to quickly rinse off, shaking my legs out as I stepped away from the falling stream of water.

"Whoa, you okay?" Cascade stepped up behind me.

"Yeah," I said, taking a deep breath. "I just started thinking about what I was going to say and I got that foot tingling." I shook my bare foot for emphasis.

"Yeah, maybe try not to think too hard about... everything going on when you're out there. Relax. Embrace the chill." Cascade grinned.

Laguna padded over, her thin lips in a straight line. "Ask your questions before we go out there." She didn't seem at home here in a gym shower with a standard swimsuit, a swim cap, and goggles. That long, red, crimped hair needed to be free, her tail the only covering she'd need, a lake or river her destination, not a stark gym pool.

"Okay," I said, shaking my limbs out more to dry a bit off. I checked both ways to make sure no other members of the swim team were present. "How come none of you came to help at Homecoming? Or introduced yourselves to me earlier?"

"You weren't our champion until the dance," said Cascade, her tone uncertain. "Prince Calder had to win you to our side first before we even knew for certain there *would* be a shot of us winning this thing." She frowned as her chin tilted down slightly. "Besides, we did see you under the lake a few weeks back. Don't you remember us?"

I shook my head. I'd been overwhelmed then, and there'd been *so many* merfolk to take in that day. That, and the fact that I'd had a tail just like theirs and could breathe underwater for the first time in my life.

My toes were tingling again and I shook off my feet until the sensation faded away.

Laguna ground a fist against her lips before dropping it to speak. "He asked us to let him convince you alone," she said, slow and direct. "I wouldn't have liked to have been overcrowded in your position. I wouldn't have been able to think clearly."

That kind of thinking hadn't stopped the vampires from popping up everywhere Ember and I had gone. But I liked the other merfolk my age. They might have helped make the decision easier.

That led me to my second question. "So why aren't any of the adults helping?" I asked. "Like why didn't they show up yesterday along with the rest of you? You have the numbers when it comes to a battle against the vampires—at least from what I've seen."

"This isn't supposed to be a merfolk versus bloodsucker conflict," said Cascade. Her feet scuffed the ground. "Otherwise, yeah, we probably could kick their butts with numbers alone."

"They're fast," said Laguna quietly. "We really only have the advantage in water. And they're savvy enough to stay away."

"Not to mention they're extra strong at night." Cascade sighed, then stood straighter, almost like she was at the ready. "And you don't want our parents and the other old people there," she spat. I had to stop myself from chuckling at the idea of people my parents' age being "old." She flexed her bicep—it was toned, but no bodybuilder's arm or anything. "We've got the speed and the strength to back you up."

"It's champion versus champion," Laguna added. "But we can keep the other bloodsuckers at bay." Her expression seemed pained. "The observer seemed to think that much was allowable, anyway."

Orin. Could I possibly go more than a few hours without remembering that traitorous faery existed?

Sighing, I gave the girls a curt nod. "You're right. You both kicked some *A* back at that empty house." A fluttery smile appeared, then vanished from my face. "I hope you'll back me up tonight," I said, and a sense of realization dawned on Laguna's face. Llyr had probably told her. "Because the sooner this all is over..."

I left the rest unsaid.

The coach's gym whistle blew again. "Sheppard, watch your arms. Keep them straight."

She wasn't doing the idea of joining the swim team any favors, I could tell you that much. My arms burned and my heart thundered as I tried to do my third lap of the butterfly stroke down one of the cordoned-off lanes. My toes were skirting the floor of the pool as the deep end met the shallow and I lowered my legs to stand and take a deep breath.

Coach's lips hit that whistle again. Yeah, I wasn't feeling this team. Relaxation? My heart hadn't beaten this hard since I'd seen that vintage reject's vampire fangs about to sink into the tender vittles of my neck.

Ignoring whatever the coach was saying, I watched as Laguna, Cascade, and the other girls made their laps back and forth—Laguna and Cascade of course looking not at all out of breath. The other half of the pool lanes were taken up by guys on the team—girls and guys practiced together, even if their swim meets were divided along an arbitrary binary, apparently.

Bay and Llyr were in the water now, but Calder was in line with some of the other guys near the diving board. His goggles were fixed pointedly my way.

Forget the toe tingles. My entire legs slammed together as if pulled by a magnet, something stretching and popping down below, which I only belatedly realized were the seams at the bottom of my borrowed suit.

Oh, rats.

The water was glowing around me, just slightly—probably only noticeably if you were looking for it, what with the lights on the floor of the pool glimmering through the water, too.

Dry. Deserts. Briskets? What else am I supposed to think of?

My tail twitched below me, causing the icy cold to shoot up through my hand again.

The coach blew on her whistle. "Sheppard? What are you doing?"

Cascade crossed over a few lanes, nearly bumping into this other girl's path, and was at my side in a flash. She grabbed hold of my arm. "Mrs. Wright, Ivy has a cramp." Her eyes narrowed at me.

Right. I started grunting in pain, though I found even my arm muscles lightened now that I had the tail, like that soothing sense of relaxation everyone kept promising was waiting for me in the water was finally seeping into my bones.

Laguna popped up from beneath the water at my other side and the coach blew her whistle again. "Don't cross lanes when laps are in progress!" Her face scrunched up and then loosened as she visibly exhaled a breath. "Get the newbie out of there," she said, then turned her back on us to watch some of the other girls moving.

With a splash, Calder dove into the deep end of the water, then started making his way toward me like a shark underwater, across lanes of boys doing laps.

The coach whistled again as he popped up beside me. She

shouted something about crossing lanes again, but he took my face in both of his hands, putting his forehead to mine.

Without meaning to, I asked through the mind read what to do to get my tail to go away right now—I couldn't exactly heave myself up the side of the pool and dry off—and that mermaid link between us showed me the answer.

Focus. Dry. Legs.

Perhaps Calder was getting something from me at the same time, some image of my own feelings—about the tail, about the war, about everything going on. But I remembered to focus, to think about being dry, and eventually, with a tingle that permeated every scale, I felt my legs returning, even in the water, my toes stretching as they kicked back and forth.

The bottom of my suit was loose and ripped and I felt my face flush.

Laguna darted out of the water, heading back to the edge with a towel as Calder and Cascade swam on either side of me to meet her.

Thanks to their nimble maneuverings, I got up the ladder just as Laguna swooped in with the towel and Cascade wrapped it around my bottom half, tucking it in and tugging to keep it tightly in place.

My skin dripped as I stared back down at the pool to find most of the team had stopped swimming and were staring at me unabashedly.

Coach blew her whistle again. "We're not done with drills!"

As if a spell had spread across the room, everyone began to move again.

"Sheppard, take five," snapped the coach. "The rest of you, back in."

"Thanks, but I'm out," I said loudly and sternly enough that I hoped would encourage no arguments. The coach had the gall to actually look relieved.

"Ivy," said Calder quietly.

I shook my head. "Why torture yourself like this? With training and drills and meets?" My voice was a harsh whisper.

"When you can swim—truly swim, as free as can be—almost any time at home?"

Calder chewed his lip. "Swim team is a tradition in our... family..." He looked to Laguna and Cascade, almost as if for confirmation. Cascade adjusted her swimsuit while Laguna tapped a finger to her lips.

"You know what?" said Calder, his voice rising. "She's got a point. Let's all quit."

"Excuse me?" said the coach. But Bay and Llyr didn't need to be told twice, their dripping selves padding over to join us by the towels.

Not a one of them actually grabbed any as we all headed to the locker rooms, the coach threatening the group with extra laps and being benched all the way.

CHAPTER THIRTEEN

In the sideview mirror, I could make out Cascade's car as she and the other merfolk high schoolers followed Calder and me in his pickup truck to my dad's house.

"I don't see why we have to do this," said Calder.

"I'm not avoiding my dad entirely for however long this war takes," I said flippantly. "Nor am I *moving* into the merfolk fortress. *Especially* if we don't have a plan."

"Ivy, the vampires want you *dead*."

"I don't believe that," I said, though something roiled in the pit of my stomach. "At least... Ember doesn't want that. And the vampires' hands are tied, even if they do. Ember has to be the one to deal a blow against me if they want to win."

Calder let out a breath that would have ruffled his damp hair if it had been long enough.

"Hey," I pointed out, reaching for his hand on the steering wheel. "We're going as a group. We'll be fine."

Calder pulled his hand away before I could grab it and I felt my chest go cold. He tried to cover the motion by running the shaky appendage over his scalp, and it was only then that I realized he might have been afraid of me prying to find out his subconscious thoughts.

That hadn't been my intention, though. I sighed.

Dad's place was coming into view.

"It's not like your fortress is even that far away," I grumbled as he pulled up to the curb. I gripped the door handle. "You won't have far to run if you bolt at the first sign of trouble like you always do."

Calder started to say something, but I shut the door before he could finish. Planting my feet in the grass on the other side of the sidewalk, I stared up at the large, light-colored house. It had hardly been "home" more than a few weeks, but still, I shrunk back from the powerful wave of melancholy that hit me looking up at it. Slinking my shoulders forward, I made my way to the front porch, almost digging for a key in my pocket that I knew was likely in the tote bag I'd come to get.

The soft movement of feet through the grass behind me made me check over my shoulder, but it was just my new friends, Calder lingering behind the four others, his hands tucked in his pockets. He was almost slinking back there.

A fluttering smile appeared on my face as I took in the jackets the guys and Laguna were wearing—letterman, and Cascade likely owned one too. "I guess Central might make you turn those back in now." I cleared my throat. "I'm sorry I convinced you all to quit the team."

Laguna bent slightly to examine a giant moth resting between the prickly leaves of one of Noelle's bushes. Cascade bit her lip, but Llyr let out a hearty laugh as he slid his arm around a sullen Bay. "You were right to," the redhead said. "Swim team is a horror show anyway. At least compared to the freedom we're usually allowed."

"Queen Nerida isn't going to be happy," said Bay quietly.

"My mother doesn't get to dictate our lives entirely," said Calder, slipping around Laguna to take the step up to the porch and stand beside me. "And we have more important things to worry about right now." He coughed, cupping a hand over his lips. "Ivy wants her life back and we owe it to her... to get this all over with."

I didn't fail to miss the look that Cascade, Bay, and Llyr all passed between them at that, though Laguna was too focused on lightly petting the moth's wings to bother.

"Anyway," said Cascade, her voice perking up and her words pouring out, "we can't stand here like idiots all day, can we? Why don't we knock and let the bloodsucker champion know now's not the time to mess with our Ivy?" She draped an arm around my shoulder, practically dragging me down, and used her free hand to knock, followed by a quick double-press of the doorbell.

Laughing nervously, I tried to straighten myself so she didn't drag me down to the ground.

Pounding footfalls echoed behind the door before it pulled open. "Ivy!" Autumn bounced on her heel as she unlatched the outer front door.

"Hey, peanut," I said, disentangling myself from Cascade's grip to pat the back of my sister's head as she tackled me with the fervor of a professional wrestler. "Oof," I said exaggeratedly as she took me in her arms.

Autumn pulled away, the curl of her lips replaced by the narrowing of her brow. "Who are all these people?"

I guided her inside and nodded to the people behind me. "My new friends from Central."

"You were here for the *boring* Homecoming pictures," said Autumn, pointing to Calder. "You were *spying* on everyone."

True. He'd been lingering nearby, looking forlorn. I didn't realize Autumn had seen him.

"Why did you change schools anyway?" Autumn asked, her little button nose upturned. "And Dad said you're only going to be living with Mom awhile, and when I tried to ask him *why*, he got all... *weird*... and confused and then Noelle was like, 'Stop questioning your father, young lady,' and *she* got confused and Ember was like, 'It's better this way,' and *I* got confused—"

"I'm sorry it's all so confusing," I said, ruffling her hair. She cringed as she went to work smoothing out her dark brown strands. "But is anyone else home?"

"*Yeah*," said Autumn, as if that were obvious. "Dad!" She padded her bare feet up the stairway. She stopped at the top and turned around. "He's still taking a crap. Only if anyone calls his phone and asks for him, I'm not supposed to say 'taking a crap.'"

I headed upstairs, slowly, caught at the top behind Autumn, who seemed to have taken it upon herself to act as Dad's home secretary.

The flush of the toilet from down the hall in the open master bedroom, followed by the too-brief rinse of hands simultaneously made me gag and feel a sense of relief, recognizing the pattern as Dad's.

"Hey, kiddo," said Dad as he appeared in the master bedroom doorway. "I see you got my message—no mean feat when you make a habit of losing your phone."

The fact that I'd also lost my phone in the woods when this had all started was not lost on me. I was going to glue the thing to me from now on.

"How was your first day at the new school?" he asked, coming out into the hallway to meet me.

"Fine," I said quickly. "So do you have my bag?"

Dad didn't seem to hear me and simply stared over my head down the stairway at the small group I had gathered there.

"I see you make friends fast." He brushed past me and held out his hand—merely rinsed, ew—to Calder. "Easton Sheppard, Ivy's dad," he said.

Calder hesitated a second but removed his hand from his pocket and shook Dad's. "Calder Poole." I noticed he didn't mention anything about being my boyfriend, but *fine*, I wasn't sure that was what was important just now anyway. "And these are my kin, Laguna and Llyr Irving and Cascade and Bay Asturias."

"*Kin*, eh?" Dad said, taking each of their hands in turn. He squinted. "I think I can see it."

Ugh. "Hey, Autumn, do you know where my phone and tote bag are?" I asked her quietly. If Dad had no interest in seeing me quickly on my way, I'd at least make sure I had them in my hands before the merfolks' favorite strategy of heading for the hills inevitably came into play.

"I think so," said Autumn. "She put it in her room." She walked over toward Ember's closed bedroom door and my heart rate went sky-high as I ran a nervous left hand over my right, bringing discomfort to the hand by squeezing it, trying to focus on keeping the ice nearby and at the ready—but not strong enough to glow bright blue and draw Autumn's attention just yet.

"Hey, is Ember home?" I asked, but Autumn was already at the door, knocking at it.

"Ivy's here," she said in a singsong tune. "She wants her stuff back."

She was home.

A crash from downstairs made me jump as Ember's door swung open, and Arty the white-and-black cat bolted up the stairs, headed straight for Autumn's own open doorway and under her bed.

The three of us stared, watching that lightning-fast cat go.

"Sorry about that!" shouted Dad from down below. "I wanted to show these guys your baby pictures and I didn't realize the cat was atop the curio cabinet. I think I scared him when I slammed the swinging door open."

My temples throbbed under my hands as I massaged them. *Dad, can you stop?*

Autumn chased after the cat, leaving me standing virtually alone in the hallway with Ember, my friends apparently distracted by photos of me in diapers.

She shook her head, brushing a tendril of blonde hair over her shoulder before crossing her arms in front of her. She had tight Capri pants on and a vintage-style pale pink blouse. All she was missing was the handkerchief bandana and she might have looked at home alongside Rosie the Riveter. "You came." With the way she was standing there, I expected her to sound snootier, but there was a sullen echo to her tone.

Autumn's gentle cooing drew my attention, and I clenched my fist at my side as I looked from Ember to Autumn and back. Wildly, my eyes darted around to see if Ember had company in her room.

"I'm alone," she said. "I hoped to speak with you. Alone."

Someone thundered up the stairs—Calder, Bay at his heels. I held my left hand out to the side of me, instructing them to hang back.

"Ow! Bad kitty." Autumn shook her hand in the air as a fluff of white vanished beneath her bed.

"You have to give him some space when he's upset," said Ember, leaving her doorway to head to Autumn's room. She didn't sound angry, but even so, I found my fingers flexing, curling and uncurling, and I darted down the hall after her.

"Are you okay?" asked Ember, ignoring me and taking Autumn's hand in hers.

A thin scratch line spread down the back of her hand, oozing the smallest droplets of blood.

Beads of sweat were forming on my forehead. If she touched Autumn's blood, then—

"Let's get it washed," said Ember, tugging gently on Autumn's arm and bringing her to standing. Ember glared at me as they passed, not letting go of my sister's hand as they headed to the bathroom. "Cat scratches can have a lot of germs." Ember flicked the faucet on. "You need to get a lather going really well."

Realizing my feet had frozen me in Autumn's doorway, I scrambled toward the bathroom now, barely registering as Calder popped out of Ember's bedroom, my tote in one hand and my phone in the other. I nodded but ignored his thumb indicating we should head toward the stairway.

Dad's hearty laughter echoed from downstairs and I realized with a sinking feeling that despite all my denials of the fact, I really was leaving my dad and sister to be used as pawns in a game they had no idea they were playing. More than anything, I wanted this all to be over—*needed* this all to be over.

The faucet shut off and Autumn shook off her hands just as I stepped in between her and Ember, yanking the hand towel off its rack and drying Autumn's hands for her.

"*Stop*," said Autumn. "I'm not five." Like eight was so much older. I let her take the towel from me as I opened the medicine chest and rummaged around for bandages and ointment.

"Here," said Ember, ducking between my sister and me to open the cupboard beneath the sink. She handed Autumn a bandage that claimed to have ointment already in the pad. "And be careful around that little panther, okay?"

"I thought he liked me," Autumn muttered as she tossed the towel on the sink and opened the bandage package.

"He does." Ember patted her on the head and Autumn squinted her eyes as she flattened the bandage diagonally over her scratch. "He's just overwhelmed with so many *people* around. He takes a while to get used to new faces."

"He liked *my* friend right away," muttered Autumn. "Curled right up in his lap."

"What friend—?" I started to ask, the use of *his*—a rarity among my little sister's friends—not lost on me, but Dad interrupted.

"Sport! Come down here and help Noelle with the groceries," shouted Dad up the stairs. "She just pulled in."

Autumn said something about donuts and then bolted out the door, brushing past Bay and Calder on the landing without a word.

It was only half a second later that my eyes flicked to Ember and I saw she had the dirty hand towel in her grip, the slightest few dots of red hard to miss among the white of the towel fibers.

"*Wait*," snapped Ember when I realized my fist was up at the ready, the ice chilling my fingers already.

She held her right hand out cautiously to me, her fingertips glowing with the faintest shade of red, then stuck out her left hand, still clutching the towel, toward the guys just as Cascade and Laguna ascended the stairs behind them.

"Calder, you said you didn't want to hurt me," she said, her round, brown eyes wide.

"I don't," replied Calder. He had my tote up around his arm as he stood at the ready for a fight, his muscles tense. "If you just surrender, this will all be over."

Ember turned to me. "I can't do that." Her voice was quiet. "But I hope you'll believe me that this house is a neutral zone, okay? You don't have to worry about your dad or Autumn..."

"How benevolent of you." A sour taste permeated my mouth.

"Your dad said you're staying with your mom exclusively for a while." Her limbs shook slightly as a nervous chuckle escaped her lips. "Hey, did you know this whole debacle got my dad to come visit me? He's still in town."

Something inside me softened. I might have felt empathy for her before Homecoming.

"He's... That is, he's..." She went silent for a moment before a watery smile erupted on her face. "Ivy, I need to win this."

I scoffed as the inaudible conversation of our family from downstairs traveled up the landing. "And doom the merfolk to extinction? I don't think so."

Calder nodded at me, and something in his demeanor, something like a sense of courage I so rarely saw in him, spurred me on. "The vampires have had their time, Ember. It's not like them vanishing would be cutting lives short."

"Their lives were already cut short," said Ember. "This second life—it might be some kind of recompense for that." She frowned, her right hand clenching into a fist at her side as she clutched the dirtied towel to her heart. "Ivy, I need you to trust me."

The laughter that escaped my lips sounded hollow. "*Who* was the first person to attack whom back at Homecoming?" I asked.

Ember's gaze darted to Calder.

No. I'd walked in on Calder surrounded, the vampires having a field day as they'd paced back and forth like lions about to assault their prey.

...I'd walked in to find the battle in progress.

And who had started the fire to get the sprinklers going anyway?

Calder shook his head as my fingers seemed to thaw, my own arm lowering.

"Ivy?" called Noelle up the stairs. "Oh, hello. Are you Ivy's new friends? Will you all be staying for dinner?"

Ember turned at the sound of her mom's voice and I let the ice flow out of my hand, but even so—I grabbed for her wrist.

She let out a startled cry, but I wasn't intending to hurt her. Instead, I focused. *What are you so afraid of?*

I saw images of a man with gold-and-gray hair, a wineglass in hand, a wide grin on his face. The room was dark, my surroundings difficult to focus on. I blinked through Ember's eyes and saw the bright blue irises first—the scores of them all around me—Dean coming into focus to the right of me.

A woman in a dark red dress drank from a goblet filled with a dark liquid, a trickle of red dripping down her pale chin.

Dad, *I thought. But Dad was nowhere to be found.*

I gasped, letting go of Ember's wrist, realizing what had gone through my brain. *Her* dad. Her uninvolved father had come to visit her in the hospital and wound up dining with vampires?

CHAPTER FOURTEEN

My fingers were barely off of Ember's wrist before it all came tumbling out. "The bloodsuckers have taken your dad hostage?"

"What?" she asked, rubbing her wrist with her other hand as if I'd burned her. "How did you...?"

"That's enough," said Calder, striding forward to snatch my elbow. "If this is a neutral zone, we need to get out of here. All of us." He nodded to his group.

"Ember? Ivy?"

I'd almost forgotten Noelle was at the bottom of the stairs.

"We're leaving, Mrs. Sheppard," said Calder as he practically dragged me down the stairs.

"Ms. Goodwin-Sheppard," said Noelle, her lips drawn tight. "Ivy, are you really going...?"

I yanked my arm away from Calder and put a flittering smile on my face. "Yes, sorry, but thanks, Noelle. I have plans."

"Ivy." Ember looked down from the second floor, her pallid figure behind the bannister too reminiscent of a specter. "You can stay."

"Don't trust her," hissed Calder into my ear.

I shook my head up at Ember, then gazed around the staircase and into the kitchen. Autumn and Dad were laughing, Autumn continually trying to keep a box of donuts out of his reach and Dad clearly just pretending to miss snatching it.

My stomach grew knotted, my regrets piling up by the minute.

"No," I said again, fighting back the tears in my eyes. "We have to go."

I led the way, brushing past Noelle without even telling my dad and Autumn I'd see them later.

"Now, wait a minute, young lady."

I stopped in the middle of the driveway, my merfolk milling about between me and my step-mother, who'd followed us out onto the porch. She approached us by cutting across the grass, her hands on her hips, the ruffled collar of her blouse slightly askew at the end of a long day. "I hope you haven't forgotten your father's and my wedding ceremony." Her eyes flicked to Calder, then the rest of the group. "Your new friends are welcome to come."

I blinked rapidly, my brain scrambling for some semblance of what my life had been before this. "Right. End of the month." That was just about a week and a half away.

"Just because you're spending more time with your mom doesn't mean you can't be there for your dad and me on this important day." She jiggled a bracelet on her wrist and the movement reminded me of her daughter just a few minutes before. "I know we already got married at the courthouse, but this is for friends and family—this is the *real* celebration of a life we're so happy to be living." She smiled and took a few steps closer, practically willing the other teens to step away. Then she gave me a hug and it was awkward, but I tried to hug back, patting her on the shoulder. My eyes darted about and locked on Ember in a second-story window above—the master bedroom. The lace curtains billowed gently at her touch, her blonde hair falling in waves over half her face, reminding me of that one old starlet who probably couldn't even see out of one of her eyes when she filmed thanks to the hairdo.

Noelle pulled back and squeezed me by the upper arms. "We need all our daughters there."

"Of course," I said, my insides quivering. "Of course..."

If this was over by then, one way or another, I couldn't guarantee all her daughters would be there.

—————

I spent the better part of the very short drive scrolling through the missed messages on my phone, my palm clammy and my heart thundering even as I tried not to think too hard about everything before me. If Ember had never joined this battle, I wouldn't have, either. I ached for the normalcy of my life, for the company of my longtime friends.

My fingers dragged over a picture Paisley had sent me of her and Lyric in history, Lyric sticking her tongue out, probably because she'd been instructed the picture was about to be sent to me. She was probably more upset about Raelynn than anything—assuming they hadn't quite made up yet—but it was clear I was also on an enemies list of some sort at the moment.

"The vampires don't know about our ability. At least—they didn't." Calder let out a deep breath as he put the truck in park in the lot outside the Poole Estate garage. He flicked off the ignition. "Now Ember is going to wonder why you know something she didn't tell you about her dad—"

"Yeah, something pretty *important*, wouldn't you say?" I dropped my phone into my tote bag, the only message sent to Paisley, about my first day at Central being okay but totally failing to make the swim team—which was fine by me, I'd been sure to add.

I'd never be one for that kind of structure in sports and exercise. I'd envied the freedom of the merfolk—though I couldn't bring myself to be *quite* so free and loose in the nudist sense like they were.

Cascade, Laguna, Bay, and Llyr poured out of the garage, suddenly gathering in a circle and playing rock-paper-scissors, one coupling at a time, until Cascade threw up her hands in the air, a grin on her face even as she shook her head.

The other three started stripping in front of the moat and I realized they'd been playing for clothes-pick-up duty.

"How is that important?" Calder's voice cracked as he slammed a palm against the steering wheel.

"What...?" I'd almost forgotten what we'd been speaking about.

"Argh," said Calder. He slanted away from me, leaning his head against the driver's side window. "Just don't... Don't tell my mom you screwed up, all right?"

"Excuse me?"

"I mean it." Calder gripped the door handle, his brain clearly churning for a minute. "Just... don't. Don't let her know you may have let Ember know about our subconscious thought touch." He opened his door.

"Oh, so it's like a proper superpower now?" I kept up the conversation as Calder reached into the space between us to grab his backpack and then slid it over one arm. "Could have fooled me that it would come in handy." I opened my own door and had to grind my teeth as Calder joined me and Cascade made her way toward us, her arms piled high with clothes and shoes. Laguna floated on her back like a painting of Ophelia, and only the very tips of fins were visible from Bay and Llyr.

"Can I get a hand with the backpacks?" asked Cascade, nodding toward the garage.

Calder growled and stormed over there, his legs practically bouncing to join the others in the water.

He was getting harder to root for by the minute. "You know, it actually *did* come in handy for once," I pointed out as Calder opened the back door of Cascade's car and started loading up his arms with bookbags. I shuffled the straps of my tote bag higher up my arm and grabbed one, the heat of my face at odds with the ice forming on my fingers. "We know something we'd have no reason to know before. Something that could partially explain Ember's motivations—at least her current ones. Something we might hold over her or use to think of a plan—"

"Let me repeat myself," snapped Calder. "The vampires *didn't know* that about us and now they'll probably figure it out. We lost an advantage."

I flailed my arms around, knocking my tote bag down to my elbow. "Like you don't already have an insane advantage in this fortress?"

"There's no way my mom is going to allow you to lure the vampires here."

"Why on Earth not? Doesn't she *want* this to be over?"

"Listen. You have *no* idea how badly my mom wants this to be over, but there are precautions we have to take."

"Like *what*?"

Cascade cleared her throat as she stood in front of the door leading inside. "Sorry to interrupt this lovers' quarrel, but can I get a hand?" There was too much in her own two for her to get a hand free.

A sigh escaped Calder's lips as he looked at his own arms, bulging with school supplies. "You get it," he said sullenly.

"Me?" Right. The scanning. I put my palm against the sensor, and sure enough, it lit up green, the door to the glass water-coated hallway swinging open. Cascade and Calder made their way inside.

They hesitated at the other end, waiting for me to do my palm trick again, but I wasn't one of the ones wearing aquatic shoes, and my poor water-logged boots had just dried out from this morning. "Just a second," I said, cringing as my toes tingled while I moved one foot in front of the other.

I laid my palm on the second sensor and the door opened again, Cascade going straight to the laundry table with all her stuff and Calder hanging the bookbags on a coatrack nearby. They both kicked off their shoes and added them to the others' beneath the table.

"You think I could get a pair of those?" I asked, cringing as I peeled away the foul-smelling leather of my boots.

"Sure," said Cascade, a bright look on her face as she started peeling her shirt off in front of Calder and me. I looked away. "Someone should have thought of that. I think we have some spares in a closet somewhere."

Calder was removing his clothes, too.

"What... are you two doing?" I asked.

"Getting ready for dinner," said Cascade, bending to peel off her pants.

"No, that's the complete opposite of what you two are doing," I pointed out.

"Come on," said Cascade, padding over to me in her bra and panties. "Get undressed."

"No thanks?" I tried not to look at Calder's bare rear end as he strolled over to the pool in the entryway. He put his arms together above his hand, ending in the point of his clasped palms, and dove, his toes shimmering into fins just before they vanished beneath the water.

"You'll have to excuse him," said Cascade, shaking me back to the moment.

I'd been thinking about how toned and sculped his leg muscles were before they'd vanished into scales. "He's... He's not taking this thing well," explained Cascade.

"This... thing?"

Cascade flourished her hands around her. "The battle. It doesn't... It doesn't feel real."

"What do you mean?"

The splashing from Calder's swim was fading now, the distant trickle of water the only indicator of movement.

"Unlike the vampires, the merfolk—we live human life spans." Cascade maneuvered her arms behind her to unclasp her bra. I took off the sweater she'd lent me and folded it numbly, then hugged the midriff-baring top I still had on after putting the sweater on the table. I wasn't going for a swim topless, if that was where I was expected to go.

I nodded. "Calder's really sixteen and De—the vampire prince is an old man. I get it."

"But do you?" She held her bra aloft and chucked it into a laundry bin. "That means the bloodsuckers have done nothing but wait with bated breath for this battle to begin. Our parents grew up without it ever being a possibility. Our grandparents even—despite the..." She chewed her lip.

"The queen's grandfather," I said, remembering that important detail.

"Yes, and even then, it wasn't the *battle*, it wasn't the real war." She shook out her long hair so part of it covered her chest. "Calder probably just thought... Well, he might have thought we'd have a chance to grow up without worrying about any of this. A chance where 'the battle to declare a winning species' is just a distant, far-off idea—like it had been for generations."

"It shouldn't *be* all on your shoulders." I looked around, but there was no sign of life from the kitchen behind me. "You have enough people here that you could all chip in."

"Maybe," said Cascade. She was working on getting her panties off now and I turned away. "But either way, Prince Calder would be at the center of it. He couldn't get out of his role to play in all of this."

"Well, he's not doing a great job of that," I muttered. "If he's supposed to be my support."

"Your consort, even."

I winced. "We're trying that... But I thought, well... The one thing I'd ask for in a boyfriend—especially one for whom I'm doing *so* much—would be to have my back. Calder doesn't have that."

A splash behind me told me Cascade had jumped in. "That's not true." Her voice was loud as it carried across the entryway. "You just don't realize what he's trying to do for you."

I arched an eyebrow. "Are we talking about the same angry, frightened merman here?"

"Trust me," said Cascade.

Sure. I just met you yesterday, but sure.

"Come on in," she said, waving one arm high above her head. I felt my feet moving toward the edge of the water. She laughed and winced. "Sorry. I'm so not used to speaking to humans in this form. I forget about the siren call."

Shaking my head, I blinked myself back to the moment. Right.

Another potential tool in my arsenal. "Does that work on vampires?"

"What?" asked Cascade, her arms fluttering around her.

"Siren call."

"Oh." She chewed her lip. "No. I don't think so. Not that I've ever tried it myself, but, like, vampires have their own seduction technique, I guess you'd call it? They don't seem to fall for mermaids."

Drat. Biting my lip, I checked for any other sign of life in the house. "So are we having this dinner meeting?" I asked. "The war council?"

Cascade's fins poked out of the water as she made little coquettish movements with her hands to swim backward, her torso almost fully above the surface. "That's why I told you to get undressed."

I blanched and pointed to the water. "It's down there?"

"Sometimes we prefer to dine merfolk-style," she said. "Come on!"

Well, I clearly needed more practice in the water anyway, if the swim team coach's ire was an indication of my skill. I waited for Cascade to make a loop around the little pool so her back was to me and then removed my leggings, skirt, and underwear. I hesitated at the top. *Nope.*

I dove, maintaining my human form almost all the way to the bottom.

Cold. Really cold.

A hazy, shapely figure appeared to my left. I blinked hard, but Cascade—I presumed—didn't come into focus, though somehow I was filled with the tantalizing promise of a mermaid rescuing me, like sailors lured to their dooms.

My mouth opened and the cool splash of sour water filled in, the panic squeezing at my chest, at my throat—

The figure seemed to speak beside me, bubbles floating from her mouth.

I closed my eyes. *Water. Calder... Calder...* That brought on a mix of emotions, but it also centered me, churning that asphyxiating water into soothing air, my lungs filling with the liquid as naturally as if I were breathing air.

A sense of warmth overtook me. A cozy feeling of home, of belonging.

"Whoa, that was a close one," said Cascade beside me, as clear as day. She giggled, and the sound was like music in the hollow echo of the pool. "Who'd have thought you'd have a hard time staying human in the water when you need to and a hard time not when you don't?"

Flicking my tail and feeling the movement stretch up from my waist to my spine, I swirled in place. "Give me a break," I said, grinning. "This is only my third time intentionally *trying* to turn mermaid."

"Really?" Cascade's voice rose in pitch. "Someone needs to give that prince a talking to."

Tell me about it.

"Still," she continued, "that's incredible that you were able to kick bloodsucker butt with so little experience." She took me in, head to fin, and gave me an appraising nod. "I think we might just win this thing."

I gave her a double thumbs-up and she laughed.

"All right," she said. "Follow me. It's a bit of a swim."

I shrugged. "I did a bunch of laps at school."

"Well, this is a longer swim than that." Cascade winked. "But you'll find your arms are much more suited to the task when in this form." She stared down at my chest.

"Sorry about the top," I said. "It's all wet. Obviously."

She shrugged. "It looks cute on you, even as a mermaid. Now let's go! Everyone is probably waiting."

She whapped her tail—hard—and took off like a shot. I followed her downward, swimming through what seemed like the fish side of an aquarium tank. Machinery at home in a basement—like a water heater, a sub pump, a furnace—streamed by on the dry side of the tank as I swam forward, and I realized we were swimming through the basement. Cascade kept flipping her fins before me, and though I didn't tire from all the swimming, I couldn't quite match her speed. A blinding light welcomed her up ahead and I blinked as I joined her, realizing we were under the glass walkway now, and there were two options for us to go—north and south.

She paused and turned upright, flapping her arm for me to follow her north—behind the house and to the trickling river.

We were headed for the park lake. I knew it at once. To that cavernous place below the little jut of land at the center of the water.

We did swim for quite a few minutes more, Cascade doing side rolls as she guided me, dodging piles of rocks and shoving aside growing algae as we made our way.

At last, the burbling chatter up ahead hit my ears and then our narrow river path opened wide, the lake welcoming us, the merfolk milling about and swimming around as if this were a bustling city center—granted, with only a couple dozen people. Merpeople.

"You made it!" Bay swam up beside us, his sculpted, flexing torso second only to his dazzling smile.

"Apparently," I said, shooting a glare at Calder as he swam over with Laguna and Llyr on his tail. Cascade whispered something in a hushed tone to Laguna and she frowned, shaking her head.

Bay scratched his scalp. "Yeah, they know. They're not happy about it."

"Happy about what?" I asked.

"Us quitting swim team," said Llyr. "Our parents, that is."

"Oh." I wondered why that was even important right now. Before I could ask, the sweet, dulcet tones of Nerida rang out across the water.

"Dinner is ready, everyone!" She clasped her hands together and squeezed them beside one of her cheeks when her eyes fell on me. "And our guest of honor is here at last."

She swam toward me and threaded her arm through mine, her bare breast nuzzling dangerously close to my skin. "Come on now, dear," she said. "I promised you a proper discussion—but first, we eat."

She guided me into the little cove below the lake's sole island.

The rock lit up in several alcoves with a blue, glowing light.

The rest of the merfolk swam into the cove from all the other entrances, gathering in a circle in the middle, though there were no table or chairs to be found.

And in the middle—amidst many collections of algae arranged to look like they might be plates—was an ungodly number of mussels, the shells piled high in a giant pile for the eating.

"Dig in!" said Nerida, nodding her head.

And the merfolk did, my stomach growing sour at the sight of them cracking the shells, leaning their heads back, and swallowing the slippery meat inside.

CHAPTER FIFTEEN

"Please, have a taste. There's plenty." Nerida guided me to an empty spot at the head of the gathering, giving me déjà vu to yesterday's dinner despite the incredibly different surroundings.

"No thanks," I said, watching as Calder slurped down a mussel beside me. "I'm not... hungry."

"Nonsense." Nerida picked up one of the mussels and held it out to me with both hands. "You'll find in this form that your tastes are different—your digestion works differently. Please. Just try it."

I never did understand the friends' moms who seemed to take personal affront to you not liking this or that ingredient in their homecooked meals, but my own mom had raised me to be polite anyway. Out of habit, I ran my palm against my thigh—only to be reminded with a start it was actually scales and I was surrounded by water anyway—before grabbing the offered shell.

Nerida turned to the mermaid beside her and chatted about something or other to do with the winter freeze and a thought occurred to me.

"What do you do during the winter?" I asked Calder, almost forgetting the tension between us. "Doesn't the lake in Standing Springs Park freeze over?"

"With climate change, maybe not so much." Calder shook his

head, sending little bubbles afloat with the movement. He snatched another mussel from the pile. "But that's up there anyway. On the surface. The water below is still passable for a water creature. There's just too much of it for it to go entirely solid."

A vague sting of a recent memory of a vampire concerned about global warming sent a tingle to the back of my neck, almost like a reminder they weren't so different after all.

Except one was already dead.

"Are you fresh water or salt water fish?" I asked, trying to taste the water I was breathing on my tongue. There didn't appear to be salt, but I remembered a slight tang of the stuff in the drink I'd had aboveground yesterday.

"Either," he said, slurping down the mussel. I cringed. "This is a freshwater lake, though we do need the salt for healthy functioning merfolk organs, so we make a point of ingesting saltwater whenever we can." He mimed the action of taking a drink with an invisible glass. I supposed we wouldn't feel thirst when we were breathing water in through our lungs. "But really, we could ride the rivers out to the ocean and from there... The world."

Laughter echoed liked a musical refrain across the water, Laguna's so alarmingly loud and beautiful as she spoke with her mom that I blinked rapidly, readjusting my eyes to the water.

"You should really try it," said Calder, sending me an encouraging look.

I sighed and opened my mouth wide, ready to get this over with. The smooth, slippery meat fell onto my tongue with a quick flick of my finger.

It tasted good, though. Not rubbery and cold like I'd expected, but sweet and succulent even. Grinning, I chucked the empty shell into the pile beside Calder's and grabbed another.

"I bet you can't wait to win this thing," I said as I dug into my second mussel. "And leave this cold, dreary suburb behind to swim for warmer waters." True, I wasn't shivering in the water in my mermaid form. But still, something was missing—the mermaids in my fantasies had always been surrounded by bright colors, flourishing in warm water. Out of the corner of my eye, I saw a couple of dull brown trout swim through the cove.

Calder stiffened and lowered the mussel in his hand, his appetite suddenly seeming lost. "These lands are important," he said, and that was all he seemed to want to say on the subject.

Nerida snorted in her conversation, the sound tinny and strange.

"My great-grandfather died here," said Calder—almost imperceptibly under the noise. Nerida didn't seem to notice, so I lowered my voice in response to his quiet tone.

"She said that after World War II, the vampires appeared again. So you retreated back here to these consummate lands?"

He nodded, tossing the uneaten mussel back onto the pile. "It's better for us to be here. We remember here—we remember what it is to walk among humans, to see the dreary world for what it is from our dreary waters."

My teeth worried at the corner of my lip. "What happened? When the vampires appeared—when your great-grandfather..."

"That was an unfortunate story," said Nerida smoothly. A shiver jolted up my spine. I hadn't realized she'd heard us speaking in hushed voices.

The glare she sent Calder then made him shrink back before grabbing another mussel and distracting himself with picking at the meat within.

"A vampire seductress tricked him with promises of peace." She slid her hands together tightly in front of her tail, squeezing one hand with the other and drawing attention to the way her hands were trembling. "He tried to end this second war before it started, and she *lied*. She cheated to give herself an advantage."

"That's awful. What did she...?"

"What did she do? How did she trick him?" Nerida sighed. I realized the room had gone quiet as her questions rang out through the waters. "She tried to convince him that blood and water could exist as one—in the same person."

The words left my mouth before I could think over them. "She tried to have a vampire mermaid baby...?"

Nerida's jaw clenched. "No vampire can conceive that way. No, they're not fertile, thank goodness." She laughed sardonically. "They have to pour venom into their *offspring*'s veins to create more of them."

I nodded, not sure what else to say. I still didn't understand.

"She bit him," said Calder, straightening his back. "She tried to create a vampire merman by injecting venom into a merman's veins."

My jaw dropped. "And he...? He let her?"

Nerida's lips pinched. "Yes. Grandfather had noble goals and sought to avoid a repeat of the past, even if our kind had done better in the conflict than hers." Her eyes shone in the water, and I wondered briefly if it was a trick of the light. Because then the shine faded. "But Grandfather thought even those bloodsuckers should have a chance to live." She snatched a mussel from the pile and ripped open the shell with such force, the crack rang out throughout the water.

A vampire merman. A merman vampire? I wondered if the experiment had always been intended to succeed, or if the vampire seductress had known it would bring a quick, easy end to the leader of her enemies.

I wondered at the possibility of fangs and fins united in one, of both salt and venom running through one person's organs, creating a super paranormal creature.

"In any case, just one more reason to despise these unnatural monsters," said Nerida. "And to hope for a speedy end to this conflict." She looked out at the gathering around her. "Ivy, we've discussed your idea and have come to a decision. You're right. We own the perfect place to have the upper hand. We'll lure the vampire champion and her cohorts to the house. We'll stage the final battle for you two champions there." She wiggled slightly in the water, her hair bobbing up and down.

Murmurs broke out amongst the crowd, and Calder stumbled backward a little, his tail quickly working to straighten himself. "But, Mom—"

Nerida closed one fist in the water above her. "I don't want to hear it from the prince who encouraged his people to drop out of swim team. Our people have led Central to swim team championships for more than half a century. And you throw that all away." Her eyes turned pointedly to Cascade, Bay, Llyr, and Laguna. The first two shirked back while Llyr ran a smooth hand through his red hair. Laguna's eyes were focused on the ceiling and I followed her line of sight to see three fish swimming languidly in a circle.

"Mom, we have more important things to consider right now. And besides, Ivy was uncomfortable, and her protection comes first—"

Really? Swim team is a thing that matters right now?

"And what better place to protect her than *in the water.*" She sighed. "*Fine.* This will all hopefully be at an end soon enough, and things like the last generation of merfolk winning swim meets isn't going to mean much anymore," she said. "We can look at it as just a reminder—a reminder of our time walking amongst the humans."

So they did plan to head to warmer seas when they won? I studied Calder, trying to read him—fighting myself not to reach out and grab his wrist and pry his feelings from him—but his focus was on the algae below him, shifting slightly in the gentle movements of the aquatic world around us.

"So how do we lure them there?" I said when it became clear a cloak of awkwardness was descending over all of us. "To the house?"

"We've talked about that, too. Right, Beck? Dathan?" Nerida exchanged a look with Calder's uncle—Beck—and he nodded, then another with Bay's dad—Dathan—and he gave a slight head bob as well.

"We suggest stealing the selection orb," said Dathan. "The one the faery is holding."

"Why...?" I asked. If I could perspire underwater, the skin prickly at my forehead would be sweat right now. "With both champions decided, what use does it have?"

Nerida's lips went thin. "The vampires won't like that we have it, I can assure you that much. Even if it's played its role."

"Okay," I said, not at all sure. Then again, what did I know about all of this? But there was another way... "What if we looked into what the vampires are up to?" I suggested. "See what kind of hold they might have over Ember?"

Calder sent me a pleading look to stop. *What? I didn't mention Ember's dad.*

"We don't need to know what the vampires are up to," said Nerida, her voice loud and clear despite its singsong quality. "We just need to steer clear of them."

"This is the safest way to get their attention," added Beck.

So the merfolk adults had already decided, then.

But they'd taken my idea to use the house to its full advantage, to lure the vampires to where the merfolk were stronger.

And this when Calder had seemed so certain Nerida would never see the value in my idea.

I fluttered my fins, feeling the soothing touch of water as it slicked across my face. "Then it sounds like a plan to me. Let's do it!"

The crowd broke out into applause, but my face fell when I noticed the crack in Bay's smile, the lack of enthusiasm in Cascade's clap. Llyr and Laguna barely moved and Calder swallowed visibly, even as his palms slapped together, the watery echo of the movements hollow and dark in my ears.

CHAPTER SIXTEEN

Bay stole his second bite of cod from Llyr's plate, then moved his fork to Cascade's salad bowl, stabbing the arugula she'd left behind. His own tray was long-since cleaned, his wandering fork distracting me in the middle of our hushed lunchtime conversation under the purple-and-gold banner of Central High.

"Orin always seems to know where the action is," said Calder hesitatingly. "So maybe we distract him..."

"He's not that dumb. He'll realize some of us are missing." Bay shook his head between bites.

Cascade seemed to finally notice what he was doing and slid her salad bowl toward him. She shivered, drawing her hands into her lap and staring down at them. "Even if we get the orb... I still don't like the idea of them being in our space. In our... home."

Llyr put a hand on her shoulder as the table went solemn.

Okay, so this had been my idea. Granted, I hadn't really thought about the fact that I was asking them to open up their fortress-like home to invasion. But they had to take risks or nothing would change, right?

"We have to let go sometime," said Laguna quietly. "For the greater good."

So she understood. Still, I shuddered at the idea of Mom's or

Dad's houses becoming battlegrounds. Though Ember had specifically told me she would keep Dad's place neutral.

Dad's place. The wedding ceremony. Ember no doubt bringing her "boyfriend."

"When we do get the orb—I know the perfect place to tell the vampires about it," I said. "My dad and step-mom's wedding ceremony two weekends from now. Ember won't want the vampires to make a scene."

Calder nodded. "Then we, what? Ask them to follow us afterward?"

"I guess?" I tapped the tines of my fork against the edge of my tray, my own lunch half-forgotten. "But I don't really get why they would care that we have it. If they needed it for something, they could steal it from Orin now." I looked from one merperson to the next. All eyes seemed to wander toward Calder, as if waiting for his cue. "Would *you* care if the vampires stole it?" I asked.

"We would," said Calder. And that was that, apparently.

I ground my molars before speaking again. They were hiding something from me. "And you think Orin will just... let you get away with having it?"

"There's no rule against taking it once the champions have agreed to battle," explained Llyr. "I think he'd let it go as part of our strategy."

I threw up my hands. "Then let's just ask him for it."

Laguna opened her mouth and then shut it.

Calder shook his head. "I don't want him to know what we're doing until we've already done it. He's too capricious. We can't count on him letting us have it willingly."

"And if he demands we give it back once we do have it?" I asked. A girl from one of my classes waved at me and I waved back. I was in my own clothes at least today, the haphazard stitches across my dark gray sweatshirt and the loose, dangling threads an aesthetic choice on behalf of the designer, manufactured into a sort of individuality repeated six times alone on the same rack. So sue me. I still felt more at home in punk.

And it'd been great to sleep in my own bed in the relative peace of Mom's townhouse, Blossom snuggled up beside me, memories of eating slippery shellfish under the lake nothing more than a vivid dream.

"Then we give it back and try to think of something else," said Calder glumly. "So he might make a rule not to steal it. He's at least fair enough not to punish us for something that's not against the rules yet."

That gross guy from near the registrar's office waggled his eyebrows pointedly at me as he walked by with his arm around a girl chattering away and I rolled my eyes, turning my back to him. "Okay," I said. "But you have to tell me: Why's the orb important again now?"

All eyes went back to Calder. They were hiding something from me. From *me*. The girl who'd turned her life upside down to be their champion.

Calder let out a deep breath. Then he straightened in his seat. "Technically, if we could get her heart and mind in the right place, Ember could drop out of this battle with the help of the orb."

"What?" My head was pounding. They'd made the "trial period" followed by the kissing-contract seem so *final*. "We can... We can still drop out?"

Calder shirked back, his eyelids fluttering. "You'd want *Ember* to drop out," he said. "Right?"

I squeezed my fork tightly in my hand, feeling the cheap metal dig into my palm as my mind raced. *I* wanted Ember to drop out. Then *I* could drop out.

But that wouldn't be what the merfolk wanted. "Without two champions, there's no winner," I said quietly. People were getting up from cafeteria tables all around us and a short bell went off overhead, signaling the approach of the end to this lunch period. But none of my group moved.

"Ember dropping out isn't our goal," said Calder quietly. "But it wouldn't hurt if the vampires *thought* it was."

"So what *is* the goal?" I demanded to know.

Calder leaned back in his chair and scratched the nape of his neck. "To get her to where the vampires can't reach her and make her surrender." His voice cracked at the end.

I supposed I could live with that.

———

"What are you playing?" Autumn peered over my shoulder at Mom's kitchen table as she set my utensils down beside my plate, then tapped her own fork slowly over her lips. "Something like Pokémon Go?"

"What?" I asked. "I'm not playing anything. I'm texting."

I went back to texting Calder, then quickly swiped it away and wrote more in a conversation with Paisley. Between classes and meetings at the merfolk mansion over the past few days, Calder and I had tossed out ideas—both for getting the orb and how to lure Ember to where the vampires couldn't reach her. We'd settled on investigating whatever was going on with her dad if we failed to obtain the orb, though the merfolk didn't seem to relish the idea of going anywhere near wherever it was the vampires congregated.

I wondered if there were anti-merfolk traps all over the vampires' home, too. Though I couldn't really think of a merperson weakness, other than the fact that they just weren't as strong or as fast as vampires.

And they couldn't see as well in the darkness.

Still, nothing as potentially prohibitive as sizzling in water or being blinded in sunlight.

Maybe the merfolk really could win this thing.

"You're texting *about* playing," said Autumn as she made her way around the table to her seat. "Collecting orbs with your *boyfriend*."

"You don't know what you're talking about." I gripped my phone a little too hard at the word 'orbs,' angry she'd been prying that much. "And stop reading my texts over my shoulder like a little Miss Nosy."

"*Mom*, Ivy called me 'nosy.'"

"I said you were *like* a little Miss Nosy. And what's wrong with calling it like I see it anyway?"

Mom brought Autumn's plate to the table. "All right, enough, you two." She grabbed my plate and hers.

"I want *pizza bagels*," said Autumn as she stabbed a spoon over and over into Mom's attempt at beef stew. Rather than eating, she was swirling the gravy into her mashed potatoes, her other palm flat against her cheek, her eyes heavily lidded.

"We don't complain about what food we're given in this house," said Mom as she returned to the table, my serving and her own in hand. A lock of her dark hair had long ago fallen out of its ponytail and hung down all wild and frizzy alongside her face. After putting the plates down, she almost sat and then turned with a start as something sizzled over at the stovetop. She ran to switch off a burner she'd left on.

"And we don't use our phones at the table, young lady," she said to me as she returned, as if she'd never taken a break to go avoid potential disaster.

Sighing, I caught sight of Paisley's reply—she'd be there and she'd drag Lyric along, she'd had enough of handling her grumpiness on her own, and she was definitely tired of being cooped up with her grounded brat of a little brother. That satisfied me enough, so I leaned backward and put the phone on the kitchen counter behind me.

We had a plan. Tomorrow—Saturday, a week before Dad and Noelle's wedding ceremony—the merfolk would sneak into Orin's cabin to search for the orb while I kept him distracted at The Hollow Tree with Paisley and Lyric. Paisley had let slip on one of our texts that Raelynn—comfortably Lyric's girlfriend once more —had preordered a book she was picking up this weekend, and, assuming Orin would have to be there since he now had zero employees, I'd parlayed it into our plans.

Besides, it would be nice to pretend this week had just been a weird dream and hang out with my best friends again. Even if it hadn't been *that* long since we'd seen each other. Even if Central High was okay.

I still wanted my life back.

"Straighten up, Autumn," said Mom as she took her first bite of her dinner. Her pinched lips betrayed her own feelings on the meal before she quickly recovered and slipped on a neutral mask. "Eat your supper. Or no dessert."

Autumn growled and put the spoon—barely covered in mashed potatoes—to her mouth, staring at me.

I sighed and did the same. It wasn't as bad as they were all making it out to be. A little burned. A crunch echoed in my head as I bit into what might have once been a carrot before it turned into blackened goo. Okay, so it wasn't great.

Mom deserved a break. "Thanks for dinner, Mom," I said, swallowing hard. I soothed my palate with a scoop of bland mashed potatoes.

"Thank you," echoed Autumn, but she glared at me as she ate another bite, like I'd betrayed her somehow.

"So," said Mom, her face screwing up with courage as she ploughed on through the meal, "I thought we girls would go somewhere nice tomorrow. Just the three of us. We haven't done that in a while."

Autumn brightened. "Chuck E. Cheese?"

"I was thinking more like the mall, pumpkin," said Mom. "So Ivy wouldn't be bored."

"No, that's okay," I said. "I have plans with my friends—I promised I'd go. I haven't seen them all week."

Mom chewed her lip a little. "Okay, then," she said, a sigh belying her disappointment. "Chuck E. Cheese's, it is." She smiled at Autumn, who let out a little excited squeal. She started scraping her plate, piling more of the stew onto her spoon and swallowing quickly, washing it down with chocolate milk every few bites.

"Are you coming golfing Sunday?" Autumn asked me after her glass was empty and her plate half-gone.

"What?" I asked, distracted by the feelings of guilt and anxiety and everything else flowing through me at once.

"Dad is taking Ember and me golfing," she explained. "Noelle is selling napkins."

"*What?*" I said. My spoon clattered with a thunk to the table.

"She sells napkins and straws and other restaurant supplies," said Mom, as if that were what I had an issue with. "And office supplies. Even to my store—despite the fact that we sell our own things in bulk." Mom grimaced as she took a sip of white wine she'd poured for herself in a coffee mug. "She sells supplies everywhere."

"Yeah, I knew that, but why is she doing that on a Sunday? Why are you going golfing without her?" I didn't know why, but the thought of Noelle being there made me feel safer somehow, like Ember wouldn't try anything with her mom there—but with just Dad and Autumn, well, there was the perfect opportunity to snatch up some hostages.

Some bait more effective than a stupid glass rock.

Bait more like the dad of *hers* I'd kept bringing up to Calder and the others, but that they'd kept dismissing. Not that I wanted to kidnap a person over an orb, but if Ember was already planning to do some kidnapping of her own...

And this was war.

"Ember said you probably wouldn't want to come with us," said Autumn. She was done eating and she traced her left index finger over the back of her right hand, not looking up at me.

"I'm coming," I said, standing from the table and snatching my phone off the counter behind me. "Excuse me," I said to Mom, gathering my dishes even as I tucked the phone under my arm. "I've got homework to do."

I felt the weight of Mom's stare on me as I quickly rinsed the dishes and shoved them in the dishwasher.

"You have to clean the sink," chided Autumn in her best tattle-tale voice. "Or the crumbs stick to it." She was just echoing what Mom and Dad had told *her* a thousand times.

Grumbling, I slammed the phone down next to the sink and went to work with the sprayer, Autumn cocking her head and smiling broadly at me from the table the whole time.

She seemed a little *too* happy with herself.

But Mom didn't notice, asking her about school and nodding as

Autumn launched into a rambling story about her new favorite book and how she was going to have a friend who was "an expert" help on her diorama for it.

Her left index finger kept moving in slow circles over the back of her right hand.

Familiar tingles worked their way up from my toes and I realized I was getting too distracted while my hand was wet. Any second now, my feet were going to become fins—right in the middle of the kitchen. *Focus*, I told myself.

My phone buzzed and I shut off the faucet, quickly wiping my hands off before heading upstairs to relay everything to my team of kickbutt mermaid and mermen teen soldiers.

CHAPTER SEVENTEEN

Meeting at Journey's dad's diner for lunch probably wasn't the best idea, considering Journey kept insisting she'd had food poisoning during Homecoming. You know, instead of vampire venom.

Homecoming. It didn't feel like a week ago. It felt like years ago.

But if I just got through this week—and I meant that literally—it might all be over.

"Still waiting on those friends?"

It was the waitress who'd been flirting with Calder the last time I'd been here, though she was too old for him, even if she was probably barely out of high school.

Something bristled in me at the idea of someone else pining after Calder, even though I could already tell that romantically, things weren't going great. He wasn't the prince I'd dreamed of—if I'd even believed in princes like that to begin with.

I sighed, not at what the waitress had asked, but she clearly took it that way.

"They'll be here any minute," I said, quickly pasting on a smile.

She nodded and went to check on a pale, blond man in a business suit sitting at the counter nursing a coffee. My first instinct when I'd laid eyes on him had been to look for a pair of sunglasses, but he wasn't wearing any.

Still, something about him nagged at me. I twirled my straw in my cream soda, clinking the ice cubes against the glass.

A man I presumed to be Journey's father—he shared her dark complexion and wore a chef's apron he took off as he came out from the back of the restaurant—stood on the other side of the counter from the man and smiled broadly, shaking his hand and leaning over the counter to speak with him. I couldn't hear what they were saying from here, but both became rather animated as they spoke.

The front door opened and I heard Lyric's voice before I even turned to confirm my friends had pulled up to the restaurant. So much for keeping careful vigil, particularly with Laguna in the restroom and the other four merfolk on my team all gathered in the woods, waiting on my signal.

"Ivy!" Paisley slid in beside me and side-hugged me as if I hadn't seen her in months. It might have felt that way.

"Hey," said Lyric, her lips pinched. Raelynn beside her seemed quite a bit friendlier, her face brightening as she exchanged a simple "hello" with me.

Buried beneath the menus, my friends didn't notice when Laguna popped up at the end of our table, her long, wavy red hair half behind her back and half in front of her shoulder.

"Whoa, hi," said Paisley. She gave me a side eye. "Ivy didn't tell us she was bringing anybody."

"We have a project to work on later today," I said, scooching over so Paisley could do the same.

"No Bay...?" asked Paisley, looking over her shoulder. I grinned. I'd rarely seen her enamored with anyone but Grey before. Maybe she had a thing for rhyming names.

"No," I replied. "He and Calder had stuff to do."

I'd never seen Paisley paste on a sour expression so quickly, not even when her brother was acting like a brat.

"Hey," grunted Lyric, not looking up from her menu.

"Hello, I'm Raelynn," said Rae, all business and reaching her hand across the table. "Lyric's girlfriend."

"Laguna," the secret mermaid answered quietly, not taking the hand offered to her.

"We go to Central together," I explained when it was clear no other explanation was forthcoming from the redhead. Her eyes weren't focused on the group, instead darting this way and that, and zeroing in on the man at the counter still talking to Journey's dad.

"Yeah, Lyric's been complaining about your transfer all week." Raelynn pinched Lyric's cheek and Lyric leaned away, her lips pressing into a fine, white line.

Paisley leaned in to whisper into my ear. "It gave them something to focus on other than themselves, I'd wager."

The waitress returned, the door to the back of the restaurant swinging open wide to reveal Journey with a clipboard talking to an old woman, and I noticed Laguna's hand clench on her lap.

We went around the table and placed our orders, and Laguna had to be snapped out of whatever she was thinking of to order her fish fry.

Merfolk certainly had no qualms about eating the denizens of the sea.

The conversation delved into something Grey and Ashton had done this week that I'd missed, but I was more focused on the moment when Raelynn turned over her shoulder to wave to Journey's dad and he waved back, patting the blond man on the back before retreating into the kitchen, slipping on his apron as he went. Our waitress refilled the man's coffee.

A minute later, Journey came out with the first couple of plates of food. She still looked sick in my opinion, a touch pallid, but her smile was dazzling, her poise as straight and confident as if she were a model on a runway instead of a fill-in waitress holding a giant sprig mix salad and a tuna sandwich. She slipped the dishes in front of Lyric and Raelynn respectively. "Hey, Rae," she said, her tone as musical as her words.

"Hey! Oh! I have a question about the Chile debate prep."

Raelynn dug into her purse to pull out her phone just as the waitress came out with three dishes balanced precariously between her arms, maneuvering around Journey and sliding them in front of Laguna, Paisley, and me.

"Babe, can you do the homework talk at another booth?" Lyric flicked through her greens with her fork. "It's getting crowded here."

Journey's eyebrows arched, but it wasn't until her eyes darted quickly to me that her expression soured somewhat. She backed up as Raelynn slid out of the booth and started chatting animatedly about GDP and tariffs and other things they discussed for Model U.N. in an empty booth a few tables away.

Laguna's fingers traced over her butter knife handle as she watched them go, and I wondered—not for the first time—if there really was something to be worried about as far as Journey and Devam were concerned.

If I could just somehow casually brush against her.

As if there'd ever be a scenario here where I needed to touch her. But I wanted to make use of that subconscious mindreading trick and find out what she really knew.

"She's not going to even eat her sandwich at this rate," said Lyric, shaking her head and taking a bite of her salad. "Whenever she gets all geeky like that, there's no reaching her."

I frowned. We were kind of on a schedule to get to the bookstore. True, I wanted to spend time with my friends, but the sooner this was all over, the sooner I could get back to all of this without worrying about a pair of fangs lurking around every corner.

Paisley cleared her throat, probably as tired of Lyric's sniping as I was starting to be. "So how are things with Calder?" She nudged her arm against mine as she dipped her chicken strips into a tiny cup of honey mustard sauce.

I opened my mouth. I'd spent the better part of the week being mad at him. I was beginning to empathize more with Lyric after all.

My instincts had been right before this. Relationships were nothing but trouble.

But whatever was going on between us, that didn't mean I'd give up on his people or what I'd promised to do.

...Right? The orb could undo the contract. They hadn't wanted to let me know that.

I shrugged. "We've both been too busy to do much," I said. I hoped that would be the end of that.

Paisley had to almost singlehandedly handle the conversation from there, Lyric throwing her a sassy bone once in a while and me snapping to answer a question whenever Paisley directed her attention to me. Laguna said nothing, only nodding once when Paisley tried to make her feel included.

Just as we were all just about finishing up our meals, Raelynn finally came back to the table, her dazzling white teeth on full display.

"You geeky nut." Lyric gently pounded her shoulder with a fist. "It's been, like, twenty minutes. Everyone else is finished already."

Raelynn's only reply was to shrug and quickly dig into her sandwich. The waitress came back just as Journey headed toward the bathrooms Laguna had used earlier.

This could be my chance.

"Anything else I can get you?" the waitress asked. "Pie? A root beer float?"

"Oo, well, as long as Raelynn's still eating, maybe some apple pie à la mode?" Paisley's tone seemed questioning.

"Oh, like you'd have passed up on that even if she hadn't still been," said Lyric. But she was smiling. Her mood was at least improving, even if she still directed cold energy my way every time she looked at me.

"Nothing for me," I said, then turned to my friend. "Can you guys get out? I need to use the restroom."

"Okay, okay," said Paisley as my movements practically nudged her up against Laguna. "Sheesh. When you gotta go, huh?"

But I didn't reply. I didn't want to miss this opportunity. I walked brusquely between the counter and the booths, only realizing after a few beats that Laguna was on my tail. I supposed backup was a smart idea, though if my worries were all for nothing, Laguna might make any attempt at casual social interaction with Journey followed by a grip of the hand—or something like that—difficult to pull off.

A crash of glass breaking snapped me out of the moment as I whipped around. The waitress had been trying to juggle all of our plates, and one now lay on the ground beside her in pieces. She tried bending over to pick it up, balancing what she still had in her other hand, but then she let out a little pained cry and flung her free hand out above her.

The girls I'd left behind at the table all stood up to look at her, Raelynn even helping guide her stack of plates back down to the table.

"She cut herself!" shouted Lyric over her shoulder toward us.

The blond man in a suit jumped up—and I hadn't even realized I'd stopped so close beside him.

He moved so quickly, he practically shoved me over, and I lost my balance, flinging my hands out, accidentally grabbing on to his arm to steady myself, that niggling feeling at the back of my mind springing into action as I then purposely seized his hand.

Ember, clear as day, in a red dress, even paler than I remembered her. The soft, old-timey music played from a distinctly vintage-style radio in a large family room. A few couples danced animatedly, while others lingered around the room. One stunning voluptuous redhead woman in particular ran a finger up and down a sickly-looking man's neck. She seemed familiar, but I strained, trying to find myself among these memories.

They weren't my own thoughts.

There were so many bright blue eyes. Not on all of the people here. But so many of them. They were intoxicating. Beautiful. Calling to my soul.

"Thomas?" said the redhaired woman languidly stroking the other man's neck. "Am I making you jealous?"

The way her lips upturned into a grin could melt me where I stood.

I snapped back to the moment, my hand dropping from the man's.

He was with the vampires. And he'd just jumped up with a bolt at the smell of fresh blood.

CHAPTER EIGHTEEN

"Laguna!"

But I didn't need to get her at the ready. As my fingers went numb, the cold taking hold of my fist, she was on her haunches ready to pounce at the blond guy with flecks of gray in his hair—Ember's dad, I realized with a start, the memory I'd seen in Ember's mind resurfacing.

But the guy ripped his hand from mine—I hadn't realized I'd been still holding it, clutching it for dear life as the ice started to form there—and rushed toward the waitress and my friends.

"Look out!" I shouted, hot on his tail, Laguna right on mine.

But Ember's dad barely hesitated by the table, where Raelynn was dabbing napkins to the waitress's hand and Lyric, ignoring the mad dash of the middle-aged man, was calling out for someone to come bring a first aid kit.

He pointedly stared at the bleeding hand, no doubt about that, but perhaps at the sound of my pounding footfalls right behind him, he kept going and ran to the entrance, pulling a Calder and speeding right out the door.

I screeched to a halt, watching him get into a car—a shiny, gray thing with a rental car service sticker on its front window—and drive away.

"He's one of them," I explained to Laguna in hushed whispers as she, too, watched him go.

She shook her head. "His eyes."

"Well, he certainly spends time with them." I looked her up and down. "Besides, you've been acting like you smelled something on him ever since we came here."

It was strange that the man had been here *before* we'd arrived, so it wasn't the result of any tailing. He did appear to know Journey's dad, but certainly this couldn't have been a coincidence?

Not with this age-old battle going on.

But if he was one of them—in some way—why had he run at the smell of blood—*away* from the blood?

My mind scrambled with possibilities. Maybe he was a baby vampire, not yet drinking blood but unable to control himself around it. Maybe he hadn't wanted to give away his cover, thin though it may have been.

"Oh, jeez, Tiff."

Whipping around, I realized my original intention of using the subconscious mind reading thing on Journey had been abandoned. And that, if my theory about baby vampires not having to wear sunglasses turned out to be true—well, Journey Slowe didn't seem to have any problem being around the blood. She cradled the waitress's hand gently, not flinching and fleeing or taking a drink for herself. Maybe she and Devam really did just think they'd gotten food poisoning. Maybe they *had* or the vampires had been clever enough to disguise whatever had gone down as such.

At least I'd gotten some intel. Something squeezed tightly in my stomach. I'd *wanted* to look into Ember's dad before, but Calder had stopped me.

True, Calder had been right to focus on some inanimate object instead. But what if tomorrow the bloodsuckers had some plans to use my own dad—and sister—against me?

What if I'd just let my best opportunity of preventing that from happening pass me by?

"I'm so sorry," said Journey, guiding the waitress toward the back room. She spoke over her shoulder as they moved. "We'll have everything cleaned right up. And the meal's on us."

"Oh, you don't have to worry about that. It was an accident," said Raelynn.

Lyric nudged her, though, and pasted on a broad smile. "Thanks so much."

I stood still a second, watching Journey go.

"Fat lot of help you were," said Lyric with a laugh. "I saw you bolting over here and I thought you were going to help us keep the bleeding down." She turned a shade of green as she spotted some red splots on the table's edge. "Anyway, can we get going? Unless you two still have to use the bathroom?"

Chewing on my lip, I shook my head. "I'll use it at The Hollow Tree."

———

Even though it hadn't been that long since I'd last been here—I'd gotten my last paycheck, so to speak, just earlier in the week—I was struck by an overwhelming sense of nostalgia as I walked through the front door, the bell jangling overhead.

Lyric and Paisley were chatting about a physics assignment—or more accurately, they were discussing the way Mr. Jones's moustache bobbed whenever he sighed, which was often, I remembered —and Raelynn made a beeline for the front counter, looking around.

Laguna lingered at my side, the door shutting closed behind us.

"Ah, Miss Kelly," said a familiar voice. The brown, curly hair with flecks of green and gold appeared above a row of bookshelves and made its way toward the counter. "Been waiting for you. Lovely day, yeah?"

I pulled my phone out of my pocket, taking a second to think about how the scuffed and chipped case could really use some replacing, and fired off the text message that would be our signal. *He's here.*

Calder sent a thumbs-up back.

I nodded to Laguna and she started wandering down an aisle, doing a poor job of acting nonchalant, with her fists clenched and her vibrant red hair whipping this way and that every few seconds. She jumped with a start at Paisley's cry of "Kitty!" Maine Coon Feilia opened one eye lazily as Paisley went to work disturbing the feline's beauty sleep atop a sun-soaked armchair, the sniffling starting almost immediately as her allergies kicked in.

The chatter between Orin and Rae melted into murmurs, punctuated by Raelynn's delicate peals of laughter and the clank of the cash register.

Feilia stood up and stretched before jumping down off the chair, pointedly ignoring Paisley, even as she chased after her.

"Let the cat breathe, Pais," said Lyric. She scrunched up her nose as she took in Paisley's puffy eyes. "Let *yourself* breathe. Remember the cat allergies."

"Oh, I remember," said Paisley sadly, rubbing her nose on the back of her sleeve. She sighed and let Lyric guide her away.

I stopped to let Feilia trot by, but she looked up at me and hesitated, then started rubbing my legs and letting out a grumbling purr.

I bent down to scratch her ear for half a minute when Orin scared the living daylights out of me.

"The little shop gaffer missed you, yeah? Though I reckon she doesn't usually show it."

I stumbled onto my backside and looked up. He was leaning over a bookshelf, his hands dangling across a line of creased paperbacks.

Feilia yawned and made her way around the shelves toward the back room.

Jumping to my feet, I smoothed my hair. "Hello," is all I said. I feigned interest in a nearby book, flipping through it and realizing with a start that it was one of those midlife crisis books where the guy drinks a lot, almost cheats on his wife, and tells off his boss before riding off into the sunset.

"Your taste in literature is surprising," said Orin as he rounded the shelf to peer over my shoulder. "Though certainly in line with most professional critics', I'll give you that."

Flushing, I shoved the book back on the shelf.

"You're a lot of fun to take the mickey out of, you know that?" he asked.

No, I didn't know that, whatever "that" was. But I had an idea.

Raelynn appeared at the other end with her The Hollow Tree bag in her hand. "I have to be somewhere at three, so I'm going to get Lyric and Paisley and get going. Didn't you have to use the bathroom?"

Right. I'd almost forgotten about that. "Yeah, uh... Okay, see you guys." I looked around for Laguna and found her halfway up the stairs to the second floor, peering down over the space below like a queen surveying her kingdom.

"How *does* a half-fish relieve herself again?" Orin pondered aloud as Raelynn turned the corner.

"Shut it," I said, my face reddening. I actually didn't know how they went in merfolk form. I supposed it must have been similar to a fish, however *they* went.

"We're going to get going," said Lyric as she rounded the corner. "Thanks for meeting us for lunch. It was... certainly memorable."

Orin raised an eyebrow as he shoved his hands into his pockets. His reading glasses dangled precariously from his front shirt pocket. "Oh? Do tell."

"The waitress bled all over our table," explained Paisley. "So we got to eat for free."

He nodded, clearly considering. "Well, that's one way to dodge a bill, in't it?"

Paisley gave me a hug, sniffing loudly, though I knew the tears were from the cat dander. "I can hitch a ride with you two if you want me to stay."

I looked up at Laguna, who probably couldn't hear anything from where she stood. "Oh, that'd be nice, but we do have that project to work on. Besides, I don't know if she could give you a lift later since it's her parents' car."

Paisley nodded. "All right, then, but don't be a stranger, okay?"

I nodded.

Lyric gave my arm a mild punch, what might have been a genuine smile darting on her lips. "See you around, traitor."

Little did she know I was apparently working subterfuge from within Central High, pulling their team's top swimmers out of the next meet. Giving her an awkward smile, I waved as they made their way to the door.

As soon as the bell over the door ceased its clanging, Orin looked from Laguna to me and back again. He cupped his hands around his lips. "Can I help you find something, fish girl? Or are you just going to stare down at us menacingly all day?"

Laguna's lips pinched and she made her way down the staircase, her feet stomping loudly with every step.

"She's just on guard since the blood incident," I explained.

"Oh? So were there vampires present after all?"

I shrugged. "We're not sure. Not the sunglasses-wearing kind anyway." I didn't know how much to tell him. He was supposed to be neutral, but he clearly had no qualms about helping stir things up on occasion.

"I see. Well, if you don't have any purchases to make, I may as well close up shop." He stretched, putting his arms straight up overhead, leaning first one way and then the other. "I feel like going home and putting my feet up before the fire."

A shot of adrenaline coursed through me, the pounding of my heart loud and overpowering in my head. *He can't leave yet. Not until I hear from Calder.* "I really do have to use the bathroom," I said quickly.

Orin chuckled. "All right. Well, you know where it is." He eyed Laguna as she shuffled over toward us and she gave me a slight, almost-imperceptible nod, as if to say she'd keep an eye on him while I dodged out of sight.

I walked briskly around the counter and to the back room, Feilia giving me a one-eye stare from her perch atop some of the boxes stacked high beside the bathroom door. Things had gotten even more disorganized in the short time since I'd last worked here. The door shut behind me, the sensor light flicking on, and I leaned against the door and checked my messages. Nothing.

Find it? I sent first.

There was half a minute before Calder entered his reply. *No. It's not anywhere.*

Are you sure?

There aren't that many places to look.

I sighed, wondering how I was going to keep stalling Orin and how much time would prove necessary before they called it quits. *It's not on the mantel?*

Huh? wrote Calder.

A thought struck me. *Did you find the cabin?* I asked. Calder had said that even the princes usually couldn't find the place without Orin's permission.

No, he wrote back. *That's what I meant. We can't find it anywhere. But I know it's somewhere around here.*

They hadn't even found the cabin yet, let alone turned the place upside down for the orb. A sigh flooded out from between my lips. This was a disaster. Why hadn't any of us thought of that?

There was a knock on the bathroom door. "Almost finished, love? I want to close up shop and your fish girl friend's cold, icy stare is giving me the willies."

Shoving the phone back into my pocket, I took a deep breath to steel myself. "Not yet. Geez, don't rush me."

I decided to actually go while I had the chance, while I needed to think.

"Okay, but yeah, she's followed me back here now, and she's got some Jason Voorhees-level blank-face staring at me going on, yeah? Please hurry."

I chuckled despite myself. What were the two of them doing out there? Did Laguna have any idea how to be subtle?

I finished up my business and gave my hands a good, long, long washing.

"Sheesh, obsessive compulsive much?" said Orin as I let myself out. "You're going to rub your skin clear off, yeah?" He was sitting at the breakroom table, cradling a mug of, no doubt, tea as Laguna stared at him from the open doorway that led to the rest of the shop.

He kept staring back at her, tugging at an ear with the hand not cradling the mug, somehow his expression both befuddled and bemused. "She your muscle now?" he asked, not even taking his eyes off Laguna.

"Something like that." I swooped into the other chair at the table and used Orin's portable water boiler and a tea bag to make myself a cup.

"Help yourself, why don't you?" Orin's brow arched.

"Thought I'd just share a cup of tea with an old friend."

"Right, right," said Orin. "That's why the last time you saw me, you had to restrain yourself from throttling my throat."

"You *were* watching movies on a garage rooftop while bloodsuckers were threatening to inject venom into my veins."

"Hey, I helped with that."

To be fair, he had.

"True," I said, holding my mug up. "So like I said. A cup of tea with an old friend."

"Well, you've got the 'old' part right anyway." Orin sipped at his mug before looking up over my shoulder. "She going to join us or just glare at me?"

I didn't wait to see Laguna's response. "Glare, I suppose."

My pocket buzzed as a text message came in, but I didn't dare check it. If they were only just now finding the cabin, they'd need at least a few more minutes to search it.

A playful smirk tugged on Orin's lips. "You know, you could have just asked, all right?"

I blew on my mug of tea, the bag still in it. "Sorry. Next time I'll ask if you can spare the tea bag and water before I just help myself." I took a sip. Too hot. My lips pinched as I swallowed to get it over with quickly, the cold tingling on my fingertips almost an automatic reflex to the fire on my lips.

"No, you're welcome to my tea," said Orin. "I mean the orb."

Splurting out my drink, I slammed the mug down harder than I'd meant to, wiping my mouth with my sleeve. "What?"

"Don't play coy with me." The corners of Orin's lips were visible around the mug as he took a slow, slow sip.

Now he was the one being aggravatingly slow as my heel bounced rapidly below the table.

"How did you know?" I asked, all games dropped—probably the best plan to get him to answer me faster.

"I have my ways. You've been planning this for days."

Laguna shuffled closer, but I held an arm out to stop her as she reached the edge of the table.

"Harming the observer, fish girl," said Orin, putting his mug back on the table. "War-losing penalty."

"She's not going to lay a hand on you," I said firmly, as much to Laguna as to Orin.

"Oy, yeah, I figured that. That's why she's settled for making the hairs on my arms stand up on end instead." Shuddering, he pushed back from the table and stood.

My mind raced as he went to a box of books beside Feilia. He'd hypnotized or whatever it was my parents into accepting him as an old family friend. Was it just a matter of calling up my mom and asking her to browse through my text messages or...? But how did Mom know my password? She could have had a parental override, I supposed.

Biting my lip, I vowed to never let my phone out of my sight. To sleep on it even—and to be careful what I wrote on it.

"Catch," said Orin, and I realized I hadn't even been paying attention to what he'd been doing over there.

Luckily, Laguna's instincts were sharper than mine. She bent over and caught something before it could hit me smack dab on the head.

The orb. The bright blue, the bright red, the darkened third section of it.

Orin slid his hands into his pockets and leaned against the stack of books like it was a wall and he was the epitome of rebel without a cause. "You can borrow it," he said. "I like the plan. Might just put an end to this kerfuffle."

Laguna handed the orb to me and I traced the blue with my

fingertips, remembering that somehow, there'd be a way to drop out of this if that was what I wanted.

My thumb stopped at the bottom of the orb, the part not glowing a bright color. It was caked in what looked like mud, the grime masking the third section entirely.

"Had a bit of an accident while doing the dishes," he said, as if noticing what had caught my attention. "Don't wipe it off, though, all right? I don't want it to get scratches."

"Okay..." I said, staring hard at the orb between my fingers.

Something was wrong. On so many levels. But Orin giving us an advantage was just the sneaky kind of thing he'd do.

I wondered what he was doing for the vampires that I didn't know about, and if they'd have some faery-given advantage at this mini golf trip tomorrow.

CHAPTER NINETEEN

Dad and Ember loitered near the mini golf entrance, Dad no doubt telling one of his lame jokes as he was about bursting into laughter while Ember pasted on an awkward smile. The day was cool and overcast, and she still looked out of place in her vintage-style, puffy, black pants and red blouse, the sleeves rolled up to her elbows. She had a red kerchief woven through her yellow hair, her skin almost alabaster even in the dim sun.

"I'm not sure it's a good day for golf," Mom said as she pulled into a parking space. She leaned over her dashboard and gazed up. "It looks like it might rain."

Good, I thought. *It'll scare the vampires away.*

I wondered what Mom would have thought if I'd said that aloud.

"Dad!" shouted Autumn from the back seat. She unbuckled her seatbelt and opened her door, across the lot in a flash.

"Hey!" called Mom as she followed suit. She stopped to grab Autumn's overnight bag from the back seat, checking over her shoulder to make sure Autumn was nearly safely in Dad's arms. "Watch for cars!" She was barely doing the same herself as she headed after her.

Letting out a deep breath, I patted the little backpack I'd borrowed from Autumn—it was purse-sized, but it slung over my back with a strap for each arm. Then I patted my pocket to make sure my phone was in my jeans. Check. Inside the little backpack —nestled against the decorative black buttons down the back of my thin, blue sweater punctuated at the bottom by a trim of black lace—were my wallet and the orb, which settled with a thunk against my spine.

Before I picked up my feet, *I* checked for cars carefully, zeroing in on two in particular: Calder's pickup and Cascade's smaller vehicle. They were here. So my backup was going according to plan.

There was no sign of Dean lingering near Ember as Mom made small talk with her and Dad carried Autumn's bag to his car, Autumn riding piggyback all the way. No sign of anyone in sunglasses—the overcast sky would have certainly made them stand out more.

But they were here somewhere. They had to be. And my team would hang back and cover the place, hopefully far enough back that chatty Autumn wouldn't notice them and let slip there was a group of teens playing golf a few groups behind us looking tense and jittery.

But even if she did let it slip and that made Ember call out her minions, that was what the orb was for. Instead of being safely secure in the merfolk fortress, it was with me. To show them not to act up because... because I could drop out of the game at any moment? Or I could force Ember to?

I really didn't think we'd have a chance of that until we lured her to the merfolk mansion, and that... That was another big plan being set in motion.

Let them know we had the orb. Make them want to get it back. Separate Ember from the other vampires and... Convince her that she could drop out as champion and leave the vampires safely standing, yet somehow actually make her surrender instead.

Without causing any injury.

I tensed as someone shut their car door, then felt my muscles relax as I realized it was just Dad putting Autumn's things away.

There was also another idea that Calder had floated. He'd

suggested that if the orb failed to act as a sufficient enough lure, we capture Dean and use him to *convince* Ember.

Let him suffer in water or surrender. Merfolk would hold him down and then she'd have to give up. Letting him die for real would be better than letting him suffer.

I felt sick. I had a week to think of a better plan than that. But I couldn't think of anything. If my end goal was the end of vampires, the only one I could really protect from harm was Ember herself.

Because if either of us dropped out and the war went into a ceasefire, I didn't imagine vampire, merfolk, or faery would just let us live out the rest of our senior year in peace.

"Hey, sport," said Dad as he walked up alongside me, Autumn's hand in his. "Thanks for choosing your old man and sisters over your friends today."

Sisters. Even after this was over, I didn't think I could ever go back to trying to think of Ember as a sister.

Nodding, I tightened my grip on the backpack straps as we met up with Mom and Ember. Ember pointedly looked just slightly over my head as Mom moved in to give Autumn a hug and a kiss and then laid a hand on my shoulder. "See you tonight, honey," she said, and she and Dad jerked their heads in unison, a cloudiness glazing over their eyes in that moment, almost like their real memories were trying to fight the soothing words Orin had pasted over them. *Why is Ivy going back to her mom's on a Sunday?* Why indeed?

I swayed slightly from side to side as I stared Ember down, waiting for her eyes to meet mine. They did.

If I wasn't just imagining things, her brown eyes flashed blue for just a moment, long enough to get her to cry out and rub at her face. She'd almost gone vampire on me and she hadn't had the proper protection in place. Fortunately, she brushed it off as if something had gotten into her eye, turning her back to us when my dad and mom glanced her way.

"Bye, Mom!" called Autumn as she tripped over her feet to get in line.

Ember was there in a flash, picking her up and stopping her stumble from turning into an outright tumble. "Careful," she said. "Wouldn't want anything to happen to you before the game even begins." Ember looked pointedly at me.

Autumn grinned and kept on moving as my heel ground into the pavement beneath my aquatic shoe.

"Nice shoes," said Ember, her tone a perfect mixture of genuine conversation and perhaps the slightest bit of condescension. Dad joined Autumn to get our tickets and I lingered behind, casually pivoting myself to get a good look around me. "Thanks," I said. Calder and the others hadn't gotten out of their vehicles yet. There was no sign of bloodsuckers, but I didn't believe that they weren't already waiting ahead of us.

"They clash with your outfit," she said, flinging a loose lock of hair behind her back under the kerchief. It had been rolled into a thin line and tied at the side of her head like a bow.

"Yeah, well, it looks like it might rain and I prefer function to fashion these days anyway."

She bristled as Dad raised a handful of golf clubs above his head, signaling us to join him.

"You know, I've honored our deal," she said as we slowly made our way toward him.

"What deal?"

"To keep my house—*our* house—a neutral zone."

Autumn took her club from Dad and practically bounced on her heels at the entryway to the course.

"Thanks," I said, and I meant it.

"So why not come back home? Mom and Easton are both acting strange whenever they think too hard about where you are." She lowered her voice. "I don't really appreciate Orin messing with my mom like that."

So the vampires did know about the faery's little useful quirk. I wondered if they'd made use of it and I just didn't know it yet.

"Here you go," said Dad, handing each of us a club and a ball. Ember got hot pink and I got dark blue. "Autumn, wait. *Wait.* You have to let the group ahead of us finish the hole."

Distracted, he took a few steps the other way, and I lowered my voice so he couldn't hear me. "I don't know if I could sleep at night there knowing I'm your target."

"If that's true, the same goes for me," she said. "And yet I'm willing to trust you."

"Thanks," I muttered. Dad waved at us to signal that it was finally our turn.

I surveyed my surroundings as Autumn positioned her ball and took the first shot. The golf course was minimally decorated but consistent with a mountain adventure theme. To one side of me, a go-kart race track thrummed with the hum of tiny vehicle engines. To the other far end of the course was an enclosed building with doors propped open, from which echoed the sounds of a multitude of arcade games, ball tosses, and laughing and screaming children.

Lights from the machines flickered from the darkness. If the vampires were hiding anywhere, it was there.

But unless they wanted to make headlines, they weren't going to be climbing up the fence that separated us to attack us in the middle of this game.

Relaxing considerably, I realized it was already my turn— everyone else had gone, even Ember.

I lined up the ball and took a shot. It soared through the first tunnel but got stuck between a rock and a wooden barrier on the other side. It took me five more hits to get it in the hole.

"You stink at this," said Autumn gleefully. She'd only beaten me by two strokes.

"*Hey*," said Dad. "Be nice. Or I'll make you wait to go last this hole."

Autumn grumbled but took her turn, exaggeratedly swinging her tush out as she went to make her first hit.

"I just want this to be over with," said Ember under her breath and I thought she meant the mini golf at first. She leaned her elbows behind her on a large fake rock, her golf club threaded through her arms. We were higher up now, overlooking the parking lot. I caught sight of Bay and Llyr making their way toward the entrance, Calder, Cascade, and Laguna behind them. I needed to get Ember's attention fast.

"So where are they?" I asked.

She turned back to me. "Huh?"

"Girls, it's your turn!" called Dad. Ember straightened and set her ball down, tapping it in a smooth, sleek motion.

"Your friends," I said as I set my ball down before Ember could head toward the hole to finish her play. "Journey, for starters. I thought you never went anywhere without her."

"Ha," said Ember. "Then you don't really know me at all. Journey has a much busier life than I do. I stay home while she has all these after-school activities and her dad's restaurant to help out at."

"That was *before* all this," I said. "Before Homecoming." I whacked my ball. It bounced off the side of the wall around the play area and went way farther than hers.

"You almost hit Ember's!" shouted Autumn from down the line. "Wait your turn!"

Leaning atop my club with one hand, I gestured for Ember to go ahead.

I waited for her to finish—Autumn screamed in delight when she quickly did—and joined them, taking far too many swings to get my ball in the hole.

"You're *amazing* at this, Ivy," said Autumn, laughing haughtily. That was how she was getting around Dad yelling at her to be nice. To *pretend* to be.

I just rolled my eyes. I couldn't care less about losing the game.

"You didn't answer my question," I said to Ember once Dad and Autumn had gone ahead to linger behind the next group, which was taking its time. Looking down the mini mountain, I could see Team Mermaid was at the first hole. Bay and Llyr were laughing and shoving each other, and Cascade was about to tap her ball. Laguna was rubbing her golf ball against her forearm as she looked around. Calder's lips were thin as he put both hands atop his golf club in front of him, looking for all the world like a medieval knight posing heroically with his sword pointed in the ground.

"Where are yours?" she asked instead. "You're the one scientifically proven not to go anywhere without an entourage."

An entourage? That would imply they all revolved around me. Though I supposed my new merfolk crew did.

"They won't do anything if yours don't," I said, rather than dodging the question. She nodded glumly, then took her turn.

The rest of the game was a lot of that. Autumn getting excited, me doing poorly, Ember and I cautiously feeling each other out between holes. There was a group between ours and Calder's, but it didn't take long for Ember to spot them, for her accusatory glare to land on me. I shrugged. I hadn't dodged her question like she'd dodged mine.

We finished the game. Ember won, and Dad came in second; Autumn gloated about getting third place. As we were hanging up our golf clubs—the last hole had eaten our balls—Autumn darted away. "I want to play games!"

"Wait!" I said, but Dad stepped in front of me just at that moment and I slammed into him.

"Hold up, sport!" he said, then patted me on the back.

Autumn was already gone, already lost into the dark, cavernous space from which colorful, blinking lights emanated on rotation. Dad was on his way after her, doing his own middle-aged, out-of-shape version of jogging to keep up.

"What's in the bag?" Ember asked from behind me.

I swirled around. Ember pointed one red-painted nail at my stomach—where the bag had been, I supposed, before I'd turned around.

"Something important," I said, gripping the straps tightly. Thinking better, I maneuvered to get it off my back and cradled it against my stomach where I could see it, sliding my arms through the straps backward.

Behind Ember, the other group began to hang up their clubs, leaving my team at the last hole. I locked eyes with Calder and nodded. He ran forward, his final play forgotten.

A huge boom sent shivers down my spine as the group of bystanders putting away their clubs all let out a little shout. Calder flinched, coming to a stop, the others on their haunches behind him.

Ember didn't so much as move.

"Come on," she said, snatching my hand before I even realized she'd unfrozen.

There was a commotion over by the go-kart track, along with smoke—and what looked like a go-kart on its side up against a fence, the wire bent and damaged.

And from the driver's seat, out jumped a pale, dark-haired guy in a dress shirt, khakis, and sunglasses.

My eyes locked on the vampire climbing through the hole in the metal fence, I didn't realize Dean appeared at my other side, his hand on my upper arm.

And then the world went still. Literally.

CHAPTER TWENTY

E mber and Dean tugged me toward the arcade, and I just sort of let them, so in shock was I at the total and utter *silence* of the world around me.

No one moved but we three. No sound rung out. The lights from the arcade had even stopped blinking.

"What's going on…?"

Then I realized *enough* of what was going on. I was being kidnapped by vampires and their champion. Maybe to be killed— at least to be defeated. And they were getting the orb, whatever it was good for, at the same time.

What was I *doing* just letting them drag me anywhere?

"Get off!" I screamed, trying to yank my arms out from both of them.

"I told you the shock wouldn't last long." Ember chewed on her lip as she fought back.

Her grip was looser than Dean's, who was threatening to bruise my arm, his fingers sliding down and wrapping tightly around the skin of my wrist.

Skin-to-skin contact.

Taking a deep breath to calm myself, I searched for his plan in his mind.

"The fishfolk don't know how we move so quickly from one place to

another," I found myself saying in a deep voice. Dean's voice. "I say we use it to ambush her. Distract the others, then grab her before they can follow."

"How do you know where the others will be?" Ember. She leaned up against me—Dean—her cheek flush against my shoulder. Her warmth was soothing, yet somehow, unnatural.

"They'll be there," said a cool, familiar voice. Though it was feminine and high-pitched, there was no mistaking the surety and poise in her tone. A pale redhead with bright blue eyes sat at the head of a long table, a glass of wine in her hand. "They may stay a few steps behind, pretend to keep their distance, but they'll be ready to pounce at a moment's notice." She drank the liquid and I realized with a shudder it was probably blood. Red stained her lips as she put the glass back down.

"She might not even come," said Ember beside me.

"She will," said Dean. "That's what Easton and Autumn are for."

I gasped and came back to the present. So this had been their plan all along? To use my family as bait to lure me here, not to use them as hostages?

I'd been so concerned with watching out for them, I'd forgotten to watch out for myself.

The bag slipped down my arms as I struggled, the weight of the orb heavy, somehow heavier in this unnatural environment.

I tried summoning the cold to my hand—the one Ember had hold of—but she seemed to notice, bringing heat and flame to her fingertips at the same time.

I screamed as the scorch of heat reached my skin. We were almost at the entrance to the arcade now, but they weren't directing me that way—they were taking me toward the parking lot.

"Ivy, just calm down," said Ember. "Just say you surrender and we'll let you go."

"No!" I shouted, and I brought my foot down hard on hers. She let out a yelp and dropped my hand.

"Ember, wait," said Dean. "Stay in the chain. I can't hold it much longer—"

Ember went still mid-movement, her face contorted with pain. I didn't wait to be marveled by her joining the stillness around us. I kicked Dean's shin. He didn't flinch, so I yanked on my arm and kicked harder, higher up, wishing I still had my boots on.

"What do you have in that bag?" asked Dean and I realized with a start that the top of the bag had become unlatched, that the orb was rolling out.

I summoned the cold to my freed right hand, fighting through the sizzling of Ember's lingering heat on my skin.

Dean's face contorted. "Calm down or you're just going to make this harder—"

I shot the ice at him and he dodged, but it still skirted his shoulder. He dropped my wrist and the world came to life.

The echoing sounds of the games in the arcade were the first things to assault my senses, though I had to shake my head to snap it back to reality, like my brain was still caught in whatever that unnatural stillness had been.

The vampire power. The explanation for their apparent speed.

"No!" snarled Ember again and she grabbed my wrist, then the world went still and heavy—but just for a fraction of a moment, like it was all an illusion. Ember's face was screwed up in concentration, but it was clear her power was still new to her. Her lips peeled back to reveal a set of fangs elongating from her incisors.

"Get off!" I yanked away, darting past Dean as he lunged for me, bolting for the dark arcade.

I looked over my shoulder to see if my merfolk were too far behind—they were across the way still back at the golf course, a crowd of people forming between them and me as the curious went to take a look at the go-kart crash. Not to mention the sunglasses-wearing driver who still stalked toward them as if he hadn't just put a hole in the fence around the go-kart track.

As my head whipped around, a shiver ran down my spine. Atop a vintage restored car in the lot nearby sat the redheaded woman, whom I realized was Union High's new "principal." I wondered how the bloodsuckers had woven their way into positions at the school like that. But flashbacks of those memories I'd stolen—of the redhaired woman demanding the room's attention, like a court enraptured with their queen—shot through me, lending some weight to her power. She was a woman who got what she wanted. To an unnatural degree.

And right now, she wanted me.

"Rain!" said Dean, but I didn't hear more aside from the curse escaping his lips as I slipped inside the darkness.

I repositioned the backpack in front of me, clutching the orb tightly as I wove around blasting arcade machines and families playing Skee-Ball.

"...crash at the go-kart track," said a guy holding a basketball and tossing it in his hands. He flung it and scored a point by getting it through the basket.

"Anyone hurt?" asked the woman next to him.

"I don't know. Ambulances are probably on their way."

As if in answer to his statement, the faint sound of sirens punctuated the noise of the arcade.

Grinding to a halt, I checked left and right. What was the plan? Rain pounded overhead, a slight tinny sound to the water droplets as they hit the roof. The doors had been propped open, the light even from an overcast day pouring in, making those brighter areas by the door less hospitable to a vampire afraid of the light. Then again, with their sunglasses, it seemed to make little difference to them.

But if it was raining, the arcade was the only form of shelter.

Dean and Ember appeared in one door, the slight, almost-imperceptible tinge of smoke sizzling off Dean's form. In the other appeared yet another vampire I recognized from the pool and back at that empty house.

Principal Horne was nowhere to be seen.

And to my left, deep within the darkness of the arcade, I caught sight of three sets of blue, glowing eyes.

Think. I bounced in place. *Find Dad and Autumn. Get out of here. Pray Calder and the others make it here before the vampires get hold of me again.*

Picking up my feet, I started moving, my mind racing through the types of games Autumn liked when she went to these things, but I was drawing a blank. The raucous rumble of thunder overhead raised my shackles on end, my mind filling with the desire to just crawl between a nearby Skee-Ball machine and a wall to hide.

I didn't know how good a look Dean had gotten at the orb, but it would do little good to let them know I had it when I had no backup and nowhere to run—they'd just gleefully grab both me and it at once and thwart the merfolk plan entirely.

I should have never agreed to bring it along.

The top of the mini backpack was still undone. I scrambled to shut it when I noticed something off. Red, blue... green.

I took the orb out of the bag. The caked-on mud had scuffed off in one small section, the green glow coming from there.

Not caring about Orin's request or anything, really, I used my nail to scrape more of the dirt away.

The final third of the orb was glowing green.

What did that mean?

A cackle of laughter made my skin crawl and I realized the arcade was filling up with even more people seeking refuge from the rain. Beyond the gathering people, red and white lights lit up the parking lot and I finally, *finally* saw Calder and Bay push through the crowd.

But there were too many people between them and me.

"Ivy," said a familiar voice.

I turned to find my dad clutching the rails of an old *Dance Dance Revolution* game, Autumn's flying feet hitting the colored arrows in tune to a semi-familiar beat.

"Dad!" I shoved the orb back down into the bag and made my way to his side. Looking over my shoulder, I pinched his sleeve. "We need to go."

"There's a bad storm right now," he said. "We should wait it out. Besides, your sister is still playing her jumping game."

"*Dance* game," corrected Autumn between heavy breaths. Her feet were flying.

"It's important," I said. "There's been an accident at the go-karts and if we don't go now, we might be blocked in by emergency vehicles."

"Is that what all the ruckus was about?" Dad grimaced. "Hope no one was hurt."

Oh, if only the driver actually *was*. That'd be one less blood-sucker to fight.

There were too many people here, though. Too many people. Surely, they wouldn't do anything. But we needed to go. Now. While it was still raining.

I couldn't just go with Calder and leave Dad and Autumn here with the vampires.

"If you need to go somewhere, why don't you ask Orin to give you a lift?" asked Dad. He frowned after he said it, like the words out of his mouth were only now just catching up with his brain.

I whipped around. Of course he'd be here. He'd probably helped the vampires out somehow, had known this was going to happen.

I spotted him a few arcade cabinets away, engrossed in some fighting game. He screamed in delight and pumped his fist in the air, never once turning my way.

Very observant, observer.

"Dad, *please*," I said.

Dad shook his head. "Well, we need to find Ember first."

Drat. I'd almost forgotten that.

"She... ran into her boyfriend," I said by way of explanation. "I'm sure he'll take her home."

Dad scratched the back of his neck. "Well, I can't exactly take off without checking with her to be sure, can I?"

I was bouncing on my heels now. The song in Autumn's game ended and she stopped moving, so I used the opportunity to grab her by the wrist and yank her away.

"Hey!" she shouted. "I still have some more time left."

"We have to go," I said sternly.

She yanked back and Dad moved to step in. "What's gotten into you, honey?" he asked.

As Autumn pulled away, she hit the backpack dangling at my front and I realized I still hadn't tightened the top flap. The orb was exposed, glowing in three colors, most of the green muted by the caked-on dirt.

"What's that?" asked Autumn, peering inside. She cocked her head. "Why do you have that...?"

I ripped it back from her.

"Mr. Sheppard," said a deep voice, a scratchy sound almost out of tune.

Dean laid a hand on Dad's shoulder, his sunglasses in his pocket and his bright blue eyes trained on me under his gray fedora hat. "So nice to see you." The slightest cloak of smoke still sizzled off his skin, but it seemed to be dying off, his jaw clenching tighter as I took him in.

Dad jumped. "Scared me there, son. Ah. I see Ivy was right." He smiled as Ember peered around Dean's side to give him an obviously-fake smile. I glanced around. Blue eyes glared at me from every corner—between other people milling about, between arcade cabinets. The only different set was the green eyes trained on me now. Orin had finished his game and was leaning against the cabinet, his arms crossed, one ankle in front of his other shin.

I took Autumn's hand and backed up against the railings of the dance game. My merfolk were harder to spot, but with an audible gasp of breath, they pulled up behind Ember and Dean, the lot of them soaked, but all the better for it.

Still, my gaze darted left and right. So many people. And my family.

I shook my head slightly toward Calder, then dropped Autumn's hand to take the orb out and hold it above me with both palms. "Stop," I warned. "Or I can end all of this right now. Take you back to where you started, no progress made."

Dean and Ember exchanged a look and her mouth puckered into a little 'o.' *She* didn't seem to know what I could do with this.

Calder's face blanched—as if my threat had scared him, when it had been meant to scare the vampires. But the others beside him —Bay, Llyr, Cascade, and Laguna—also seemed on edge, their eyes focused on the orb with bated breath.

One champion could drop out and this war might never end.

The merfolk seemed actually terrified I might do it.

"Ivy, what are you talking about and what is that toy...?" Dad. Let him think I was roleplaying. Whatever.

Dean held up the hand he'd had on Dad's shoulder. "Go," he said, then he nodded to the vampires on either side of me.

"Dean, what are you doing?" hissed Ember. "We're so close. We can do this, we—"

He shook his head and laid a gentle finger on her lips. His eyes roved from one corner of the arcade to the next, perhaps giving them a signal.

"Go," he said again, his bright, bright blue eyes falling on me. "But should you do what you threaten, there will be nothing to hold us back right now... *Nothing.*"

I didn't have time to argue about that or wonder if he'd really follow through on his threat. Orin was right there, but if I dropped out of the war, would his status as observer still keep them from harming innocents?

I wasn't waiting around to find out.

"Dad, let's go," I said, shoving the orb under my arm and taking his hand in mine.

"I'm not finished," whined Autumn. I nudged her forward, glancing over my shoulder as we made our way to the doors and the sheet of rain outside.

I had a feeling Ember and Dean were thinking the same thing as my sister.

CHAPTER TWENTY-ONE

"Okay, you're going to have to explain what sort of nonsense that was—holy cow!" Dad flinched as a big flash of lightning tore across the distant sky, surging into a riotous growl of thunder. He grabbed hold of Autumn's arm to keep her from heading out into the parking lot as we lurked under the overhang. "We're waiting this out."

Calder appeared behind us and I jumped as his hand slid gently onto my elbow. The other four formed a line at our backs, their own backs turned to us as they readied themselves should any of those bright blue eyes come closer.

"We need to go," whispered Calder.

I took in the state of the parking lot. Every once in a while, a family would burst out from the mini golf area or the go-kart area to run to their cars or to the relative shelter of the arcade, laughing and pinching at their clothes as they pushed past us to go inside. The red and white lights of an ambulance, a firetruck, and a police car congregated near the go-karts, their sirens silent. The police officer was taking notes speaking to someone in an employee uniform as they huddled under the very small overhang at the go-kart entrance. The employee pointed our way as the firefighters took a look at the hole in the fence, another police officer setting up yellow caution tape.

And then there was that vintage car parked on one side of the ambulance—trapped until the emergency vehicles went on their way.

A woman with a scarf over part of her head, a fluff of red bangs popping out like a beacon over her sunglasses, watched us from the front driver's seat.

I nodded and handed the backpack with the orb to Calder. We needed to go before the rain let up and the vampires' vehicles were no longer trapped.

"Dad," I said, my voice lowered, "it's a mess here. Why don't you take Autumn out for dinner? I'll get a ride home with Calder."

Dad bounced in place as he took in the strapping, tanned athlete. "Hello! Did everyone invite their boyfriends?" He gazed around me. "I have to make sure Ember wants to get a ride with hers."

"She does," I said, looping my arm through his. "She told me. Back there? It's kind of like a scavenger hunt we're all playing."

"A *what*...?" asked Dad, but he flinched as we stepped out into the rain. "C'mon, sport," he said to Autumn, who squealed in delight as they both ran to his car. I followed behind, trying in vain to shield my eyes with my arm, my sweater going heavy and sticking to my skin.

Autumn scrambled into the back seat and I lingered at the driver's side door as Dad slipped in.

"You're going to catch your death of cold," Dad said. "Hurry up and get into that beach bum's car."

"*Dad*," I said, blinking rapidly as the droplets stuck to my eyelashes.

"See you, honey," he said, then his gaze went kind of blank again. No time for that.

"Don't tell Noelle or Ember where you're going if they call and ask," I spat out.

"Huh?" asked Dad, snapped back to the present. "Does this have to do with your scavenger hunt?"

"Yeah. You don't want to be responsible for me losing, do you?

Just have a nice, quiet dinner with Autumn and then go *straight home*."

"Yes, Mother." Dad gave me a sideways glance and then started up the car. It was unlikely he'd actually follow my advice. "Now get someplace dry," he ordered as another grumble of thunder sounded out. I stepped back so he could shut the door.

I waited until his car had pulled out and maneuvered around the emergency vehicles to exit the parking lot. Staring at the vintage vehicle still trapped behind the ambulance—a car brought here by their own machinations—I grinned.

"Come on!" said Bay as he appeared beside me with Llyr in tow. They took position on either side of me as we made our way to where Calder's and Cascade's cars were parked.

The rain made their hair stick to their skin like paste, their clothes darkening as the fabrics clung to their muscles. The set of Bay's jaw as he took inventory of our surroundings made me wonder if they were struggling to keep their legs intact.

With a little tingle in my toes, I realized I might be, too.

Calder had the passenger door of his car open as wide as it would go without hitting Cascade's car beside his. "Let's go!"

I slid into the seat. The backpack with the orb brushed against my feet. I dug into it to make sure it was still there. As Calder made his way into the driver's seat, I took it out of the bag, holding it on my lap, my fingers tracing the green portion and its faint glow.

Bay and Llyr jumped out of the way and into Cascade's vehicle as Calder started up the truck and put it in reverse. His arm shot out to the back of my seat as he looked over his shoulder and guided us out of the spot. "Well, now they know we have the orb," he said, shifting back around and putting the truck in drive.

His tires squealed as we took off, kicking up water from the puddle that had accumulated at the end of the lot. I stared into the sideview mirror. Cascade's car trailed behind us. In her bright red top, Ember was unmistakable as she darted out from the arcade to the middle of the lot, standing there, staring out at us. No vampires flocked to her, the water probably deterring them.

It would have been the perfect opportunity to snatch her as she'd tried to snatch me.

But before I could say more, the sight of Ember and the flashing lights of the emergency vehicles behind her grew smaller and smaller as we turned and made our way down the highway that would take us back to town.

"So what the heck happened?" asked Calder.

I snapped back to my surroundings, staring at the orb. Digging a nail into the dirt beside the glowing green portion of the orb, I started scratching at it. "It was a trap."

"Well, we figured it would be. That's why we all went." Calder sniffed, running a palm over his face and pulling it away, dripping with moisture. "But I mean, how did Ember and that bloodsucker get you away from the golf course so quickly?"

"Oh. Right." The more mud I scratched away, the more brightly the green shone.

What did that mean? And why had Orin clearly tried to hide it from me?

"They have some kind of time freezing power," I said, my heart only half in this conversation as I stared into the orb's light.

"What?" Calder slammed on the brakes and my seatbelt dug into my shoulder. I glanced up, my heart pounding, and realized at least that we'd come to a stoplight.

"I take it you didn't know," I said. "Or you would have warned me."

"No..." Calder tapped his fingers on the steering wheel with one hand as the other cupped his mouth for a moment. "So that's how they move fast?"

I nodded. "And it looks like if they touch a person, they can make them move fast with them."

Calder let out a curse and pounded on the steering wheel, making the truck honk. "This isn't fair. Nothing about this is fair!" He growled. The light turned green, but he wasn't moving.

"Calder," I said, laying a hand on his upper arm.

Honks behind us made him snap back to it, moving the vehicle forward as another flash of lightning sparked across the sky.

I checked to make sure Cascade's car was still behind us. It was, Bay up in the front seat twitching, looking over his shoulder at the third lane for turning vehicles.

"This time freezing thing won't matter when it comes to our plan of getting Ember to your house," I said. "Once there, that won't give them any advantage."

"Really? Because I call being able to move when your opponent is immobile a pretty big asset."

"I just mean—" But my throat went dry as I realized what I was looking at in the sideview mirror. "Watch out!"

A gray car was barreling past Cascade's vehicle in the right-turn-only lane, clearly not letting up as it approached the next intersection. It passed Cascade's car and now pulled up alongside us.

A man with blond hair—no sunglasses, no bright blue eyes—leered at us as his car sped faster and faster, the lane in front of him about to end.

A flash of Ember in a similar manic driving position reminded me of what I should have realized earlier—I'd seen this *rental* car before. I'd seen this man.

Ember's dad was driving like a maniac in the rainstorm, preparing to mow down our vehicle.

"Get to the left lane!" I screamed, reaching across the console to push on the steering wheel.

"Wait, Ivy! There's a car there!"

The orb slipped from my fingers and tumbled onto my feet as Calder slammed on the brakes.

CHAPTER TWENTY-TWO

The car in front of us careened into our lane, mere feet from hitting us, just as the lane it had been in ended and the driver was supposed to make a right turn. Fortunately, Cascade was on the ball behind us, screeching to a halt in time with us and avoiding hitting the back of Calder's truck—though she did jackknife just slightly.

The van that had been in the left lane kept driving past.

Ember's dad opened his car door and got out.

"That's Ember's dad," I said quickly. "This isn't just some average car accident. Calder, we have to get out of here!"

Grim-faced, Calder checked over his shoulder and then floored the car, steering right. It bounced as it went over a patch of grass and down into a ditch to get into the turn-off. A scream escaped my mouth as I took hold of the dashboard, but somehow we made it through, the truck's tires squealing as we hit the pavement once more. Stretching my muscles, I turned around to see what was going on behind us. Ember's dad was making his way back to his car as another vehicle swerved past him, honking the whole way. Cascade's car was going in reverse, just narrowly missing hitting another car.

I gasped, my lungs going still until the need for air seized up in my throat.

Cascade and the others fell in line behind us as we took the ramp off the highway onto a back road I was unfamiliar with.

Hyperventilating, I had to consciously slow my breathing until I could finally speak again. "What was up with *that*? Was he going to try to kidnap me in the middle of a highway?"

"Or worse." Calder swallowed visibly.

"But *he* can't do that alone, can he? It's supposed to be champion versus champion, not champion versus... champion's dad. Holy cow, she's involved her *dad* in this. How on Earth did *that* happen? I thought she wasn't even close to him." I was rambling now, but there was so much my brain was attempting to process at once, and none of it was making sense.

"He's not a vampire," spat Calder, his mouth curling around the last word. "Yet."

"So the rules don't apply to him?" I sighed. "But what happens if...? What if...?" I didn't want to say it.

"Either you or Ember die, but not by one of our hands?" Apparently, *someone* had no qualms voicing my concern aloud. "Then we're back to square one. So no, I don't think the vampires want anyone but Ember to kill you."

That was... reassuring?

"So he wanted to kidnap me for his daughter."

"I guess."

Vampires certainly didn't know how to fight fair. What did Orin think of pulling highway stunts like that? Unless he didn't know.

That reminded me of the orb. I moved forward to grab it, only to be choked on the seatbelt.

"Stay still," said Calder, revving up the truck's engine. "We're going to shake him."

The rain picked up its relentless pace and Calder increased the speed of the truck's wipers.

"I think he's sufficiently shaken," I said, checking the sideview mirror again to be sure. "He had to get back into his car and turn around, for starters."

Calder nodded, his foot letting off the pedal slightly. He shifted in his seat to grab his phone from his back pocket, handing it to me. "Dial my mom, will you?"

"Okay," I said, brushing aside some notifications to get to his contacts. Once I dialed "Mom," I put it on speaker phone and rested the phone in the drink holder between us.

"Yes?" snapped Nerida's voice, clipped and irritable.

"It was trouble, just like we thought," said Calder, his focus on the road ahead. "They almost got Ivy."

"She okay?"

"Yeah." He sent a quick glance my way with a fluttering smile. "She can hold her own and then some. She showed them we have the orb—that made them back off."

"That and the rain," I added. "Bad day for a vampire plot, if you ask me."

Calder and I exchanged a look then and my heart skipped a beat. It was hard to focus on how handsome he was when he and I kept clashing and there were vampires potentially around every corner.

Nerida went quiet for a moment. "Anything else I need to know?"

"Oh"—Calder turned, taking us down a back road I started to recognize as an alternative route toward Standing Springs Park—"there was a human who chased after us. Tried to run us off the road."

I was about to add the fact that he was Ember's dad, but Calder did the little "zip the lips" move as he turned to face me and I closed my mouth.

"Probably one of their meals," said Nerida. "Looking to win their favor and get granted an undead existence. They can prove useful before they turn, before water and sunlight bothers them. Though their exposure to even small doses of vampire venom can make them a bit... *irritable* around blood..." Nerida's voice drifted off, perhaps lost in thought.

If the vampires had a whole army of these people, maybe our merfolk fortress plan wouldn't keep them away. Then again, if they were only human, they wouldn't pose that much of a threat regardless.

"We lost him on the highway," Calder continued, "but I need to know if they're near the house and if we should take an alternate route there."

"Just take the lake," said Nerida. "No human or vampire can follow you that way. Report back to me when you get home." The call cut out.

"We're *swimming* home?" I asked, pointing out the window. "In this storm?"

"We'll be fine," said Calder, then he asked me to dial Bay. I did and he relayed the plan, but as I went to end the call, one of the notifications I'd dismissed earlier popped up and I caught sight of the first line.

From "Mom."

End this before she finds out.

Putting the phone back carefully in the drink holder, I bent slowly, the seatbelt slackening, to hold the orb between my fingers once more.

———

Calder tossed his keys to Llyr as Cascade picked up the damp clothing Bay and Laguna were leaving behind. "Just circle the block to be sure. Watch out for any hiding in the woods. They might have walked there." Calder peeled off his shirt and put it on Llyr's pile.

Llyr grinned. "I'll be in a truck. I can run them down."

I raised an eyebrow, the rain battering my nose, making it look like it was running.

Llyr shrugged. "Hey, the faefolk can't get upset about a little self-defense, right?"

Who knew what Orin would allow anyway? That reminded me to scratch more at the orb, but there was no denying it—the faint third color was glowing.

I wanted to ask Calder about it. But that text bugged me.

"I'll take that," said Bay, fully nude as he reached for the orb between my fingers.

Luckily, no one in their right mind was visiting the park in a downpour.

My face reddening, I almost just handed it over to have him go on his way, but it felt... Too important. Not until I was sure what was going on.

"Give it to Bay and get undressed," said Calder, working on his own pants.

I couldn't look at him now, either.

"Laguna and I will get the orb back safely," said Bay. "Calder's got your back." Bay took the orb from me before I even noticed, all because I couldn't look at the parts on full display.

Gritting my teeth, I peeled off a layer of sweater but left my shirt on. I put the sweater and the borrowed backpack atop the pile in Llyr's arms. Behind Calder, Bay was submerging himself into the water, the blue and red coloring the water around him, showing him off underwater like a beacon that drifted deeper and farther away. Laguna's red hair bobbed as she took a leap through the rain-soaked air like a fish, her full half-person, half-fish body on display before she dove in, the tips of her fins the last thing to vanish.

For a moment, I was in awe. Of the mermaid. Of this fantasy I was actually living.

"Pants, Ivy," said Calder, snapping me out of the moment. "You have to at least part with that much."

I glared at Calder's upper half. "Meet me at the water."

A hand behind his head, Calder gave me a soft smile. "Okay."

Llyr tilted his head toward Cascade, who was leaning on her car, her head back, just soaking it all in. "Why don't you give her your slacks?" he suggested. "See you back at the house." He grinned. "Good job back there."

"Thanks," I said, moving back so he could get into Calder's pickup.

Shuffling toward Cascade, I sighed as I slipped out of my pants and handed them to her. "Do you ever get embarrassed?" I asked. "Having your cousin and other guys see you in the nude?"

Cascade's eyes snapped open and she laughed. "No. None of us care. We just know that we have to wear clothes to go out because humans have this thing called shame." She gave me a onceover. "Why you'd be ashamed of such a cute pair of legs, I'll never know."

"It's not the legs part that bothers me." I took in a deep breath as the sky rumbled overhead and took my panties off, dropping them atop my pants, phone in my pocket, in Cascade's hand. "See you later!" I said, scrambling to the shore of the lake.

"What about your top?" Cascade called from behind me.

Yeah, no, still not doing without that part, so long as it doesn't rip off me.

Calder was already in the water and I felt my face flush despite the cold of the rain as I ran, my hands covering the area below my bellybutton as best as they could.

Unfortunately, the water pounding my bare skin, the thought of Calder checking me out, and the stress of everything came together too early and my legs snapped together, sprouting scales, my feet morphing into fins.

I stumbled forward, flat on my face in the sand.

"Ivy!" called Calder from nearby.

"I'm okay." I spat a mouthful of sand out from my lips as I pushed myself up. It tasted like sandpaper and vomit. "I'm okay," I said, wincing as I shimmied forward. I was so close to the water.

I finally got there, whipping my tail around to submerge it entirely, gasping as the soothing touch of the waters seemed to relieve all my muscle soreness. Calder had swum out to meet me by then and he wrapped a protective arm around my shoulders as he pulled me deeper into the lake.

I took a last gasp of air but found no reason to expel it as my head joined the rest of me down below. Blinking, the water went from fuzzy to clear, if tinged with a bit of murkiness. My lungs felt refreshed as I somehow took in the water through my skin, got my oxygen needs from the molecules.

It felt peaceful down here, the thunderous echo of the rain above us like a waterfall, offering protection from above as well as below.

In water, a mermaid felt at home.

"Let's go," said Calder, shifting his grip to my hand.

My shirt felt heavy and sticky and I had to fight my instincts to rip it off and leave it behind. It was nothing Calder hadn't seen before—but he hadn't seen *mine* before and... Something felt off within me. To be honest, I didn't know where we stood anymore.

"Can we talk first?" I asked. I searched around for a sign of any other merfolk, but the most company we had was an eel and a couple of skittish fish.

"Of course," said Calder. His face seemed to go ashen, though that could have been the dim light.

I swam toward the little palace of sorts under the island in the middle of the lake. As Calder swam up to join me, I took a moment to admire the giant bubbles making their way from floor to ceiling in an endless cycle.

My fingers reached out to touch one, and Calder slipped in beside me, his arm cradling mine, as he gently pulled my hand away. "They're decorations," he said. "But they break easily."

He looked about ready to cry—if one even *could* underwater. Letting go, he drifted slowly over to one of the rocks doubling as a chair. "We shouldn't linger too long. They'll think something happened to us."

"In the water?" I asked. "Like your mom said, no vampire or even human could follow us here."

Calder nodded slowly, chewing his lip. "So what do you want to know?"

That was an odd question to ask. Not what did I want to talk about. What did I want to *know*.

I got right to it. "What does your mother not want me to find out?"

Calder's shining eyes found mine. "I don't know where to start."

CHAPTER TWENTY-THREE

"Start with what your mother doesn't want me to find out." I flipped my fins, finding it harder to focus on staying in one place with nothing else to distract me than I would have thought. "Did you... Did you think about the fact that I might see your texts when you had me dial for you?"

Calder's face twitched. "I was a little shook from what happened on the road."

"This is war—apparently," I said. "I've only been in this business officially for just over a week. You should have had a lifetime of getting ready."

Calder directed a long, pained look at me, then hung his head.

A sigh escaped my lips. "Look, I didn't mean to make this like I was lecturing you about accidentally letting me see something you shouldn't have. Considering I don't want any important secrets being kept from me, I guess that actually worked out in my favor." I clenched my fists at my sides. "What bothers me is... It seems like Ember just has to sit back and let her dashing vampire guide her. I can't always count on you to have my back."

Calder's form seemed to crumple in on itself, as he no longer flapped his fins to stay seated in one place, letting himself float into a nearby alcove.

"I don't..." I swallowed in a large gulp of water, letting the cool comfort of the liquid soothe my worries. "I don't mean you let me down today. You did as good as you could. We all did."

"No. I just let you down every other time you fought a vampire."

It was my turn to go silent. I swam closer to his alcove and slipped inside beside him, resting what would have been my rear end on the hard surface.

"I tried to keep you out of this. I really did." Calder threaded his fingers through his short hair. "At Homecoming, I attacked the vampires on my own. So long as you weren't my champion, I figured the faery wouldn't call foul if I took a few out in self-defense."

I nudged my arm against his. "Self-defense? From what I hear, you lured them to the pool and set a fire before they laid a hand on you."

Calder's shoulders slumped. "That may be true, but I didn't do more than cause some water to sizzle on them. They had me cornered in that pool and it was up to them to run or hurt me."

It made sense now—and was more in line with what I believed. Timid Calder wouldn't have gone on a battle rampage. He'd have waited for the vampires to make the first move. But I just hadn't realized he'd had it in him to force their hand—to make it so they had to walk away or take the first shot, absolving the merman of blame.

"You didn't even call your friends in to help," I said quietly, the mermaid voice making even the soft-spoken sentence seem airy like a song. "You didn't invite me to meet them. You were doing everything all alone."

"Much to Mom's chagrin," he said. He opened his mouth, a bubble bursting forth, but then closed it, clearly thinking a moment. "Ivy, I don't want... So much of me doesn't want any of this. Not for you. Not for my friends. Not for anyone."

"Then why?" I asked. "Why fight at all?"

"You're our champion now." A flittering smile passed over his lips. "I'm in this fight whether I want to be or not."

I thought about that for a moment. "But apparently, I don't

have to be your champion anymore. We have the orb. You dropped that little bit of news on me that there was a way out of this..."

He grimaced. "Ivy, I... I've run away from this for too long."

I waited for him to speak more. He took my hand in his.

"I can't force you to stay—now that you know," he said. "Mom... Mom doesn't know you're already aware. She wanted me to keep the fact that you could drop out with the orb a secret from you."

So that was what that had been all about? "If I *know*, she thinks I'll drop out."

"Won't you?" He made a *hmm* sound deep inside his throat.

"And with no champion of water, the war is back to a stalemate."

He nodded, shifting so he could get a better grip on my hand as he clasped it to his chest. "That might mean we couldn't find another champion for a generation." His face seemed purposefully left blank. "There could be decades before two young women lived in the house at the same time. Or whomever my descendant preferred to make a champion."

By the time Autumn was our age, both Ember and I would be out of the house, and since it was Noelle's house, on the off chance she and Dad had divorced by then, he and Autumn wouldn't be the ones to stay there. She'd have to move or have twins with Dad or some other new guy or marry a new guy with two teen daughters. He was right. The chances of two potential champions putting down roots on those consummate lands were slim.

Still, it would make this all somebody else's problem. For both of us. Dean might still be the prince of vampires by then, but Calder would be king—or gone by the time there were two champions there. We both could be.

"When your mother was princess, were they waiting for a young man and a young woman to live there?"

Calder lowered my hand, nodding. "An old widow with a daughter lived there the first couple decades. Then the daughter moved out and the widow just kept... staying there for decades. No chance of fresh blood in the house."

"I'm surprised no one staged a haunting or something to get her to move out."

Calder's grin practically reached his ears. "Maybe we would have if we'd have had your guidance back then." The smile dropped. "But the faery was very clear. No harming or frightening the house's inhabitants."

If Orin was so sick of waiting for this battle to begin, I was surprised he'd even had that rule in place. "But Ember..." I cocked my head.

"She had an older brother on her father's side, but he rarely set foot in there," said Calder. "Besides, by then, Mom had already married my father. She couldn't spend her whole life waiting for something that *might* happen. She thought it better to have a child and see if the young couple that moved into that house could bear a new set of champions for him or her."

"They had Ember," I said.

"And then they got divorced." Calder's lips pinched. "That woman was stubbornly single for too long afterward. I got so used to hearing my parents complain about it that it all felt like a distant dream. This destiny I was supposed to bear. Like my mother and her father before her, I was convinced I could live a normal life, that this war wouldn't start when it was my turn to be prince."

I giggled a little at the idea of a "normal life," considering our surroundings. Once more, I took in the subtle beauty of the bubbles going up and down in the wide-open space around us.

"So Mom and Wilhelmina... Came to a truce."

"*What?*" I must have heard him wrong.

"They scouted single fathers with a daughter the right age and they... they set them up on a date."

"*What?!*" I ripped my hand from Calder's, pressing back against the wall. "Vampires and merfolk set my dad up with Noelle?"

He shrugged, like he hadn't just blown my mind with the fact that these warring species had set aside their differences to purposely drag *me* into this. "Your dad and Ember's mom were in business together anyway. All it took was a vampire going in as Ember's mom's secretary and planting some ideas in her head..."

"Wait, wait, wait, wait, wait." Both my hands were waving in front of me. "They don't even love each other? This was all a trick? Some brainwashing?"

Calder shook his head adamantly. "No. We didn't think the faery would allow that—besides, he's the only one who can outright convince someone of something that isn't true. The bloodsucker just nudged them to come together, that's all."

"Well, it certainly worked." I scoffed. I'd always thought Dad had been a bit nuts to rush headlong into this relationship so quickly. Brainwashing might have explained the whole thing. Though apparently if my merman boyfriend was to be trusted, it was just my dad being lonely after too many years "focusing on his girls" and barely dipping a toe in the dating waters.

He kept talking. "Mom and Wilhelmina clashed a bit that night of the trek into the woods. Mom got angry the vampire prince had even been there on what was technically our property and called up the school to yell at her about it, but the vampire queen reminded her that Orin's cabin was neutral ground and, in any case, it was hardly fair to expect them to stay out of the woods if it was necessary for them to be there to declare a champion." He swallowed visibly. "The little truce was over nearly as soon as it began."

It did seem bogus that the merfolk would insist Dean never set foot on their land—especially if they *wanted* him to get a champion and wanted this whole thing to begin. Frankly, I was surprised vampires and merfolk had ever gotten along long enough to concoct the whole marriage thing.

They'd been united in one desire: to pit one hapless girl against another for a chance to finally eradicate each other once and for all.

"During the first war," I began, "if the vampires lost, why was one still left?"

"We didn't know there was." Calder shrugged. "But it didn't

surprise us that much when they came back. The mermaids didn't win that first battle."

"Huh? But your mom said—"

"No one won. Not really. Not like we hope to now."

"I don't understand. Your mother explicitly told me the merfolk won that ancient battle."

A deep sigh escaped Calder's lips, turning into airy bubbles that spread up and to the surface. "Maybe we did beat them into submission—enough to keep them away. For a long time."

"How did your people do that?"

Calder grimaced. "We took out their champion."

A grim image of Ember lying lifeless flashed before my eyes. "Isn't that what you're supposed to do?"

"Our champion didn't take out their champion. *We* took out their champion. The merfolk. Then we wiped the vampires out, or so we thought..."

I gasped.

Calder's mouth popped open and hung that way for a moment before the words started tumbling out of him. "But you have to understand—we didn't know. This.... This proxy war thing, it wasn't fully established. My ancestors saw a danger in these undead creatures and found the champion versus champion thing too slow-moving. Too unsure. They were *dangerous*—and we didn't know if they would stop biting humans while we fought by proxy. They *didn't* stop biting humans, didn't stop adding to their numbers."

I didn't know what to say to that. It wasn't like Calder or his family and friends had had a role in all of that. But his mother had kept the truth from me. Just like she'd wanted to keep the truth about the orb from me.

"But if we had really won, once and for all, champion versus champion... Things would be different now."

"And what does *that* mean?"

Calder's head snapped up, alert to the point where I had to peer over my shoulder to make sure there wasn't any threat. The sky rumbled overhead.

"Just, look..." he said, practically pinching his scalp as his fingers wove between the follicles of his hair. "The vampires didn't win, either. Or we would have been gone for good." He nodded, but it seemed as if that was to convince himself as much as it was to convince me. "Merfolk had the upper hand. We got to spread out, enjoy the peace of living in the oceans without the threat of bloodsuckers snatching it all away... And then Wilhelmina resurfaced and tricked my great-grandfather into trying to settle their differences 'peacefully.'"

"The vampire merman," I said, my breaths slowing as I tried to focus on it.

"Right," said Calder. He grabbed my hand again. "Ivy, I know this is a lot. I wish it didn't have to be you who has to deal with it all."

Our eyes locked and I felt my resolve softening under the eagerness in his irises. It couldn't be the siren call. Not when I was a mermaid, too.

"I wish none of this was happening," he said. "Really, I do." He broke our gaze and swallowed noticeably. But then his grip on my hands tightened. "But if we don't win this war, my people will die. I can't allow that."

"And if I don't win this war for you, you'll just be left in limbo for generations to come."

His hands moved from mine to cup the sides of my face. The way he looked at me... It would have sent tingles to my toes if I'd had them. "And vampires will keep breeding in the meantime, killing humans to make them walk among the undead. Even Ember's own father seems poised to be one of them."

"You need this to be over," I said, my fingers tracing his arm as he kept his palms on my cheeks. "And the vampires put people in danger—"

His lips moved forward and pressed against mine.

My insides were a jumble of feelings. The kiss felt great—amazing under the cozy comfort of these waters' depths. But there was so much that weighed on my mind. And I realized suddenly with a start that if he were just some swim team boy and I were just some average girl, these brief blips of passion... they wouldn't last.

We didn't have what Ember and Dean did.

I pulled away, gently, letting him tease my lips once more with a little nibble before we parted.

I couldn't look him in the eyes.

"Let's... Let's do this," I said, not ready to tell him I would probably be walking away when it was all over. "Time to kick some vampire butt."

He was a good guy. He did what he thought was best. And he cared—about me, about his friends, about inconveniencing other people.

But this was about saving the merfolk to him more than it was about me.

So I would help him out. As a friend.

I met his eyes again as his hands fell from my face, retracting back to his torso as he put a little extra space between us in this tiny alcove. His face sunk at my unspoken rejection.

"We have less than a week to plan the battle that will end this thing," I said. "So let's focus on that."

He nodded silently, the bob of his Adam's apple eliciting a slight swallowing noise that made me want to sweep him up in my arms again and kiss his hurt away.

Forget my brain. I was a teenager. Hormones came with the territory for a good chunk of us, right?

We spent a few more minutes kissing, his lips traveling down my neck, pushing aside my shirt slightly to access my shoulders, before we finally broke away and swam back to his house, hand-in-hand.

He was my merman boyfriend for one more week at least.

CHAPTER TWENTY-FOUR

The past week had been suspiciously quiet. After school, the merfolk and I went over the different parts of the house the people might defend. The youngest merkids were going to wait it out with some of their parents and the few older merfolk in the lake during the conflict. Everyone else had a place and a role to play.

Mine was getting Ember there—with Calder's help. Cascade and Bay would be on standby back at the house. Laguna and Llyr would mingle amongst Dad and Noelle's guests to act as our backup.

Good thing because now that the wedding ceremony was here, I discovered there were vampires up the wazoo at this party.

"Yvonne!" said Noelle as she touched her cheek lightly to the cheek of a pale brunette wearing, no surprise, some dress more at home at a costume party. "So glad you could come! We owe this all to our own little cupid."

The woman laughed, a theatrical, overly loud laugh. "I wouldn't miss it for the world. You don't know *how* happy I am everything worked out between you two." She didn't wear sunglasses. Instead, her eyes were unnaturally black, even over the whites of her eyes. She trained those eyes right on me and the chip I had brought halfway to my mouth started shaking in my hand.

"Some wear contact lenses," whispered Calder in my ear. He had on a dress shirt unbuttoned at the collar and a pair of khakis. He hadn't swapped his aquatic shoes for dress shoes, though. "But they're still easy to spot, right?"

As if the paleness and clothes alone didn't give them away. I looked around the kitchen and out into the back yard. It wasn't really warm enough for an outdoor party, but Dad and Noelle had a wooden arch brought out back and had decorated it with autumn leaves and colors anyway. Folding chairs were divided into two sections in half a dozen rows. Food was set up buffet-style here in the kitchen and people were supposed to take their plates to the rest of the downstairs—the family room, the dining room—to mingle.

The party was just getting started, but there were already four people who looked like they'd stepped out of a 1945 celebrity-studded affair, two of whom wore sunglasses. The other, a guy who seemed vaguely familiar as the one who might have wanted to take a bite out of me before, had those same black eyes.

A pair of shiny, small irises peered out at me from the cracked door to the basement, Artemis's ears pasted back in a perpetual show of displeasure. Whether from the fact that the house was so busy, period, or because bloodsuckers walked among those gathered, I could only guess. The skittish thing had barely warmed up to me during the short time I'd lived here.

But things would be back to normal soon. Ember would have to forgive me. She'd understand.

And besides, Calder had been right to keep the news about Ember's dad from his mom, now that I knew how she made a habit of dancing around the truth and trying to keep things from me. We had the orb. It would have to do as bait. If they knew about Ember's dad, they might have used *him* as bait, and I wasn't going to let anyone else get hurt, even if he had almost run us off the road.

If he was being used as a bloodbag, he may have been similar to an addict. If I got Ember to surrender, I'd cut off the source of his "fix"—vampire venom—and save him, too.

Ember had to come around.

Whenever she showed up to her own house.

"You're sure your friends aren't coming?" asked Calder quietly. "What about your mom? She might have been safer here, if this is really neutral ground."

Mom *had* been invited and hadn't made a stink over it or anything, but I could tell by the way her jaw clenched just slightly as she dropped Autumn and me off that the idea of going *this* far to celebrate Dad's remarriage wasn't on her list of priorities. "She wore her workout sweats and took off," I said. "Are you sure Cascade's dad is keeping tabs on her today?"

He nodded. "But we don't have enough people to spare to watch all of your friends."

"Paisley got sick and Lyric has some track thing." My lips pinched. "If Lyric and I were on better terms, she might have stopped by after her meet."

"Rather than spend time with her girlfriend?"

I finally remembered to dip the chip that had been trembling in my hand. "Raelynn would be welcome to come with her, too, but according to Paisley's text, she has a Model U.N. thing today. They took a bus to Milwaukee this morning."

Calder narrowed his eyes as he surveyed the crowd. Llyr clutched a cup he never brought to his lips a few feet away from a vampire in shades who grinned over and over as he made small talk with some not-vampire woman Noelle had greeted heartily. The woman kept fanning herself with her hand and taking furtive sips of her drink, even though it could hardly be called hot in here.

"Hey, sport."

Dad made me whip around, even though I recognized his voice almost immediately.

He smiled as he ladled himself a cup of punch. "Whoa. Jumpy."

I laughed nervously and hogged another chip.

"You look nice," said Dad, slipping in beside me and kissing me atop the head. I had on a flowy, long black skirt for instant mermaid tail generation, paired with a tight navy blouse under which I wore a bikini top instead of a bra. I was ready.

Out of habit, I smoothed the hair he'd mussed and Dad chuckled. "All right, all right. Your old man will stop embarrassing you." He shifted his plastic cup to his left hand and held his right out to Calder. "Nice to see you again, kid."

Clearing his throat, Calder took Dad's hand. "Yes, sir. Thanks for having me. Congratulations."

"Well, we've actually been married about a month, but let's keep that under our hats." Dad winked. "Who doesn't love a proper excuse to party, right?"

"Oh my gosh! Lacey! This can't be Dante." The echoing footsteps of Noelle in her tight-fitting, lacey lavender dress, turned our heads as she ran toward the door. She exchanged a hug with Journey Slowe's mom, whom I recognized from the pre-Homecoming fracas, followed by the cook from the diner I figured must have been Journey's dad, and Dante Johnson, one of the guys from Union High. Journey's cousin, now that I thought about it. But Journey herself was absent.

"Hey, Mrs. Goodwin," said Dante. His hands were in the pockets of an oversized puffy jacket at odds with his dress shirt, tie, and pants.

"It's Ms. Goodwin-Sheppard now," said Noelle, beaming and giving him a hug. "But you can call me 'Noelle,' dear." She held him by his arms. "Gosh, I haven't seen you since you were this high." She held a hand out to her side.

"Excuse me, hon," said Dad, patting my arm and going over to join his wife.

"What about the team you hung out with?" asked Calder in a low voice once Dad had stepped away.

"Baseball?" I shrugged. "That was mostly due to proximity to Paisley. Not sure I'm close enough to any of them to invite them to my dad's wedding ceremony."

Calder's deep inhale startled me. He gripped the edge of the table. He hadn't snacked on anything.

"Relax," I said, sliding my hand over his. "Nothing's going to happen for a while yet."

Calder took inventory of the areas around us—the outside, the family room, the small bit of the dining room we could see from where we were standing. "That's *if* they don't start something sooner."

Right. I wandered over to the door in the dining room that led out to the back yard. Autumn was out there near the edge of the woods, her hair in a fancy French braid Mom had styled for her this morning, her green dress at odds with the way she hunkered down in the grass surrounded by her pony and dinosaur toys. Laguna stood nearby, staring down at my sister, whose mouth was moving a mile a minute as she kept holding one toy after another up to Laguna, shaking it as if to tell her the entire made-up history of each plaything. Laguna seemed fascinated, but she also didn't seem to have the instinct to know how to play with little kids. She clenched her fists at her side as she kept staring down at Autumn, nodding once in a while, and then taking another look around at the few guests mingling outside. One man shivered as a short blast of cold air ruffled the leaves decorating the arch. He pulled his suitcoat tighter, but the pale, vampire woman Noelle had greeted as "Yvonne" didn't so much as flinch in the face of the chill.

"Hey," said a familiar voice in an unfamiliar manner behind me.

Lyric stood there in the hallway, clutching her purse, awkwardly wiggling her fingers. She looked a little dressed up in her tight capris, flowery blouse, and white denim jacket, but Lyric always looked nice.

My body tensed before my eyelids blinked rapidly and I fully understood who was standing in front of me. "Hey!" I gave her a quick hug, my head coming up to her shoulders. "I thought you had a track thing."

She embraced me back, patting me. "I finished this morning. Took a quick shower, changed..." She stepped back, frowning. "Unless you didn't want me to come?"

"No, no—of course I do!"

Calder's eyes narrowed at me over Lyric's shoulder. I gave him a slight shrug, as if to say it didn't really matter, did it? We weren't going to break out into a fight during the ceremony.

I locked eyes with Lyric. "I'm always glad to see you."

"Right," said Lyric. She cleared her throat. "It's just... I'm sorry. About kind of giving you the cold shoulder since you said you were transferring."

"Kind of?" I asked.

She chuckled. "Okay. Full-on cold shouldering. But it's not like I *totally* ignored your texts, right?" She slid her arm through mine and guided me back to the kitchen. "Can I get some grub? I'm starving."

Calder and I shared a nod as he walked around the house and I went with my friend to the buffet. Dante was picking at the hummus with a carrot stick and he and Lyric exchanged *hello*s while I kept looking around the place, taking note of where the vampires and merfolk were in my head.

"Didn't you transfer or something?" he asked.

Snapping back to attention, I realized he was talking to me. "Ah. Yeah. Central."

"Weird time to be transferring to a school practically down the block," he said.

Shrugging, I took another chip. "It's in my mom's district."

"That's right. This is your dad's thing, huh?" Dante loosened the knot of his tie and then grabbed a celery stick. "Your dad married Ember's mom."

"Yeah." I studied his face to see if he had any particular reaction when mentioning my as-yet missing step-sister, but he was fully focused on getting as much hummus on the veggie as possible.

"Isn't Journey coming to this?" I asked, glancing over my shoulder for any sign of her—or of Devam. I supposed if they'd stopped dating, Paisley would have probably told me. She'd kept me pretty up-to-date on the inconsequential details of the life I'd left behind.

Dante shrugged. "I guess. She had that Model U.N. thing." His sparkling white teeth shone as he sent me a grin. "I'm just here because Auntie invited me and I thought I'd come for the food."

"Oh, sure," said Lyric, nudging his arm. "And seeing little nerdy Ember all dolled up isn't another one of your reasons for coming?"

I did a double-take. "You have a thing for Ember?"

"Shut it," said Dante, but he was laughing as he nudged Lyric back. "I kept waiting for her to get a clue. I'm over that. She's got that zombie pale boyfriend now anyway."

Hmm.

"I'm surprised Journey never set you up," said Lyric, grabbing a carrot stick and only slightly dipping it in the hummus.

"She tried—sort of." Dante cleared his throat. "At some dances and stuff. But anyway, I told her to lay off." He shrugged. "Then we all just grew apart."

How did Lyric know this anyway? How close was she to Dante Johnson? They talked a few times, sure, but…

"Oh! Hello! I remember you from Homecoming." Noelle swept into the room, her face perpetually lit up. "Did you ever try that salsa?"

"Yes, ma'am," said Lyric, putting on her "friends' parents" face. "It's *amazing*. Thank you."

Knowing Lyric, that was probably all for show.

"Thanks for coming, dear." Noelle reached the fridge and pulled out one of the juice boxes Autumn liked. "Ivy, have you seen your sister?"

"She's out back," I said, grabbing another chip.

But Noelle was pulling a phone out of her pocket. "I sent Ember to the store this morning for another vegetable tray."

Both Dante and Lyric looked at each other with a veggie stick halfway to their mouths, as if they were afraid they'd be accused of eating Noelle out of house and home. Then they chuckled.

Noelle's head popped up from her screen. "Ah! Okay. There they are."

The moment ground to a halt. Turning around, I looked past Calder, who'd meandered into the family room, to see Ember and Dean headed down the sidewalk, arm in arm, perfectly ready for the costume party that Noelle's vampire guests were all suited up for.

Dean had on his sunglasses, a suit, and a fedora all in burgundy, and Ember wore a similar deep red color in a vintage long dress with long sleeves, her hair half down in front of her face. Though the skirt wasn't skintight, it was close, a slit that ran partway up her thigh allowing her a little better movement.

Still, she didn't seem ready for a fight.

On the arm not entwined with Ember's, Dean carried a large paper grocery bag with a handle.

Noelle brushed past, juice box still in hand, to greet them at the door.

Llyr wandered closer, sharing a curt nod with Calder, who looked pointedly at me.

Clenching my fists at my side, I almost flinched when I heard Dante whisper, "*Daaaaaang.*"

Ember did look like a million bucks.

But if things went my way, her glamor was going to wear off fast.

CHAPTER TWENTY-FIVE

These folding chairs weren't helping. I was plenty nervous, which could account for the fact that I kept fidgeting, but a plush armchair might have gone a long way right now.

Autumn was on my right, clutching one stuffed My Little Pony. But Ember was on my left, an empty chair beside her, and on the other side of that, Journey's parents and Dante. Behind us were my friends and Dean, with Lyric fortunately serving as an unintentional buffer between vampire and merfolk.

Ember's hands clutched the knee of her dress, and at first I thought it might have been to keep that slit up one leg from sliding. But from the way her knee bounced as her back went unnaturally stiff, it seemed like she was a wreck like me.

"Easton," said Noelle, her hands clutched in each of Dad's between them. "Before I met you, I didn't believe in romance or second chances. Now I couldn't imagine ever doubting again."

The gathered people let out an elicited *aww* as more than one person blew their nose. It was at least ten minutes into the ceremony, but it felt like much longer. My head was pounding, and the fluttery sensation in my stomach was threatening to make me sick. What kind of daughter did that make me? That I was wishing for my dad's wedding ceremony to be over with already?

"Noelle," said Dad. "I'd been determined to focus on being a dad before you walked into my life. You showed me that I could do both—make being a dad my priority and welcome a new love into my arms." He choked up, bringing one of Noelle's hands higher up, almost as if he were going to use it to wipe his face. "As a *family*, the five of us are going to have so many happy days ahead. Thank you, thank you." He kissed the top of her knuckles.

A flurry of whispers down the row got my attention. Ember turned to look, too. Dante was showing his phone to Journey's dad, who tried to bat it away, but he was adamant.

At the same time, a phone buzzed incessantly behind us. Glancing over my shoulder, I saw Lyric, her eyes glistening with moisture, look puzzled as she pulled her phone out of her little clutch purse.

"Well, about that..." said Noelle, snapping me back to attention. "We're not going to be a family of five anymore."

That got Ember's attention, too, even if there were still hushed voices coming from beside us.

Dad's head jerked back as his mouth fell open.

"I'm pregnant!" said Noelle.

So much happened then, my brain didn't even compute. The small gathered crowd exploded, most rising to their feet to clap and jump excitedly. Dad swept Noelle into his arms, kissing her face over and over—I hadn't even known they'd been trying for a baby, assuming this was sort of planned. They'd spend practically their whole lives being parents at this rate, considering Ember and I were on our way out the door. Autumn was squealing and kicking her legs out next to me, clutching my knee. "I hope we get a brother this time!" she said. "I'll share all my toys."

Patting Autumn's arm, my gaze fell on Ember, who was looking right at me. I nodded stiffly. Her head bobbed back. We'd share blood someday.

But it was Journey's mom's gasp that rose above all the noise, followed shortly by one from Lyric.

They weren't joyous sounds.

"And with that," said the woman acting as a sort of ceremonial head, "I welcome you all to celebrate Noelle and Easton's good news. Congrats to the happy family!"

Journey's mom flew right up to Noelle's side, her face drained of color. She whispered to her, and the glowing smile dropped off Noelle's lips. Dad took a few seconds more, but he, too, stopped smiling.

What had happened?

"Raelynn might be hurt," said Lyric loudly from behind me.

I whipped around.

She was shaking uncontrollably, her fingers flying across her screen. "She texted me that their bus crashed on the way back and she felt sick and—" She went quiet, her lips thin.

"I have to go," said Lyric, sliding past Llyr, Laguna, and Calder.

Calder's eyes met mine, but I couldn't read the message there. It was almost like he was saying it was time, time to get Ember alone and... But there was another crisis going on here.

"Lyric, wait!" I jumped up, just as Ember did before joining Noelle and Journey's mom. Her mom bent slightly to whisper something in her ear, and I figured Journey's absence had been explained by her involvement in the same bus crash as Raelynn.

The murmurs throughout the crowd of people died down as Dad stepped away from Noelle and Ember to address the crowd. "There's been a bus accident just off the Interstate," he explained. He rubbed Noelle's shoulders, his lips trembling. "Noelle's best friend's daughter was on it..." He embraced both Noelle and Ember at once as Journey's dad and Dante joined them, her dad clasping his hands and closing his eyes in prayer as he started walking back and forth.

Lyric was already in the house and I had to shove past people in my way to go after her. "Lyric! You can't just go to a crash site."

Someone grabbed my wrist. Calder. "Let her go."

"She's my friend!" I said, yanking my wrist out of his grasp. "And she needs *friends* right now." She was probably already out the front door by now. I needed to go.

"You have something more important to do," said Calder as we both made our way through the dining room.

A shiver ran up my spine. More important than being there for a friend? I looked out the front door and saw Lyric climbing into her car down the road. She must have run. I had seconds to get out there and flag her down. Seconds.

But I hesitated. The plan. Putting an end to all this.

"Her girlfriend isn't the target," said Calder. "She's probably fine."

Wait, what?

My heart thundered, nearly exploding out of my chest, as something like a scream caught in my throat. Lyric left and it took eons for my brain to catch up, to turn around to face Calder and ask what he meant.

But somehow, I knew what he meant.

"*You* caused this accident?" I said in a hushed whisper.

Before he could reply, the dining room burst to life with activity as Noelle strode in, followed by Journey's family. "Get the hospital on the phone," she said, all business, and I realized the dark-eyed Yvonne trailed behind her, her phone in hand. "And then try the police department." She whipped around and took both of Journey's mom's hands in hers. "We'll find her. She'll be okay."

That was the cue that let the dam loose. Mrs. Slowe started bawling, her shaking limbs causing her to slip down, and Dante and Mr. Slowe swept in to support her. They guided her past us, as if we were invisible.

"Auntie, Journey texted me," he said. "She said she was fine—"

"And then she stopped texting back," snapped Mrs. Slowe. Her tight features softened as she laid a palm on Dante's cheek. "I'm sorry, baby, it's just—"

"We know, dear," said Mr. Slowe. They continued guiding her to the family room and lowered her onto the couch as Noelle kept rattling off instructions to Yvonne, who nodded and brought her phone to her ear.

"Calder—" I started.

But I jumped as Dad slipped in behind me and put a hand on my shoulder. "Is your friend in the accident too?" he asked glumly.

Even though part of me wanted nothing more than to lose

myself in my daddy's arms, I needed to get away from him—keep him away from vampires and merfolk right now. "Yeah, I think..." I said. "Raelynn. Lyric's girlfriend?"

Dad's head bobbed absentmindedly, but his focus was on Noelle.

"Go help her," I said. I glanced around. Most of the crowd was still outside, whispering amongst themselves, even though the cool breeze was blowing on the foliage on the arch and on the ground around it. "I'll go check on Autumn," I said, taking hold of Calder's hand and dragging him into the kitchen. Dad didn't even notice I didn't go outside to check on her.

I opened the basement door, flicking on the light and sending a wary Artemis scurrying down the steps, dragging Calder down with me. "Talk," I said, crossing my arms at the bottom of the steps.

"We don't have time," he said, practically bouncing on his feet as he looked back up the stairs. "This is the distraction."

"What distraction?" I flung my hands in the air. "Nobody told me about a distraction."

"We said when everyone was distracted, we tell Ember she needs to come with us or you're going to use the orb yourself."

"Yeah, when, like, people were talking amongst themselves over hors d'oeuvres and stuff." My stomach soured. They'd purposely kept me out of the loop. I stared at Calder, wanting to grab him by the face and shake him, but I settled for clenching my fists, focusing on the cool snap of ice forming on the fingertips of one hand.

"You lied to me," I managed to grit out.

"Look, it was my mom's idea," he said, his Adam's apple bouncing. He looked back up the stairs over his shoulder. "And we need to act *now*—"

"What did you mean before when you mentioned 'the target'? What exactly happened out there?"

"You were the one who suggested involving Ember's dad—"

I shook my head rapidly. "What? I didn't mean to *kidnap* him, per se! Was he your target? But how—was he even *there*?"

"Not him," he said. He cleared his throat. "I just mean, I thought you were okay with taking hostages if need be."

"*What?*" I paced back and forth, my hand growing icier and icier. "What are you even—?" I stopped and glared at him. "Someone crashed into the Model U.N. bus and took Journey Slowe captive?"

Like the telltale heart, Calder's phone buzzed from his pocket. Before he could so much as blink, I reached over and pulled it out of there, not even caring about the brief moment of intimacy the move brought between us.

It was from Bay.

Target secure, but we had problems. That crazy bloodbag and some bloodsucker cronies were tailing the bus and got out to try to stop us. We just barely got the girl out. They took another girl with them for some reason. Don't know who.

The phone slipped from my fingers and clattered to the ground, eliciting a hiss from the small space between a tower of boxes.

Calder scrambled to pick up his phone. The screen was cracked when he brought it up, but it appeared to still work. He didn't say anything as he read the message.

"Your plan was to take Journey hostage," I said, as slowly as I could. "And the vampires took another girl? Who?"

Calder's shoulders shifted upward slightly. "I don't know. Vampires are so foul, they probably thought we'd drop Journey to save any old person they'd subject to injecting venom through their veins—"

"Raelynn," I said, gasping. "They knew I'd care about her more than anyone else on that bus, thanks to Lyric..." I let out a growl. "We have to go save her."

"No!" Calder's head snapped up. "Absolutely not."

A shadow flitted across the basement stairs from up above as I bounced on my heels. Llyr and Laguna slipped quietly down, lingering halfway up.

"You knew, too!" I said, pointing at them. My hand was bright blue now, my fingers shaking, aching to unleash an icy spell.

Llyr glanced away guiltily while Laguna picked at a loose paint chip on the wall.

"What's going to happen to Journey?" I demanded to know.

"She'll be fine," said Calder. "If... If Ember cooperates."

"And what if she *doesn't*?" I asked.

"A threat wouldn't be very effective if there was no actual danger behind it," said Laguna, her meek voice carrying across the basement with an almost ephemeral quality to it.

I snapped. Launching my hand back, I shot out a stream of ice, larger than any ice ball I'd produced before. It nicked Calder in the side as it shot up the stairs, pinning Llyr and Laguna against the wall. Before they could think, I launched myself up the other side of the stairs, shooting an ice ball behind me without looking where it was hitting, praying at least that the poor cat stayed hidden and out of harm's way.

CHAPTER TWENTY-SIX

In the kitchen, I looked around like a wild animal, left and right, assessing my surroundings. I'd effectively iced three-quarters up the basement doorway. It was already cracking, so I had to get moving. Through the window, I saw Dean and Ember deep in conversation at the side of the house, some distance away from the rest of the party gathered in the back yard.

One vampire was with Noelle, and the others—I didn't spot any just yet.

I let up on the ice blast—Dad would probably explain the moisture with a basement leak—and charged out the sliding door and around the side of the house to face my foe.

Ember immediately responded to my sudden rushed appearance, flinging out her right hand and gathering fire to her fingers.

"Wait!" I said, lifting both hands above my head, as if to show her I was unarmed. My right hand still stung with ice, but I was forcing deep breaths through my system, causing the blue color to fade. "We need to get out of here. Now."

"*We?*" asked Ember. There was no disguising the disbelief in her voice.

"They have Journey," I said, my voice a harsh whisper. "I didn't know they were going to..."

Ember and Dean exchanged a look. Dean laid a gentle hand on her upper arm. "Where are your friends?"

"Detained… for now," I said. "But I don't know for how long."

"Come on," Dean said, turning on his heel and pressing a hand to Ember's back.

Her flames went out. "With us?" she asked. "Dean, have you lost your wits?"

A slight shake of his head.

Ember went quiet.

I could guess at what kind of unspoken conversation was going on there. Even if they didn't trust me, they'd already proven last week they'd wanted to take me somewhere alone.

But the horrible thing the merfolk had done might backfire on them if they tried anything funny right now. Ember wouldn't risk Journey's safety. At least I hoped. So, as angry as I was at Calder and everyone else… I supposed I could be thankful for that.

We jogged over the front lawn, headed down the block and to a fancy-looking red vintage car. It was sleek, but practically as big as a boat. Way to not stand out.

Dean held the passenger's side door for Ember and she climbed in.

He held the back door open and stared over at me. Right.

Glancing over my shoulder, I saw two pale vampire men heading our way.

"No!" I said, taking hold of the car door. "Just you two." I stepped back.

Dean's chin jutted upward and he made a hand signal to the other two. They stopped.

I climbed into the enemy's vehicle.

It took Dean another moment to get around the car, climb in, start it up, and pull away. No one spoke for the first minute.

"So what do you two want to do?" Dean asked, like we were just hanging out instead of potentially at each other's throats.

"Do you have Rae?" I asked.

"Who?" said Dean.

Ember's mouth opened in profile. She seemed to be waiting for Dean to say something.

"Raelynn Kelly," I said. "My friend Lyric's girlfriend. She was at Model U.N. with Journey, on the bus. Cal—He said your dad and some vampires got her."

"My *dad?*" said Ember. She turned over her shoulder. "Again, how do you even *know* about him?"

Not *it couldn't have been her dad*. Not *they didn't have Rae*. Just how did I know.

"We bumped into each other," I said. It wasn't a lie. "But I just want to know the truth about Raelynn right now."

Ember looked to Dean again. "We don't know anything about that," he said at last.

The way she waited for him to answer for her... Was that a lie?

I sighed. One innocent at a time, then.

"We should go to the merfolk mansion," I said, clutching my elbows tightly against my abdomen. "Before Calder and the others catch up. A few less to contend with to free your friend."

"Now hold on a minute," said Ember, grabbing hold of the back of her seat and practically climbing over it. "So you claim you didn't know anything about them taking Journey—what *were* your plans then?"

I opened my mouth and closed it.

"That's what I thought." Her eyes narrowed as she turned back around. "This is all just a part of her plan," she continued to Dean. "Get me to the merfolk fortress—"

"Yes," I said, my voice rising, "but now you *have* to go. And you have to work with me if you want a chance of getting Journey out safely."

Ember whipped around again. "Is that a threat?"

The car came to a sudden halt. Dean coasted off to the side of the road and put the vehicle in park. "Let me show you something," he said, looking over his shoulder straight at me.

I sunk back into my seat as he opened the door and went to the trunk, propping it open.

Ember glared daggers at me over her shoulder.

"Is that an invite to get in the trunk?" I tittered nervously.

"Do you want us to cooperate with you or don't you?" Ember sneered.

I reached for the car door with a shaky hand and let myself out. I could always run if need be. Even if they pulled that time freezing trick. I could fight back.

Ember got out of the car after I did, trailing behind me as I shuffled my feet the slowest I possibly could to join Dean.

"Oh, for Pete's sake. Come on." Ember grabbed hold of my arm, the bare skin of her hand sliding up my loose blouse sleeve.

I tried to focus. Find out what she knew about Rae.

"What if they try something at the wedding ceremony?" I—Ember— asked. Dean was sitting beside me in Dad and Noelle's back yard, on a bench facing the woods. I looked down to see a pair of tight pants on—so not what she was wearing today. Of course, she'd invited her vampire boyfriend to the place she'd declared a "neutral zone."

"You both agreed not to fight at your ma's house," he said.

I—as in the real me—hadn't agreed to that, really.

"But she'll lure me away—"

"Then don't let her." Dean squeezed my—Ember's—hand in his. "Or do. Just because you're cornered doesn't mean you can't end this. Let it happen."

I gasped as I came back to the present. Ember gave me a slight head shake. "What?"

"Nothing," I said, ripping my arm away. She let me go. So she was prepared to go along with whatever I planned for her today. Maybe she didn't believe I was even genuine about wanting to save Journey.

Dean held a long, rubbery thing out from the back of the trunk. It took me a second to let it sink in. I glanced into the open trunk to spot an oxygen tank, a set of dark goggles, and a pair of flippers.

A diving suit.

"Are you kidding me?" I asked, shuffling back a step.

"Well, this is an argy-bargy I didn't quite expect to chance upon. Oy, care to give me a lift?"

I whipped around so fast, even Ember jumped back from me in fright.

Orin strolled out of the nearby woods, foliage snapping beneath his feet with each step. He picked a dry twig out of his curls as he approached. "Heading to where all the action is, yeah?"

Orin. The diving suit. Dean. Ember. My eyes flitted between all of them.

"Truce until both of our friends are safe?" I proposed.

Dean tossed the diving suit back into the trunk and slammed it shut. Sliding his hands into his pockets, he looked at Ember.

"Fine by me," she said, clenching her fists at her side.

"Well, this is a downright shocking turn of events," said Orin, his smile wide.

"And we're not done here, either," I said, pointing to him and me. I thought of the way he'd tried to hide the green on the orb, but I wasn't sure if I should bring it up in front of Ember and Dean or try to keep at least *one* thing out of my enemies' hands. "You have some talking to do."

"That's a first," Orin said as Dean went to get the front door for Ember again. "Most seem to want me to keep my laughing gear in check, talk less."

There was no arguing with that.

———

We parked on the grass right outside the moat in the merfolks' front lawn. After getting the door for both Ember and me, Dean was back at the trunk, removing his hat and suitcoat and suiting up.

I clung to the car door warily as I crawled out, on alert for any sign of a merperson. But the place was eerily quiet.

The UV lamps buzzed overhead, but Dean didn't so much as flinch. Ember did, stumbling to the back of the car and putting her back to them. Orin squinted his eyes and held a hand up above him as he joined us at the trunk. "Blimey. That's going to leave a nasty burn on you lily-white types." He pointedly gave both Ember and me a onceover.

We weren't going to be standing there long enough to get a tan.

"So the light doesn't work on you?" I asked Dean, swallowing. His legs were in the suit now—and his sculpted, bare chest was exposed. Talk about lily-white—this guy was two shades past snowfall.

"Just the eyes," he said, gesturing to his face, where a pair of sunglasses rested. He grinned at me as he took them off and tossed them into the trunk along with the rest of his clothes.

I expected him to scream or vanish into smoke or... something. But he stared at me with those black, black contact eyes. He'd worn contacts under sunglasses in anticipation of fighting with me today. And I couldn't forget the suit. So much for all my plans about this being the perfect place to get Ember alone.

"Now what?" asked Ember as she tried to take the place in. She had to raise her voice to be heard over the trickle of the moat and the sizzle of the UV lamps overhead.

My chest constricted as I thought I heard sounds of a vehicle some distance away. Calder, Llyr, and Laguna couldn't have been caught in the ice for too long—I'd tried to paste them back against the wall, but I hadn't covered their faces in it. Then there was the fact that there could be more diving suit bloodsuckers on their way for backup. Either way, we needed to get in—fast. Get Journey, get out.

Convince Ember to surrender.

Right? That wouldn't be breaking our truce if she did it willingly. I tugged on the collar of my blouse and my fingers went to work unbuttoning it. I might not have appreciated what the merfolk did, but that didn't change the fact that the vampires were undead—that they'd had their chance to live. And that they posed a danger to people.

Merfolk needed to win and then I could put this all behind me.

But there was no question that Calder and I were done now.

"I don't even know if the front door opens," I said, peeling my blouse off and tossing it in Dean's trunk. Everyone stared at me—

Orin's eyes particularly lingering as his eyebrows shot up—but I unbuttoned my skirt and flung that off, too. I had panties on—no sense in making it a bikini bottom when it was bound to be shredded regardless—but it didn't look that much different from a slinky bikini at the beach regardless.

I decided to ignore the eyes on me. Actually, I couldn't really tell what Dean's were doing. His diving suit included a cap and he was adjusting his dark goggles over his contacts. He had frozen in place a moment as I'd undressed, though.

"Through the garage," I said, pointing the way. "And stay away from the moat," I added. I couldn't tell for certain with the bright, bright light, but there was movement in those waters—either a fish or a merperson.

The garage door was closed, but I had an idea. I approached the parked cars in the lot outside the garage, my aquatic shoes swishing through the grass. I tried the first handle and then the next until I discovered a minivan that was open.

Reaching for the visor, I found what I was looking for and clicked the garage door opener.

Ember and Orin glanced around the van as I did so, Dean several steps behind them as he waddled in his flippers.

His hands were still bare and there were slight pieces of skin exposed under his visor and around his lips. But I supposed he'd been able to stand the slight sizzle of rain before.

"Come on!" I said, climbing out of the van and pointing to the open garage door.

No one moved after me. Ember was frozen to the spot.

She ripped open the back door of the van and *sniffed* the seat, then patted it, lifting those fingers to her lips and licking them.

As if I weren't already doing some of the weirdest things imaginable, that still made me feel unclean. I moved back to the van to peer closer at whatever had gotten her attention.

Red on the seat. A small but unmistakable circle of red. Blood.

Ember hissed—like a cat, a guttural sound of anger. When her lips parted, a set of fangs stuck out as she trained her eyes on me.

"That's Journey's blood." The words were sharp and slithery in her mouth. Her eyes flickered blue just briefly. "You *hurt* her."

"Ember, no," I said, backing up a step. "You have to believe me. I didn't know. That's *why* I ran off with you."

The sound of the approaching vehicle got louder, the crunch of the gravel beneath its tires.

I backed up until something caught me, a set of hands clamping down around my bare arms. I felt the rubber against the flesh on my back.

I tried to move away, but the hands grabbed me tighter.

"Get off me!" I screamed, fighting, trying to kick at diving-suit Dean behind me.

Orin laughed and ran around the front of the van, jumping up on its hood and crossing his legs as he took this all in, like this were some movie instead of my life potentially being in danger.

"Ember!" I said, my wrists clamped tightly in Dean's grip. "We're here to *save* her, remember?"

Ember stepped closer, faltering as she did—as she stepped closer into the UV beams. She cried out and held an arm over her eyes.

She was in vampire mode right now. The light and water could hurt her.

Calder's truck braked hard as it burst through the tree-lined driveway, skidding to a rough and squeaky stop.

Laguna and Llyr jumped out of the truck bed even before it fully stopped moving.

"Ivy!" screamed Calder through the open truck window. He honked his car horn once, twice, three times.

The sound only made Ember growl more and she leaped at me, her mouth wide open, the hiss emanating from her throat like something out of a horror movie. Her eyes shone blue, her fangs bared, heading for my throat.

And then with a click, click, click the grass around us erupted into upward showers as a sprinkler system I hadn't even been aware of started up.

CHAPTER TWENTY-SEVEN

In his elaborate protective suit, Dean only flinched at the assault, but Ember released a high-pitched shrill scream from her throat as her skin started smoking.

Dean dropped one hand off me to rip his mouthpiece out of his lips. "Let go, Ember. Stop feeling the venom."

I didn't need to stick around for his little pep talk. I used the opportunity to send an ice ball at his flipper and tear away from his grasp.

My toes tingled in the aquatic mesh as I stumbled forward, Ember's cries ringing in my ears.

No tail now. No tail now. No tail now.

I heard a rip as my legs snapped together

No. Tail. Now.

The tingling lessened.

"Stop!" I said, whipping around. "I'm trying to help you—"

"Looks like an ambush to me," said Dean. His exposed skin was smoking, and he kept shaking his head every few seconds like he had a tic.

Ember let out one last scream and then all at once, the smoke stopped sizzling off her skin.

She straightened herself, the blue bloodlust gone in her eyes, her teeth retracted back beneath her lips. "Let's go," she said, as if nothing had just happened.

She took my hand in hers and I nodded, running toward the open garage.

Orin jumped down off the van's hood and shook his head quickly like an animal caught in the rain. He caught up to us. "I thought I was about to witness the most epic of fights, yeah? Though I wondered how fair it would be with the champion of water flopping about the lawn like a fish." His eyes darted downward and I knew my panties were hanging on practically by a thread.

"Don't say it," I growled.

Behind me, a whistle rang out across the sky. I looked over my shoulder just as we arrived at the garage to see Dean with his fingers to his lips, Calder, Llyr, and Laguna closing in on him.

"What's he doing?" I asked.

"Never mind him," snapped Ember, tugging on my arm. Just as we slipped past the vehicle parked nearest the door, I saw something... weird.

"Wait!" I said, tugging my arm from Ember's grasp. I ran back to the garage entrance. Orin stepped back, his hands in his pockets, a grin on his face.

"Will you look at that?" he proposed.

More diving-suit-people were stomping out of the woods surrounding the merfolks' property. Five of them—based on the shapes, two women and three men. Only they weren't wearing flippers like Dean was—and Dean himself was peeling his off.

They sprinted toward my merfolk friends, who quickly figured out what was going on and shifted back-to-back as they faced the assault from two sides.

"Ivy, come on!" called Ember from behind me, her voice practically bursting with her impatience.

"So what'll it be?" asked Orin as casually as if he were asking me to choose between a slice of pie and piece of cake for dessert. "Help your team or lead your target into the lion's den?"

"She's not my—" My mouth snapped shut. I'd gotten Ember here alone, exactly as we'd planned.

Once we made sure Journey was safe, ending this could be so easy...

I'd save the merfolk and I'd never have to speak to them again. Surely, even if she lost, Ember wouldn't want Raelynn to pay the price for that. Rae was Journey's friend, too.

"Make sure they don't kill each other," I said, not wanting the merfolk to jeopardize my chances by super-killing a vampire—how *did* one double-kill the undead?—any more than I wanted the vampires to end my friends.

My... comrades. I couldn't say if friends would keep something like this from each other.

"When am I ever not on the job, yeah?" said Orin, shuffling his feet. "Though I can't be everywhere at once."

I shot him a grimace and scrambled back to the door at the back of the house, where Ember was practically bouncing on her feet.

"It won't open," she snapped.

I laid my palm flat against the sensor beside the door. After a whirring, the door latch unlocked, revealing the long, glass walkway with the coating of water at our feet.

"Oh," said Ember, taking a look at it. She frowned but kicked off her red dress shoes and waded forward, the sloshing echoing in the narrow space. "They thought this would stop me?"

"Not you," I said, feeling the coolness seep through the aquatic shoes and to my toes. "Them."

She snorted. "Dean found an easy enough way around that, though, didn't he?"

I wasn't sure why none of us seemed to have ever considered vampires in diving suits. Maybe because picturing them out of that showy attire was an impossibility. Subtle, they weren't. But parading around in diving suits went right along with that.

Ember tugged on the door handle. "Locked again."

Shaking my head, I reached my palm for the second sensor.

"That's an abundance of caution," said Ember as the sensor

read my palmprint. "What, they thought someone would get past the first door and then lose whatever hostage they were using in the short amount of time it took to cross this thing, so they couldn't get the second door open?"

"They're a cautious people," I said as the door lock snapped open. I pushed on it and stepped through, rotating one ankle and then the other in the air to get the excess water off my shoes.

"Maybe, but their traps are easy enough to work around," said Ember. "Even for vamp—"

With a great splash from behind me, Ember went quiet.

"Ember!" I shouted, swirling back around to face the glass walkway.

The water that had coated the walkway was growing, the flooding area splashing out and onto my ankles.

"Ember?"

A hole had opened up at the end of the walkway, a trap door beneath the metal panel I hadn't even thought about being there. She had to have fallen in.

"Hey!" called a voice from behind me. It wasn't Ember's.

And Ember couldn't breathe down there like I could.

I spared a glance past the laundry machines and to the sparkling pool at the bottom of the dual staircase. Someone was floating on the middle of it on one of those inflatable toys—a fairly big one fashioned to look like a plastic paradise, complete with fake palm tree.

Journey Slowe.

"Did you say 'Ember'...?" she called.

I wondered why she didn't just jump off the float and make her way over to me.

In any case, she was confirmed to not be in danger right now. I pasted my arms together straight above me in a diver's pose and jumped headfirst down into the hole, thinking of water and Calder —how I wanted to maybe throttle Calder—and willing my feet to tingle, my legs to snap together, and my tail to grow. A thunderous echo rang out above me and I spared a glance upward to see the trap door swinging back shut.

Someone had set that thing off. Unless it somehow knew to drop for anyone who wasn't escorted by a member of the family.

I snapped back to business, looking this way and that. Feeling the water hit my lungs through the gills I'd sprouted, I didn't even have time to feel the sense of relaxation the water usually offered, to let my muscles unwind as I scoured the waters for my stepsister.

At the end of this moat, where the waters branched off into the river, there was a flash of red dress, blue fin.

Someone had *taken* her.

Those idiots! Merfolk weren't allowed to hurt the champion.

Or I supposed it was more like merfolk weren't allowed to deal the final blow to the champion?

I didn't have time to worry about that just then. Flipping my fins as hard as I could, I torpedoed after them, the moat obnoxiously long. When I reached the river and I turned, I looked for the telltale bright, red fabric, but I couldn't find any.

Instead, all I saw was Cascade peeking around a corner, a turn-off from the river that led back to the house. To the underwater portion of the basement. I went after her.

"Whoa," she singsonged, flipping her tail to float a bit backward as I approached. "What's the rush? We got her."

I waved a hand through the water. "Where is she?"

Cascade looked over her shoulder. "My cousin took her to join the hostage."

"Yeah, about *that*..." I bit my tongue. Not now. "Did you know vampires are attacking Calder, Llyr, and Laguna in the yard?"

She nodded. "We turned on the sprinklers, thinking it would get that vampire away from his champion. How did he think to wear the suit?"

Shaking my head, I swam past her into the narrow entryway leading to the house, past the water heater and furnace and all the other normal basement equipment on the other side of the glass. Cascade was at my fins, following me silently.

I startled when Bay appeared just as we approached the bright blue glow indicating the pool beneath the dual staircases.

Little had I known that I needn't have taken this long way around.

"Queen Nerida sent reinforcements outside," he said. "We need to make this quick." He locked eyes with me. "Whatever you're going to do to make her surrender—do it fast. Before…"

"Before?" I asked.

But Bay just shook his head.

My stomach roiled as a tingling spread through my chest. I swam past him, popping my head out of the water and gasping, letting my lungs take in air as they expelled the need for water.

"Ivy?"

Floating in place, I rotated around, wiping a lock of hair out of my line of sight.

Journey was on her knees and crawling across her plastic island floaty.

A pale leg dangled off the side, leading up to a soaked and mussed deep red dress.

"She's not breathing!" said Journey, and I realized with a start that her hands were clasped together over Ember's sternum, pressing hard in rapid compressions. "Ember!"

I swam over as fast as my tail would carry me, grabbing hold of the side of the plastic island and trying to lift myself up, though it was cramped enough with two people.

"Stop!" called a commanding, feminine voice from above me.

Nerida snaked down one of the stairways, clutching the bannister with a poised, delicate hand. She had a sort of seashell crown on her head, her legs breaking through a gap in her pale blue crinoline dress that hung off her shoulders like a waterfall. "If the vampire champion falls—"

"If she falls *now*, it won't be because I beat her," I snapped. "How dare you?"

Journey was ignoring us both, blowing air into Ember's mouth as she moved back to the compressions.

"Back up!" I shouted at her, then I grabbed hold of the side of the floatation device to lift myself higher out of the water before raising my right hand up, summoning the cold to my fingertips.

"Ivy, think about what you're doing—" started Nerida.

But I had. I flung a massive ice ball straight at Ember's chest.

CHAPTER TWENTY-EIGHT

Ember sat up with a start, water spewing from between her lips. My ice ball had gotten her breathing, just like I'd intended.

"Foolish girl," snapped Nerida, her feet flying down the rest of the steps. More of the adults sauntered out to the entryway from the kitchen, a couple of others appearing at the top of the staircases and heading down after their queen.

Bay and Cascade emerged a short distance behind me out of the water. That brought the total up to eight merfolk—and me—surrounding both Ember and Journey in the water. The others were either back at the lake, as we'd planned, unable to provide support, or outside helping Calder, Laguna, and Llyr—the "backup" Bay had mentioned.

I had a brief thought to thank the vampires for distracting some of the merfolk—then shook my head at the absurdity.

But it was true. I felt outnumbered. And not at all ready to menace Ember into submission.

What was the plan again? Threaten the orb—threaten to *use* the orb—no, they'd made Journey a hostage and—

Ember's gasps and Journey slapping her on the back over and over echoed out hollowly throughout the indoor pool-like entryway. I took stock of them both—they seemed worse for wear.

Ember was soaked, naturally, and still spitting. Journey had a bump on her head caked with dried blood and the muscles in my chest tightened at the thought of whether it had been caused by the accident or a conk on the head.

Delivered by my allies.

"Are you okay?" asked Ember through coughs.

"Am *I* okay?" repeated Journey. "What about you?"

"Fine," she said, training her eyes on me specifically. "Caught unawares is all. I'm not opposed to a swim." She sneered at me as she rubbed her chest absentmindedly.

Maybe it was best she didn't know exactly *how* we'd gotten her breathing again.

"Well?" asked Nerida as she neared the edge of the pool. "Are you going to proceed or do I have to get in there and *make* you?" Her nostrils flared, completely at odds with her goddess-like appearance.

I clung to the thick plastic behind me, a jagged seam digging sharply into my palm. I'd never seen the queen so unhinged.

"So..." said Journey from behind me. "Mermaids."

"You didn't know?" I asked her.

Journey and Ember exchanged a look. They were hiding something...

I reached out and grabbed Journey by the wrist, ignoring her startled cry.

"Ember and Dean asked that we not repeat the night of your Homecoming dance," said a voluptuous, pale redhead as she poured me—Journey—a drink in a wineglass. It was red, but too dark to be blood. Still, I shuddered as the scent of iron in the air hit my nostrils.

I recognized the woman as Principal Horne again. I'd never forget the way she'd peered at me—the real me—in the mini golf parking lot. Like she'd let her underlings handle all the dirty work, but she was confident enough she'd see me soon. She'd gotten away unscathed from the go-kart crash. The paper had reported it as an accident, and the vampire driver must have made his way back to the authorities and with Orin's help or something, convinced them to let him go without treatment. All while Ember's dad had been chasing us down the highway.

Speaking of, Ember's dad was near me—Journey—lying on a plush chaise lounge, his head rolled back and a dazed expression on his face, looking for all the world like he was high on some kind of drug. "Wait until you're a little older," he slurred. "Then you can decide for yourself. You're just a kid."

Principal Horne tittered, her fingers dancing across her lips as she walked behind the chaise lounge. "Thomas, you forget the age at which I turned so many of my finest family members." Her hand danced atop his head gently, lightly. "You may be one of my oldest one day." She bent over and whispered something in his ear I couldn't hear.

My—Journey's—dark hand reached out to grab the drink with shaking fingers. Looking around, I spotted a familiar face among the unfamiliar people stretched out on furniture much like Ember's dad was. Across the way sat Devam, a dreamy smile on his lips. A pale, bright-blue-eyed seductress stood behind his chair, clutching his shoulders.

I clutched the goblet tighter. "When Ember wins this thing, we'll talk." The words past my lips rung out in Journey's voice. "Until then, both Devam and I are off the menu." I drank the drink quickly.

Principal Horne's prickly sweet laughter reminded me of an old-timey moll's. "Are you sure that's what your little boyfriend wants, dear? To wait?"

The vampire behind Devam leaned closer to his neck—

I snapped back to the present, the glistening blue lights of the pool being lit from below, the sharp smell of the lake water filtered inside this home.

"Where's Devam...?" I asked, still adjusting to the present. "He's on his way to being one of them?"

Nerida was barking out something behind me, but for a moment, I couldn't make out the words. "...dive in."

Journey and Ember were communicating something silent between them. Then Journey asked, "Her mindreading thing you all guessed about?"

"Does she have to touch someone for it to happen?" asked Ember.

Calder had been right. By revealing I knew about Ember's dad, I'd made them suspect.

Journey reached over and grabbed my hand. "Ask me what the mermaids plan to do if they win," she said.

"What?" I tried to pull away. Like she would know any better than I...

But the merfolk had been proven to be keeping some things from me.

"Just read my mind," she said. A splash—and then another—behind me. I looked over my shoulder to find Beck and Dathan, Calder's uncle and Bay's dad, jumping up from the water, piles of clothes on either side of the pool. Shadows below me indicated there were more merfolk out of sight.

"It doesn't... work like that," I said. It was supposed to be a subconscious memory. Not actively reading thoughts.

"Then however it works, do it," she said. Ember crawled closer. "Or I can just tell you they're going to flood the world and drown the humans—animals, plants, *everything*—if they win this."

...What?

"You didn't know," said Ember, a bit of the edge gone from her voice.

"Vampires want to turn humans into bloodbags," I hissed, my back now to Ember and Journey as I took in the merfolk approaching me. Bay and Cascade were part of this—trapping me in a semi-circle along with the older men. Then there were the ones I couldn't see below.

"Yeah, *a few*," said Ember. "A few *willing* participants. That or everyone dead? Doesn't take a genius to see who's on the right side here."

Without even turning around, I raised my arm up and grabbed the nearest wrist—wet, so I assumed Ember's.

"They want to what?" I—Ember—said, pushing away from a soft, cold chest I'd rested my cheek on.

Dean's bright blue eyes met mine in the darkness. We were at a park—Standing Springs Park. It was night, and my eyes took a moment to adjust to the dim light from the moon and stars as they twinkled over the surface of the lake. Me—the real me—wondered what they were doing here, so close to the underwater castle of sorts. Did they know it was there?

Dean gave me—Ember—a side hug. "That's why we want to stop them. We'd have no qualms about live and let live to begin with if they hadn't wanted to wipe us out first. We were just about the only thing standing between them and claiming the power of the consummate land to raise the waters and turn the whole world into a fishfolk wonderland."

The reality sunk in for a good, long moment. "Calder didn't seem that evil," said Ember through what felt like my lips. Her voice was quiet. "Why would he do this? Does Ivy know?"

Dean shrugged against me. "That's above my pay grade to figure out. Maybe... Maybe from his point of view, he's not so evil."

"But how—?"

"Are humans really the best custodians of this world?" a familiar voice with a slightly British lilt to it said from behind us.

Orin was wandering over from the parking lot—not that I'd ever seen the guy with a car. He just sort of... appeared places. He slipped a phone giving off a bright light into the night into his pocket and nodded as he approached. "Just saying. Climate change and war and poverty. Humanity seems kind of snookered to me."

"No," said Ember—I—as I dug my nails into the arm of Dean's suit-coat. "I won't let you people give up on all of humankind."

"The fact of the matter is, the planet might be better off without most of you," said Orin, slipping on top of the picnic table beside us.

I squeezed Dean's arm harder. He lifted my face, gentle fingers beneath my chin, and my cheeks flushed as I fought the urge to move forward and kiss him. "But there are people you love," he said. "And we vampires aren't keen on the idea of water everywhere, either." A smile flitted across his lips. "Don't worry, doll. We'll win."

"She's going to the golf outing," said Orin, just as the memory started fading away.

Of course that wily observer had been the one to tell them.

He might have been using my brainwashed mom as a spy.

In any case, I shook my head to clear it, a headache pounding beneath my temples, perhaps from overuse of this mindreading gift. My hand slipped from Ember's arm.

"Well?" she said as the merfolk swam closer. "Do you believe me now?"

"They could be lying to you," I gritted out past my teeth. Right now, I didn't really feel like the merfolk were my saviors.

Ember let out an exhausted sigh. "Or *they* could be lying to you."

Whipping around, I grabbed hold of the float, rocking it and sending Journey and Ember scrambling backward a bit as I hoisted myself all the way up. My tail still dipped in the pool, my fins fluttering below.

"Whoa," said Journey, taking in the sight of me as a mermaid, I supposed. "Kind of awesome in a way."

"Did vampires take Raelynn away?" I asked Journey, ready to grab her and do a mindreading, even if my head was pounding, if she said *no* or feigned ignorance.

"Yeah," she said instead, her chin dropping to her chest as her whole body slumped. "I didn't know they were following me, let alone that they'd do that."

"How do I know she'll be okay?" I asked Ember.

She was still soggy, her hair clinging to her face like a wet dog's. "We're not going to hurt her if we win," she said, tossing a damp strand of hair behind her back as she straightened slightly.

Was that a threat?

I didn't know what to do. Make her surrender? She never would if she believed she'd be dooming the planet if she did.

...And what if she would be?

I stared at the merfolk approaching me—and realized Beck was missing.

"Look—" I started, but he jumped up from the water at our side, reaching up to grab hold of Journey and yanking her below the water. She screamed.

"Journey!" Ember shrieked.

I went to dive after her, but with a crash, one of the windows leading to the front lawn—the part surrounded by the moat—broke, the dark curtains keeping the light to a minimum in here so the underwater light fixtures could shine ripping to the ground. A man in a diving suit and Calder went tumbling as one inside the room. Nerida stepped back quickly, flinging off her dress and diving into the pool.

Calder rolled and rolled with the diving suit vampire to the edge of the pool, then rolled on top of him, panting, Calder's skin flecked with little streaks of blood from tiny cuts.

Journey gasped as she rose to the surface and I jumped back into the water to help shove her back to the floating island as Ember scrambled to pull her up. When Beck appeared again, tugging on her legs, I slammed an ice ball underwater at his head. With a great thunk, it made contact with his temple, chilling the water as a trickle of red dyed the water around him.

With a mighty grunt, Calder ripped the goggles and hood off the vampire he was fighting with—Dean, of course.

Then he grabbed him by the shoulders and stood up on shaky legs, dragging him into the water headfirst. He let go.

"No!" screamed Ember just as we succeeded in pushing Journey back onto the floatation device.

She dove into the water.

"Ember, wait!" I said.

The water was turning red now, radiating outward heavier from where Dean sank, that red, steaming blood coming thickly from his facial and hand pores. I had flashbacks to when we'd gotten him into the school pool.

Ember swam at the surface, gasping for air, and Bay grabbed hold of her easily, Cascade snatching her legs.

Queen Nerida laughed as more merfolk bobbed up from the water at her side and Calder stepped back from the pool unsteadily, hunched over, staring down at it. He was still bleeding, still panting.

Her laughter was too loud, the sounds of more conflict from the front yard and Ember's futile struggles the only other noise, both overpowered by that laughter.

The laughter of an evil queen, if you asked me.

"Well, this is something," said Orin as he stuck one long leg through the broken-open window and then the other. He was slightly wet from the sprinklers outside and he shook his curly mane out like a cat. "What do you reckon, Ivy? Merfolk for the win?"

Ember struggled and struggled in Bay and Cascade's grasp. Dathan moved closer to help them keep her from moving, and between screams of "Let me go!" and "Dean!" she started choking, sputtering as water kept getting onto her face.

Red steamed out from the other end of the pool as Dean sank. Blood dripped, dripped, dripped into the water from where Calder stood looking down at it. And blood... Blood should have been seeping into the water at my side, where I'd conked Calder's uncle.

Only there was a trail of the blood-like steam instead when I looked down, leading to where Dean had gone into the water. I stared down.

Dean was moving underwater and it looked like his lips were on the wound on Beck's temple. He lay unconscious, unmoving, as Dean had his snack.

"Uh-oh," I said, just as Dean shot upward and broke through the water, his hands and face still sizzling steam, his red, red lips twisted into a grimace, like it was taking him great effort to stay afloat. Every time his hand reached up out of the water and back down again, he let out a grunt like he was touching fire.

"Dean!" shouted Ember, and she went limp in the merfolks' grasp.

And just then a cry from the broken window grabbed my attention and Laguna went soaring through, landing in a heap with a thump. A vampire woman in a diving suit jumped after her, her breathing tube knocked aside as she bared her fangs. She turned instantly toward Calder, cocking her head like a shark smelling blood in the water.

And then she leapt for him, letting out a bloodcurdling, predator-like growl.

CHAPTER TWENTY-NINE

Without even thinking, I hurled ice ball after ice ball straight at the vampire woman and hit her dead-on in the chest, flinging her back against the wall.

Calder turned from staring at the vampire as she slumped over to looking at me. His mouth opened as if he were about to say something, but he slouched more, one hand cradling his other arm, which was pouring more and more blood forth. He staggered and fell headfirst into the pool, causing Nerida to finally cease her laughing and shriek.

I stared at Dean for a moment to see what he'd do and he stared back, the grimace still on his face as he paddled hard to stay afloat.

"Ember," I told him, then I dove to the bottom of the pool, following the blood trail to Calder's sinking body. His eyes were closed, his head lolled back, and I saw the moment his legs snapped together, his dress pants ripping as his tail formed, his top still loaded down with his dress shirt, ripped and half-unbuttoned.

It was an odd look for a merman.

As I scrambled to reach him, Nerida popped into view beside me, sending me a wicked glare as she reached her son first. "You could have ended this!" she snapped, her singsong voice at odds with the anger in her tone.

I took Calder's other arm and helped Nerida to right him upward. "It won't work," I said, my own voice bubbly and mermaid-like once more. "She'll never surrender. She believes you're going to flood the world if you win."

Nerida sneered as she tugged on her son. His head lolled back and forth and his eyes began to flutter. "So kill her, then!"

"No!" I said. Some blood-tainted water got in my mouth and I sputtered. Calder's eyes were wide open now.

"Then what use are you to us?" hissed Nerida. "Calder, get her the orb and be done with it!"

"Done with what?" I asked.

Calder shook his head, his eyes blinking hard. He ripped his arm out of his mother's grasp as he seemed to get his wits about him. He winced as he did so, the majority of the blood coming from that same arm.

"Fine, I'll do it myself," she snapped, more merfolk swimming up behind her as if to belie her point. She glared at me, her brows furrowing. Swimming off with the others, she turned around and pointed to a body at the other end of the pool. "Your uncle could be dead right now!" she shrieked. "And it'll be *your* fault! Just like it was with your father!"

Splashing above made me flinch as I gazed up to see three sets of fins thrashing about with two sets of legs—one in a diving suit, one in a soggy red dress.

"Did you ask Mom if we plan to flood the world?" asked Calder, sadly, his melodious voice somehow melancholic. "Or was I delirious?"

"Ember told me," I said. "And I confirmed that's what she's been told—by both Dean and Orin." I went quiet. There was room for doubt there. Orin might have claimed not to have picked a side, but I knew he'd helped us—"motivated" us at times. What was to say he wouldn't do the same for them?

Calder floated back a bit and cradled his bleeding arm, removing himself from my gentle grasp as he did. "It's true," he said. "That's what I meant when I told you we didn't *really* win that first time millennia ago. If we had, humanity..."

"Humanity what?" I said, slight tremors taking over my hands.

"It wouldn't exist anymore."

"You knew?" I said after a beat, my eyes darting to the struggle above us, then to the tunnel leading to the basement through which Nerida and the others had disappeared. More muffled cries rang out as figures moved alongside the edge of the pool above.

"Of course," said Calder—though his voice was monotone. "We all do. It's why Mom didn't care too much about us dropping out of swim team—none of it will matter soon enough."

"*I* didn't know!" I shrieked. "Do you think I would *agree* to such a thing?"

"As champion, you could have still lived among us as a mermaid. The change could be permanent once we won and this war was over."

"And you think I'd *want* that?" My voice was rising now, like an operatic crescendo. "What about my family? My friends? The rest of the several billion *good* people in the world?"

"Good people don't wound the planet like humans do." Calder slouched back against the side of the pool.

"You're going to make *billions* pay for the sins of thousands at most."

"They're all complicit," he said. "And things have only gotten worse since the last war the merfolk participated in." He winced and closed his eyes tightly together. "The planet is dying, Ivy."

I wasn't about to float here and debate world crises with him.

Above us, that steamy red was emanating outward again as Dean started sinking below the fins above him.

"What's your mother doing?" I snapped at Calder. "What did she want you to do?"

He shrugged. "Get the orb and get you to drop out, I guess. It was a backup plan."

"Backup plan if what?"

"If you refused to win this thing. If there was no hope of you defeating Ember your way and you didn't have what it took..." He drifted off.

"To kill her? Say it, you coward! Say what your kind wants me to do!" My hand grew colder and colder as my fist clenched at my side.

He turned his head up to face me. "Will it matter if she's going to die once we win anyway?"

That was it. I flung out another ice ball, and I kept it going, creating an ice belt of sorts across his abdomen and pinning him to the wall.

He cried out in pain but fought to keep his eyes open, to stare me down. "Again, Ivy? Will you just *listen* to me?"

He had absolutely nothing more to say that I cared to hear.

I swam off toward Dean, who was sinking now, his little doggy paddles slowing and not accomplishing much. I grabbed him under the shoulders and winced as I realized how heavy he was—heavier than his skinny frame looked, perhaps weighed down by the water and the equipment. I kicked and kicked my tail, my muscles practically tearing with the strain, and got us both to the surface.

I took a breath of air as my lungs shifted from water to oxygen. I realized with a start that Dean had no need for air—he wouldn't have drowned underwater, just steamed and been in pain. Maybe the oxygen tank had just been to protect his insides from the moisture. He was wincing now. "You believe us?" he said.

I didn't have to ask what he meant.

"Then help," he said, tilting his head toward Ember, who'd somehow made it back to the edge of the plastic island. Journey was scrambling to lift her up.

I gripped Dean under the armpits again even tighter and power-swam as hard as I could toward the little island. "Get up!" I screamed. "Quickly!"

Journey managed to pull Ember all the way up then, the water dripping from her dress onto my face and splashing Dean, who groaned. "Him, too!" I said, heaving him toward Ember and Journey, who each took an arm and tugged.

"What are you doing?" asked Bay from nearby. He had a black eye and Cascade had a scratch down her cheek. Dathan was nowhere to be found.

"Don't huddle them together," said Cascade. "Get the blood-sucking champion away from the rest."

Behind them, Llyr fought against another diving-suit vampire just as more of the merfolk crawled in through the broken window, panting. We were running out of time.

"Stay back!" I cried. Dean was up now, the steam still rising from his hands and face, though the red color started to fade as he got out from the water. I turned and launched myself up onto the small plastic island, causing Journey and Ember to let out a little "whoa" as they scrambled to make the thing stay balanced. But I yanked myself up and Dean grabbed hold of me, pulling me up the final way.

Then I told that mermaid tail to go away, my muscles searing with the effort as the scales fused back into flesh and the tail split back into legs. I stood and Ember yelped, reaching a hand out to cover the area below my abdomen as I turned back to face everyone.

I caught sight of Orin sitting atop a washing machine down the hall leading to the garage, a little smirk on his face.

Let them see. Whatever.

Reaching my arm back, I screamed, calling forth the ice, pouring it out from beneath my fingers. "STAY. BACK!" I screamed again, shooting the ice at every inch of water I could see.

Bay and Cascade shrieked as they tried to get away, but I kept icing the water, turning it to winter in here, my legs almost buckling. Ember slid in to hold me by the upper arm and lift me, Journey taking me by the other side, dodging my extended arm to grip me by the waist.

The ice kept pouring from my hand, the water snapping and cracking as the crystals spread. I shrieked, feeling all of my energy slipping, but I was quickly bolstered by the strength of the girls at my side.

The ice caked half the pool now and the additional merfolk who had entered—two men and one woman—shouted incomprehensibly as they dove toward the water.

"The prince!" yelled one.

They could breathe underwater. They'd be safe.

Right then, I didn't fully care if they wouldn't be.

I kept screaming like a woman in childbirth as I poured my all into my hand, gripping my elbow with my other arm to keep it steady as it shot out my power. Just as I reached that final, farther edge of the pool, the queen popped to the surface, flanked by Dathan and Beck, who evidently hadn't died. She raised the orb above her head, and I could see it clearly—glowing blue, glowing red, glowing green.

Though she trained her eyes on me for half a second and glared, it was toward the laundry room that she quickly directed her attention. "Fae, you sneak!" she shrieked. "I see what you've done!"

But she didn't have a chance to say more as I hit her arm with my beam of ice, knocking the orb toward the front door, and she shrieked, diving below, the mermen following her. With one last grunt, I sealed the rest of the pool in my layer of ice.

Then I collapsed, even with the girls trying to hold me steady.

My breaths were ragged, my vision going blurry.

Someone was laughing, someone familiar. A deeper, yet somehow more childlike laugh than had echoed in this room before.

"Must you, fae?" said some other guy, a twinge of that New England accent to his tone. "That sound's messing with my head." A vampire in a diving suit at the edge of the pool held a palm up to where his ear was beneath his diving suit cowl.

"Quiet," said Dean from behind me. He brushed past the three of us, balancing on the nearby plastic palm tree to get past. Only the island wasn't rocking with the movement anymore.

There really was a coat of ice across the pool, a cold steam sizzling to the surface that chilled me to the bone.

I was only wearing a bikini top for one. I shivered as Journey started massaging my limbs. "We need to get her some clothes or a blanket or something."

Ember sneezed then, as if to point out that she could do with a change, too.

"It's just the surface," said Dean as he took a tentative step on the ice. He flinched. "I can see their forms moving underneath—hurry! We leave now!" He gestured widely and the diving-suit vampires moved, coming around the edge of the pool to get closer.

"Come on," he said, helping Journey down from the island onto the ice and guiding her to the edge, where the other vampire hoisted her up off the slippery pool beneath her feet.

Ember was still rubbing my arms, but her fervor was ebbing, her movements slowing.

"Ember," said Dean, and he nodded. Then he took hold of my ankles, his eyes darting carefully away from my exposed waist. He didn't pull to help me down, though.

With a start, I felt Ember's clammy skin go even colder on mine as her mouth opened with a hiss.

Turning my head just in time to look up at the sight of Ember's fangs coming out of her mouth, I was too weak to do more than push meekly at her to get her away.

"No," I said quietly. "No..." Pain seared through my flesh as her fangs sunk into my throat.

EPILOGUE

I shot up with a start, my breaths heavy, the chill that hit my arms causing me to shiver immediately. I hugged myself, my fingers sliding through a plush, oversized sweater. My feet were warm. I stared down to find a quilt over my legs, a fire roaring toward the end of the bed.

And a snarky faery stoking the fire from one of the rocking chairs beside the hearth.

"Why am...?" My voice croaked as I tried to speak. I grabbed at my throat. "Why am I here?"

I looked around the cabin. There was no one else to be found.

"You were zonked. Vampires thought it best that I watch you for a bit," said Orin, as calmly as reporting the weather on a sunny day. "Let you recover. I wouldn't let them take you to their place. Not after you saved their hides and they thanked you the way they did." He chuckled. "Seemed a bit unfair, if you ask me."

My fingers hit two bandages, and poking harder, I felt the outline of punctures at my throat, like an animal had bitten me.

She'd almost seemed like one in that moment.

"Is it over, then?" I asked quietly. My mind raced over the day's events, a sudden thickness in my throat overpowering me as I loathed myself for not seeing it all sooner.

Calder.

Laguna, Llyr, Cascade, Bay... The little innocent merchildren.

I hadn't wanted them to die, even after I'd realized what letting them win would do.

"Are you dead?" asked Orin.

I snapped back to the moment. "Excuse me?"

"Wager not, since you answered me. Though you could argue a vampire is dead and could have answered me too, yeah? But they'd be honest and say they were dead. Why not? Bit of pride never hurt a vampire." Orin put the poker down beside the fire with a clang. "You're not a vampire—not a full one. Just had your first experience as a bloodbag, all right? Ember stopped short on purpose. Then again, she is a fledgling, part-time vampire. Might not have known what she was doing, how much venom to send through your veins to stop your heart."

My hand moved instinctively to my chest, and I didn't know whether the sharpness I found there was from anxiety over all that had happened or if I was feeling the poison burn me up from the inside.

"Did you surrender, then?" continued Orin.

"Huh?" I asked, letting my hand fall to the blanket. My limbs felt weak.

"Do you remember surrendering?"

"No," I said, clutching the quilt tightly.

He stood and shrugged. "Then nothing's changed, has it?"

My grip on the blanket slipped. For a moment, a feeling like joy soared across me—the merfolk I cared about, mad as I was at them, were alive.

But then I found myself swallowing over and over as I filled with dread. But they would have to die. They would have to. Or... Or I could drop out, make it so there weren't two champions, and the war would be delayed until one day when there could be.

As if I could live the rest of my life knowing the potential danger that awaited humankind one day if this war started again.

A sour taste hit my mouth as my chest went cold. Autumn. And Noelle was pregnant...

It could happen again. And much sooner than I'd initially thought.

"So I gather a dozen things are flooding your mind right now," said Orin, meandering closer to the bed and gripping one of the small bedposts at my feet. "Should you surrender, then? It'd save your life and the lives of everyone you care about, yeah? The world and all that?" He casually strode around and sat at the foot of my bed. "Other than those pesky little merfolk who wormed their way into your heart. But you've only known them weeks, right? And besides, it's them or a total nearing eight billion other people, all right?"

I flinched backward, pulling the quilt up. It was green and seemed worn, but somehow it was comforting, like I was a tree and the quilt was the sea of moss at my roots, cushioning the tender parts from the footsteps of nearby creatures. "I thought you were neutral," I said, though I didn't really believe it.

He raised both hands and lifted them up and down like a representation of scales. "Eh, I suppose. When it comes to vampires versus merfolk anyway. Couldn't care less which side won, though I'd have to be honest and say I'd miss my films if the merfolk won. Can't picture them putting underwater cameras to good use like that." His face wrinkled. "Too busy scraping coral off the sea floor and chugging down mussels or whatever it is they all do down there."

My heart beat faster at the memory of doing the latter—whatever nonsense the former example might have been. It was gross, now that I wasn't *in the moment*, living as a mermaid did.

"But I'm just laying your options out here. Let's see… What else? Using that orb to drop out as champion, thinking then you'd save everyone, yeah? Sure, history would be doomed to repeat itself, but maybe you'd be super old by then. Maybe you'd prefer to live on beaches in your old age—never mind that it'd be on the wrong side of the beach. The wet side. The side where you can't breathe." He waggled an eyebrow at me.

I took a deep breath, not sure whether or not to bring up my fears about Autumn and the baby on its way. It wasn't his place to know my mind.

Besides, there was... The thing Nerida had said. She'd been angry at Orin. At the "observer."

"Then there's the option of killing Ember—let's be real, she's not going to surrender peacefully, all right? But you don't want that for many reasons." The corner of his lip twitched as he took a good, long look at my neck. "Ask her to drop out and you're back to the problem of this whole thing repeating someday anyway. Maybe the two of you would be gone by then—maybe it'd be another hundred or more years. But then I hope you better not have kids or grandkids you care about or just, like, you know, care about humanity in general."

"Do you have a point you're getting to?" I snapped.

Orin lifted one finger up beside his head, his mouth opening, then shutting. Then opening again. I wanted to throttle him.

"There are some things I'm sure you're not considering," he said. "And I'm just wondering if I need to spell them out...?"

I pushed my back up against the headboard now. My own mouth fell open, the green light on the orb immediately jumping to mind. "No," I said quietly.

"What are you on about?" said Orin, cupping his ear as he leaned toward me.

"You... Who...?"

Orin chuckled and leaned back. "I'm Orin, prince of the faefolk," he said, doing a mockingly showy half-bow as best he could from where he was seated. "So yes, the green light on the orb means I've had a champion pledge to fight for me."

"*What?*" I shrieked. "But you're—!"

"The observer," he said, shrugging. "But the faefolk are tired of observing, all right? Tired of all this water and blood tosh. We were a part of it right from the start. It's just most of us don't interact much with human society." He turned and looked out the cabin's small window. "Doesn't mean we're not here—*observing*. Get it?" He grinned as he turned to me.

"What are you talking about?" I said. "Why didn't you tell me this before?"

His laughter was childlike, airy and full of mirth. And somehow untrustworthy. "Why would I tell *you*? I didn't tell anyone."

"So why are you telling me now?" My heart rate was out of control, my ears ringing in my head.

"Well, the merqueen seems to have figured it out and whatever. Time to come out of the shadows, I suppose." He gave me a stern look. "Granted, I recognize I can't be impartial when it comes to my own actions, but think of me more as a referee anyway, yeah? I step in when things get unbalanced, but it's the magic more than me. The magic of these consummate lands requires a champion to make other champions surrender or the champion to kill other champions with her own hands for there to be a victory. That's why there hasn't been a proper winner yet, not even a millennia ago."

"But now you're telling me there are *three*…" My words died. Three young women from Dad's house.

Autumn fascinated with my hand—with her own. Trying to get me to go to the golf outing. Her new book expert "friend." She was the only other girl it could be. "Autumn!" I shrieked.

Orin leaned back. "Yeah, well, sorry about that—the ceremony was just a quick peck, not a proper kiss. She's too young to be my ty—" But he didn't get to finish because I had launched across the bed at him, wrapping my hands around his throat, pushing him back on the bed.

Orin made choking sounds and I just clenched tighter. "You all said Autumn was too young—that it was only Ember and I who could do this!"

Orin continued to spurt and spurt, his eyes bulging exaggeratedly, and then he just laughed. Laughed without having any trouble breathing, even as my fingers were wrapped around his throat. He'd been acting before. "Didn't mean they *couldn't* use Autumn, just the other two princes weren't keen on the idea. Having a child for a champion makes this whole thing significantly harder, I must tell you. Kind of have to keep up the charade that it's just one happy-go-lucky game."

My fingers were having no effect on him. I let him go and leaned back on my hands on the bed, surprised at my bloodlust, even if that didn't mean it was fading away.

I wanted to kill him.

"Right," said Orin, getting back up. "I'll let that game-losing penalty go since your weak little fingers couldn't really harm me."

"You're not the observer," I spat. "Not if you're in the game. So no game-losing penalty."

He held his palms up as if to say it was out of his hands. "I don't make the rules. The consummate lands do. And I'm telling you, you lose if you hurt me. Even if I have a champion in the race."

"That's not *balanced*," I said. "Not *fair*."

"Yeah, well, it is what it is." He scratched his cheek. "So let me alert you to another thing you hadn't been thinking about. You drop out or by some miracle get Ember to, and the war isn't over. It's Autumn against whoever's left standing."

"*No*," I hissed.

"Yes," said Orin.

I slammed my fists against the bed. "Then how does anyone win, you traitorous little—"

"You have to get both champions to surrender," he said. "Or you can kill them both, but I don't think you want that, do you?" He yawned. "Seems the blood and the water forgot about the bloom after all these years for some reason. Forgot that neither side could truly win unless there were three champions in the game, unless their side vanquished them both. But if anyone drops out instead of surrendering all proper like, the battle is still on between the other two. Even if no one can really win without that third champion." He got up and stretched. "So I don't know if you really want to drop out as the champion of water, you know? Then you can't really help protect your little sister from the bloodsuckers. You'll lose your ice powers, plus your ability to turn into a mermaid, though I can't honestly say the latter will come in handy again, considering the vampires' little clever show back there." He lowered his arms and stared down at me. "Though they wouldn't have gotten the upper hand without you, so who can say?"

I blinked hard—again and again. Trying to make sense of everything he'd told me. Trying to think of the best course of action.

Lose. Stay the champion of water and surrender. It would be the end of Calder and all his people, but...

It was the only way.

But I still had to convince Autumn or Ember to surrender instead of killing one another.

And for that, I'd need to keep my powers as long as possible.

Orin hitched a thumb over his shoulder at the door. "So your merman prince has been out there—with my permission, not crossing the threshold—waiting for you to wake up. Says he's got something for you. Should I fetch him?"

I bit down on my tongue hard, the taste of copper hitting my mouth, a strange and ravenous hunger flooding me as it did. "What does he have?" I asked at last.

"Let's invite him in and see, shall we?" he asked.

He opened the door and shouted out. "'Kay, you can come in. She's up. Don't know if you figured that out from all the yelling and shuffling and such." He rubbed his throat exaggeratedly. "Your champion almost broke the rules and pasted me—practically snapped my neck, all right? Rein her in, maybe?"

I glowered at Orin, almost missing Calder entirely as a figure walked past him. Orin shivered as he shut the door and then cradled his arms. "Oh! Bollocks-bursting cold out there. Must be pretty darn devoted to wait outside in that frosty air, yeah?"

Calder sat at the foot of my bed, the colorful orb between his fingers. One arm was bulky beneath his letterman jacket sleeve, bandages probably covering his wound there. "Here," he said, not meeting my eyes. "I'm sorry. Drop out. Just hold it and..." He glanced over his shoulder at Orin, as if to ask if he were doing it correctly. "Say you don't want to be champion. Tell it you don't love me."

I raised an eyebrow at that. I'd considered myself his girlfriend for a few weeks, but it had hardly been *Romeo and Juliet*.

"I don't," I said, glowering at both Orin and Calder. But only Orin met my eyes, his green irises twinkling as he went to pick up the poker and stab at the fire once more. "But I'm not dropping out."

That got Calder's attention. "You're not?"

I shoved his arm away from me, careful not to touch the orb. "No," I said hoarsely, my heart thundering as I turned the opportunity away.

"Ivy, you could have died back there helping out the vampires—"

"But I didn't." I rubbed my bandage again. "Because Ember doesn't want to kill me, either."

"She may have to at this rate, yeah?" said Orin. He *tsked*. "Such a pity. Sister against sister against sister."

Calder stared down at the orb in his hands. "Mom said... She wanted me to take this to you. Wanted you to drop out. Said you'd never kill your sister, and I thought she meant..."

"Autumn," I said. Orin tittered at that, but I ignored him. "But I won't kill Ember, either. Just so you know. You're not going to win. But you're stuck with me because you can't force me to drop out."

Calder let go of the orb and reached a gentle hand to my cheek. I flinched but didn't recoil.

"You have to do what you have to do," he said. "For your family. Just like I will for mine." He pulled back and stood. "So for now... Let's compromise."

As those childlike chuckles filled the cabin between the snapping and crackling of the fire, I went absolutely still, a dizziness overtaking me even as my body was overcome with chills.

I was surrounded by enemies. But I had no choice but to keep fighting alongside them.

A beguiling vampire. The besotted girl who agreed to be his champion. The ongoing battle to save not only the vampires, but also the world.

Ember Goodwin didn't realize that falling in love would mean sometimes transforming into a vampire—or that she'd be able to shoot fire from her hand. Though she never wanted her step-sister to be her enemy, she can't just stand aside and let the merfolk proceed with their wicked plans. After walking amongst the undead, she knows that vampires are the true heroes of the ancient conflict, and she'll do what it takes to make sure they win —even if that means going against the sibling who got caught up on the wrong side of the war.

The third book in the Blood, Bloom, & Water series takes the war between fangs and fins to new heights as betrayals and secrets threaten to unravel even the best of intentions.

Coming in 2019!

ABOUT THE AUTHOR

Amy McNulty is an editor and author of books that run the gamut from YA speculative fiction to contemporary romance. A lifelong fiction fanatic, she fangirls over books, anime, manga, comics, movies, games, and TV shows from her home state of Wisconsin. When not editing her clients' novels, she's busy fulfilling her dream by crafting fantastical worlds of her own.

Sign up for Amy's newsletter to receive news and exclusive information about her current and upcoming projects. Get a free YA romantic sci-fi novelette when you do!

LOOK FOR MORE YA SPECULATIVE FICTION READS FROM SNOWY WINGS PUBLISHING

DECEPTION SO DEADLY
CLARA KENSIE

Winner of Romance Writers of America's 2015 RITA© Award for Best First Book

RUN. It's all sixteen-year-old Tessa Carson has ever known. Hunted by a telepathic killer, Tessa and her family have fled home after home, hiding behind aliases to survive. Her scars are more than just physical, and as the only one in her family without a psychic ability, she lives a life of secrets, lies, and fear.

After the Carsons flee to a new hideout and take on new identities yet again, Tessa meets confident, carefree Tristan Walker. Their attraction burns fierce, but she runs from him too, knowing their love can never be true when she can't even tell him her real name.

But Tristan has secrets as well—secrets that will either save Tessa, or destroy her. The only way Tessa can save her family—and uncover the real reason they've been hunted all these years—is to forget everything she's learned from a lifetime of running away, and run straight into danger head-on.

Book One in the YA paranormal thriller Deception So series, Deception So Deadly was originally published as the Run to You serial parts 1 – 3, and is the winner of the prestigious RITA© Award for Best First Book.

"A dark, suspenseful, and romantic ride!" - USA Today

"The perfect blend of mystery, romance, paranormal thrills, and danger." - Mundie Moms

"A well-written YA paranormal read, with welcome dashes of thrills and plot twists, Kensie has written a gripping and engaging series that features great family dynamics and the enormity of first love." - RT Book Reviews

"A thrilling story, packed with twists, secrets, and swoon-worthy romance. I couldn't read it fast enough!" -Erica O'Rourke, author of the Torn trilogy (Kensington) and the Dissonance series (S&S BFYR)

PHOENIX DESCENDING
DOROTHY DREYER

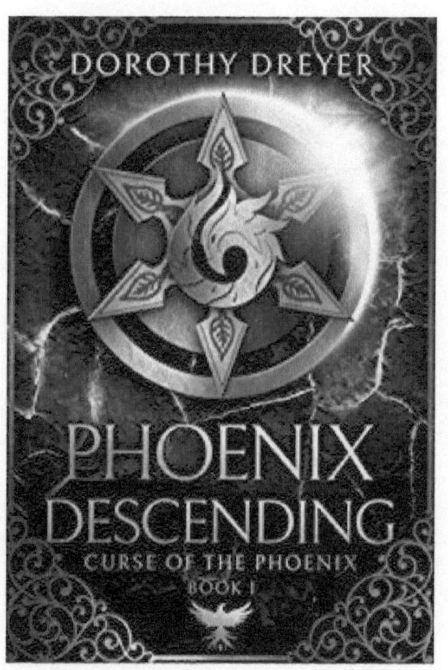

Who must she become in order to survive?

Since the outbreak of the phoenix fever in Drothidia, Tori Kagari
has already lost one family member to the fatal disease. Now, with
the fever threatening to wipe out her entire family, she must go

against everything she believes in order to save them—even if that means making a deal with the enemy.

When Tori agrees to join forces with the unscrupulous Khadulians, she must take on a false identity in order to infiltrate the queendom of Avarell and fulfill her part of the bargain, all while under the watchful eye of the unforgiving Queen's Guard. But time is running out, and every lie, theft, and abduction she is forced to carry out may not be enough to free her family or herself from death.

READ MORE FROM AMY MCNULTY

THE NEVER VEIL SERIES

"The story is fun and engaging, featuring a female protagonist who will resonate with young teens." -School Library Journal

"...A whirlwind of time-bending adventures that immerse readers in a maelstrom of plot twists and allusions to "Beauty and the Beast" and other fairy tale love stories, while Noll's understanding of gender-based social and cultural dynamics develops." -Publishers Weekly

Nobody's Goddess (Book One in The Never Veil Series), <u>winner of The Romance Reviews Summer 2016 Readers' Choice Award for Young Adult Romance</u>:

In a village of masked men, each man is compelled to love only one woman and to follow the commands of his "goddess" without question. A woman may reject the only man who will love her if she pleases, but she will be alone forever. A man must stay masked until his goddess returns his love—and if she can't or won't, he remains masked forever.

Seventeen-year-old Noll's childhood friends have paired off and her closest companion, Jurij, found his goddess in Noll's own sister. Desperate to find a way to break this ancient spell, Noll instead discovers why no man has ever chosen her. She is in fact the goddess of the mysterious lord of the village, a man who refuses to let Noll have her right as a woman to spurn him.

Thus begins a dangerous game between the choice of woman and the magic of man. The stakes are no less than freedom and happiness, life and death—and neither Noll nor the veiled lord is willing to lose.

The complete The Never Veil Series is out now and is free on Kindle Unlimited!

FALL FAR FROM THE TREE DUOLOGY

Terror. Callousness. Denial. Rebellion. How the four teenage children of leaders in the duchy and the neighboring empire of Hanaobi choose to adapt to their nefarious parents' whims is a matter of survival.

Rohesia, daughter of the duke, spends her days hunting "outsiders," fugitives who've snuck onto her father's island duchy. That she lives when even children who resemble her are subject to death hardens her heart to tackle the task.

Fastello is the son of the "king" of the raiders who steal from the rich and share with the poor. When aristocrats die in the raids, Fastello questions what his peoples' increasingly wicked methods of survival have cost them.

An orphan raised by a convent of mothers, Cateline can think of no higher aim in life than to serve her religion, even if it means turning a blind eye to the suffering of other orphans under the mothers' care.

Kojiro, new heir to the Hanaobi empire, must avenge his people against the "barbarians" who live in the duchy, terrified the empress, his own mother, might rather see him die than succeed.

When the paths of these four young adults cross, they must rely on one another for survival—but the love of even a malevolent guardian is hard to leave behind.

The complete Fall Far from the Tree duology is out now and is available widely.